I0632835

VICE

Book 1 Vegas Sins Series

Rosanna Leo

VICE

Copyright © 2017 by Rosanna Leo.
All rights reserved.
First Print Edition: September 2017

Crave Publishing, LLC
Kailua, HI 96734
http://www.cravepublishing.net/

Formatting: Crave Publishing, LLC

ISBN-13: 978-1-64034-209-5
ISBN-10: 1-64034-209-5

No part of this book may be reproduced, scanned, or distributed in any printed or electronic form without permission. Please do not participate in or encourage piracy of copyrighted materials in violation of the author's rights. Thank you for respecting the hard work of this author.

This is a work of fiction. Names, characters, places, and incidents either are the product of the author's imagination or are used fictitiously, and any resemblance to locales, events, business establishments, or actual persons—living or dead—is entirely coincidental.

DEDICATION

For my mother, Louisa.

This book was dedicated to her, even before I
started writing it.

Chapter One

"Mr. Calvert. I need you to remove your hand from my ass."

Despite the clear tone of her voice, her boss's hand continued to rove over her behind with an intimacy that was as revolting as it was inappropriate. In truth, Howard Calvert wasn't really her boss, but he was the Calvert behind Calvert's Used Automobiles, and she was supposed to be recording his radio jingle in this small Las Vegas recording booth. For that reason, and that reason alone, Kate Callender bit her tongue, determined not to overreact.

And she would have been successful had the man not leaned in for a closer grope. She hissed and pushed him away.

"No need to get snippy, darlin'. We're both consenting adults here."

"I *consented* to singing your jingle." She peered through the glass into the producer's booth. Where was Klein, anyway? Probably getting another roast beef sandwich while she still reeled from the effects of her new gluten-free diet. Someone said she could fix her various health complaints by ditching gluten, but after a couple of sin-free weeks, she was willing to endure festering boils for the sake of some white pasta and garlic bread.

Mr. Calvert's paw appeared once more on her hip, and did a finger drum roll on her ass. "Come now, Kate. I saw the way you looked at me. Don't be shy."

She stepped back. "I don't know what you thought you saw, sir, but it's not what you think." Why the hands all of a sudden? She'd sung for Calvert numerous times, becoming the voice of his radio campaign. He'd always given off a curious vibe, appraising her from a distance, but this was the first time he'd let his fingers do the talking.

She'd worked hard to get the stupid gig, auditioning numerous times before Calvert signed on the dotted line. One would think it was tryouts for *Les Miserables*, not a commercial for a fricking used car dealership. But the gig paid well and regularly. Calvert seemed to think car commercials needed the voice of a sexed-up woman to be effective.

Mind you, she wasn't all that sexed-up, and hadn't been for some time, but she put on a good show.

The man tried again, maneuvering closer to her. She had to give him points for determination. "I, uh, sent Klein on an errand so we could get to know each other better. I felt it was time."

Kate calmed her nerves and realized she was about to cause her immediate financial ruin. "We do know each other, sir, and I know *Mrs*. Calvert would be very upset at your behavior. Now, unless you keep your hands off me, I won't record the jingle."

"Darlin', please. We both know you will. You need this job."

He was right, of course, but if she had to walk away with empty pockets and her integrity, she'd feel better about it in the morning. Probably.

"I don't need it so much that I'll put up with your sausage fingers."

"Christ," he muttered under his breath. "Do you always argue so much?" He reached for her breast.

"Back off. I swear to God, I'll kick you in the nuts!" She vaulted out of the way, ran around a couple of chairs and music stands, and grabbed her purse.

"Come on, Kate. I've seen the way you look at me. Stop playin'. Don't you think you owe me? I've sent a lot of royalties your way."

"Last I checked, I wasn't rendering *that* kind of service. This is Vegas. If you want a hooker, stand on the street corner and someone will hand you a card with a picture on it. Call her." Without a look back, Kate put her hand on the recording booth door.

She should have seen it coming. Calvert was the kind of man who didn't let people say no to him, let alone insult him. The man copped a feel of her breast before she could make her exit, grinning like it was all part of the game.

Kate turned, unthinking, and brought her knee into his family jewels.

"Aw, *fuck*!" Calvert grunted and dropped to his knees as Kate opened the door to leave. Despite his pain, Calvert had enough presence of mind to aim one last threat. "I'll make sure you never get another job in this town. I bloody guarantee it."

"Go to hell. I'll take my chances." How much pull could the Lord of Lemons have in the Vegas entertainment world, anyway? As she hurried out of the recording studio, she experienced a measure of calm at being out of his grip. She stood still on the sidewalk and allowed the hot sun to beam down on her face.

Only then did she begin to grow nervous. What if Calvert *did* know people in the singing world? What if he spread the word she was uncooperative and mouthy and unprofessional? God knew it was hard enough getting a gig in this city that didn't require her to drop her drawers, and she wasn't built to play showgirl. Her ample sized knockers would never fit into those skimpy little bras they wore. Plus she couldn't dance. The Calvert jingle had provided her with the steadiest singing job she'd ever had, and she'd likely never land anything like it again.

Maybe Celine Dion would ask her to join her next tour as a backup singer. Right. And maybe the pop icon would also ask to be her new BFF.

"Nuts." She began walking toward the bus stop. Her royalties would at least keep her in gluten-free snacks for a while until she figured out what to do next. And she still had her volunteer job. It meant more to her than those dumb jingles, anyway. There she made a difference. She was always saying she wished she had more time to devote to New Horizons. Now she had a chance. She could concentrate on helping the folks there, and Karma would provide.

She had to believe it. After all, Karma had stolen everything else from her.

***

"Hi. Um, my name is Audrey, and…well, my boyfriend Darren is a compulsive gambler." The woman looked down at her lap and smoothed out a few wrinkles in her jeans. After a moment, she raised her head, looking to Kate. "What else am I supposed to say?"

"Whatever you want to share, Audrey. This is a non-judgment zone. You can talk about your life with Darren, about his gambling, or about the weather. It's your first time in group, so anything's fair game. We're not head-shrinkers here, just friends."

Kate could see Darren had trampled on her trust. She wore the same expression every arrival to New Horizons did, one of pale disbelief. No matter how much good the program did, no matter how it was lauded by its supporters, no victim of gambling addiction ever thought it would work for them.

Audrey's eyes narrowed. "I'm sorry, but I still don't see how this is going to help me. I mean…I'm not the gambler. I don't waste my paycheck at the casino the moment it's earned. I don't lie and cheat. I'm just the poor schlep whose money he stole time and again. Darren should be here, not me."

"Does Darren realize he has an illness?" Kate asked in a gentle tone.

"Are you kidding? He thinks *I'm* the one who's crazy."

"That's why it's important for you to be here," Kate replied. "Look around the room, Audrey. This program is for the loved ones of compulsive gamblers. We've all known gamblers and we've all needed support. Of the sixteen of us here, not one has ever sat at a craps table or placed a bet."

Rod, a long-time participant, chimed in. "Hell, I've never even bought a lottery ticket."

"Exactly," continued Kate. "And we all know what it's like to love someone who is buried in denial."

Rod took a bite of his gingersnap, quickly swallowing. "Yeah. I'd bet my special someone is busy at one of Liam Doyle's slot machines right now."

Kate bit the inside of her lip as a few whispers traveled through the group. *Here we go again.*

Liam Doyle, owner of a couple of top Las Vegas casinos, was the author of many a compulsive gambler's destruction. An enigmatic entrepreneur, he'd become the most lauded businessman to hit the Strip since Steve Wynn.

Defying Vegas tradition, Doyle had created a number of casino hotels that resembled the finest of New York boutique properties. The young and hip lined up to get a peek inside his establishments. No gaudy neon signs for Doyle; rather he'd built sleek, modern properties that catered to every whim and created brand new ones. If you wanted gourmet foods, Liam Doyle had them delivered, plus a bag of chips. If you wanted fancy cocktails, Liam Doyle offered them in flavors and colors invented by the top mixologists.

Oh, and you didn't just play the slots at Liam Doyle's casinos. You played them in the most upscale gaming rooms in the city. Sure, folks lauded him as a visionary with the upcoming opening of his newest hotel, Vice, but she saw Doyle for what he really was…an enabler.

The whole town was full of enablers, but she bore a special hatred for Doyle. His sexy hotels brought in a whole new clientele, gave it a unique veneer of respectability. She knew several people who'd never entered a casino before or played a game of poker who were drawn to Doyle's properties like they emitted a Siren's song. And he grew richer every year off their losses. It was hard enough living in Sin City without Doyle making sin so tempting.

Dammit, she'd already had a shitty day with Calvert. Hearing about the casino impresario again just set her even more on edge.

"I understand the grand opening for Vice is coming up," said Patti, another participant. "It's supposed to be his most elaborate venture yet."

"How much more posh could it get?" asked Rod. "His other properties have already brought in more winnings than the Venetian and Caesar's Palace combined. I can't pry my boyfriend away from Doyle's clubs. He says it's not about the money, it's about the character and ambience. Right. Personally, I think he's hoping for an eyeful of the big man himself."

No doubt Liam Doyle would end up richer than Croesus as he indulged everyone from disgraced heads of state to Hollywood starlets once it opened. She wondered if he'd built a special little chamber where he spun straw into gold as well, or paid the Devil his cut.

"The Chronicle says he is 'single-handedly revitalizing the Las Vegas entertainment scene,'" said Audrey. "They printed his picture. I had no idea the dude was so fine. He almost makes me want to take up gambling myself."

"Fine doesn't even begin to describe him," Patti chimed in. "He makes Adam Levine look like one of the unwashed masses."

Kate put up a hand. She hadn't seen the photo, and didn't care to. It seemed so many of their meetings began this way. Instead of diving into the issues they needed to address, they spent the first few minutes talking about people like Doyle and the celebrities who frequented their casinos. Sometimes it felt as if the loved ones of compulsive gamblers were just as obsessed with the industry.

"Okay, everyone. Our conversation is derailing. I'm sure Liam Doyle has a very pretty face, but that's not why we're here." She let out a breath. "Audrey, are you comfortable sharing more of your story?"

"I don't know. Maybe you could tell me yours first?"

All eyes turned toward Kate. Of course, any of the regulars could recite her ridiculous history. She braced herself for the familiar ache that never quite went away, the one that haunted the deepest part of her gut. Even though her life had taken a tragic turn ten years ago, that hurt had never disappeared, it had only numbed.

She sat up straight and took a deep breath. "Of course. I am the daughter of a compulsive, unrepentant gambler. I don't have a single memory of my dad when he wasn't holding a pack of cards or dice." She let out a little laugh. "It's funny, for most kids, the sound of dice clacking together conjures up images of board games and fun. For me, it meant he was betting on something, anything. He'd bet on whether or not you took your next breath. His addiction led him down some dark paths, and I kept expecting him to just not come home one night. Deep down, I always believed it would be the death of him."

"Is he still alive?" Audrey asked, her voice a whisper.

"To be honest, I'm never sure. Once I left home, I couldn't allow myself to obsess over him anymore. I had to put him behind me. We don't really keep in touch. Most of the time, I can't be certain he's not lying in a ditch somewhere. But then every so often, he pops up again...usually to ask for money. And on the worst nights, when I'm not my better self, I prefer thinking he's in a ditch." When she spotted Audrey's frown, she twitched her lips into something she hoped resembled a grin. Got to keep the spirits up.

"That's the problem with our gamblers," Rod joked. "They refuse to die."

Audrey shuffled in her folding chair. She clearly

didn't share his black humor, a defense mechanism.

"Anyway," Kate continued, "Despite my dad's issues, my mom never divorced him, no matter how I pleaded with her. I'd hoped, maybe if he knew he'd lose her, he might…"

The door to the program room swung open and Lisa joined the group, her face pale. Her oldest friend from New Horizons, Lisa had warned her she might not make their session that evening. It was ultimatum night for her husband, and she'd planned to offer him a choice: his family or gambling. From the haunted look on her face, he'd made the wrong choice.

"Group, take ten," said Kate, standing. She rushed over to Lisa. "Well?"

"I did it. The kids are at my mom's. We're staying with her for a while."

Kate drew her in for a hug. "Oh, sweetie, I'm proud of you. I know it's hard."

Lisa stood still for a moment, her spine as straight as a ballerina's. But then she sucked in a breath and collapsed into her, weeping into her shoulder. "Donny acted like he didn't care. He just raided my purse and walked out. He didn't even look back."

"It's better this way, I swear."

"I know. I just…I didn't expect it to hurt so much." She raised her head and wiped her face with the back of her hand. "I've spent the last few years wishing he'd fall off the face of the earth, and it pisses me off to be so upset." She let out a bitter laugh. "After I dropped off the kids, I had a hunch and decided to look for him. He was exactly where I expected him to be—one of Liam Doyle's poker tables, joking with the dealer as if he didn't have a care in the world. He didn't even notice me."

It seemed she heard the words 'Liam Doyle' in every New Horizons meeting lately. Frankly, she was getting sick of it. If she ever met the bastard…

"Kate, what am I going to do? There's so much to think about. Bank accounts, the mortgage. And the kids keep asking for their dad." She ran a hand over her pale, wet face. "I can't do this alone."

She held Lisa by the shoulders and looked into her friend's eyes. "You're not alone. I will be with you every step of the way. And you'll get through this, I promise." She sighed, but rather than lightening, her heart felt heavier for it. "Come have a coffee. It won't fix anything, but it'll make you feel more human."

Her friend offered a watery smile. "I wouldn't have been able to do it if it hadn't been for your example, Kate. Every time I wanted to cave, I remembered how you cut your father off. How you told him no and stopped giving him money. I kept thinking, 'I need to be strong like Kate.' He needs to hit rock bottom."

She stared at Lisa as an insidious sick feeling wormed its way through her.

Strong like Kate. What a laugh.

Lisa hugged her and wandered to the coffee table, where the rest of the group flocked around her, eager to help.

It took Kate a second to realize her hands were shaking, and by that time she knew she was good and angry. It felt better than feeling guilty, and she'd stopped being sad a long time ago. Sadness didn't help, but anger felt good. Anger helped her focus and forced her to see clearly.

What she saw in her memory was a seven-year-old girl crying as her parents argued outside her bedroom. She heard her mother's voice, begging her father not to go to his usual haunts.

But her father always went out, and some nights he didn't even come back. Instead, he'd stumble home the next morning, or days later, usually with his wallet empty. Granted, he'd never frequented luxurious casinos like Liam Doyle's. Her dad had been more the type to lose himself in a dingy back room card parlor. Not that it mattered. Different location, same vice. Kate had seen it again and again, and now she had to watch her friend experience the same misery.

The most ridiculous part was Lisa regarding *her* as a fucking role model.

Most days, she vacillated between blaming herself and blaming Vegas. It was so much easier to blame those who made gambling possible. Then she didn't have to examine her own actions. Her own choices.

As her fury once again took root, she sought an outlet, *any* outlet that turned the spotlight away from her past. As a newly-unemployed jingle singer, she didn't have the resources to launch a full-scale war on Vegas. God knew the casinos would be there until the end of time.

But she knew how to cause a stink. She'd always had a bit of rebel in her.

As she searched her brain for a target, she found

only one. Suddenly, her anger had a face. A pretty one with devil's horns, much like how she imagined Liam Doyle's.

***

Liam stood alone in his office suite at the newly-built Vice, his crowning achievement. In five minutes he would head outside, cut a big ribbon, smile, and welcome Las Vegas into what he knew would become its hottest property.

So why wasn't he pumped? When he opened Sin, he'd been delirious. When he opened Luxe, he'd been happy. But now?

Maybe the novelty had worn off.

Yet for some reason his pulse felt erratic. He took a long look at himself in the full-length mirror in the office bathroom and breathed deep, hoping to steady his off-kilter heartbeat. Dr. Chan said he worked too hard, and it was taking its toll.

No, it was just a strange case of nerves. Preparing for a grand opening forced his body into a state of hyper-awareness, like a runner before a track meet. Hell, he hadn't had a good sleep in weeks. Between dealing with designers and kitchen staff and suppliers, he was bound to be on edge.

He just couldn't afford to show it.

He looked himself up and down. The well-dressed, serious man who stared back from the mirror showed no outward signs of nervousness. His suit, ordered from Cad and the Dandy, his favorite Savile Row tailor in London, was pressed to perfection. His shoes gleamed, and his silver cufflinks shone under the office lights with what his stylist Xavier called "understated elegance." Damned if he knew what that meant, but apparently he was supposed to be the embodiment of it.

He adjusted his signature navy silk tie, chosen from his armada of navy silk ties. Xavier was always trying to get him to expand his color range, but Liam liked navy. If he had to wear a suit, it had to include a navy tie. Sure, he would have been more comfortable in jeans and cowboy boots, but Xavier demanded he look the part of a shark today. As the stylist had stated, "You can go back to being scruffy tomorrow."

Today, as he opened Vice, even he conceded scruffy wasn't appropriate. Vice would be his greatest achievement yet in the town where he was born. His other casinos did very well, but his marketing team had ensured the hype for this new property would launch him into the stratosphere. Already people demanded to get in, and after today, *everyone* would know Liam Doyle.

The build had gone off without a hitch. His designers had delivered on their promises of excellence. Everything was ready. The dealers, poised on the floor, waited for the first customers to flood in. The catering heads stood at the ready, with the finest of Vegas fare on their menus.

They just needed to open the door.

He almost allowed himself a small smile of satisfaction, but then he heard *her* voice in his head.

I don't want you. I never wanted you. The sooner you get used to the idea, the better.

Fuck. How was it she always managed to cut

through his pride and savage his serenity?

Now her face appeared in his mind's eye, smiling but cold. As in all his visions of her, she shut the car door that final time, leaving him alone on the sidewalk, her perfume lingering like a fragrant insult.

Liam clenched his fists, forcing the memory away. *Why are you thinking about her now? She's nothing to you.*

He wiped at the perspiration on his brow and took a few cleansing breaths. He could do this. He'd done it before, and he'd do it again, creating avant-garde casino-hotels the world would remember long after he was gone. His properties would be his legacy, and a hard-won vindication to the one who deserted him all those years ago.

If only he didn't feel her name was secretly inscribed on the cornerstone of each of his hotels. If only he didn't feel they were secretly hers, that he owed her his success.

No, he owed no one. No more dwelling in the past. He had a casino to open.

Finally granting himself that one little smile, he turned away from the mirror and headed for his office elevator.

The elevator opened before he could summon it. Wade Kennedy, his head of security, normally took care of problems before they ever got to his door. A capable and intimidating man, Wade didn't come to him like this unless he felt an incident warranted his special attention.

"Uh, Liam. We seem to have a situation outside." Wade nodded toward the office window, the one with the best view of the front entryway.

From his fourth-floor kingdom, Liam could survey all who would enter Vice. He liked it that way, and had all his casino offices designed in similar fashion. He liked the energy, liked seeing the crowds as they lined up to get into his hotels, especially at night when the city lit up. He got up from his desk and walked to the window, with Wade following.

He might have expected to see any number of interesting sights: impatient crowds, brawling drunks, cabbies fighting over the best spot. Hell, he might even have expected to see Shania Twain riding up on a horse. The last thing he expected was a picket line.

Or rather, one picketer, standing off to the side, motioning at the waiting customers.

He spared a glance for the hand-painted message on the picket sign:

GAMBLING DESTROYS FAMILIES. SHAME ON YOU, LIAM DOYLE!

He turned to Wade. "Seriously? This is our situation? Just get rid of him."

"Her. It's a her."

"Okay. Get rid of her then." He stepped around Wade's bulky body and headed for the elevator.

"Liam, I tried everything short of throwing that little hell raiser over my shoulder. She won't budge." The man threw up his hands. Liam had never seen him so frustrated before. Wade had broken up numerous fights between enormous, inebriated men in his casinos. Why should he be flummoxed by a lone, female picketer?

"Call the police and get her off my property. It's that simple."

"I threatened to do that, but she's not actually *on* your property. She's on the sidewalk."

In an attempt to preserve the boutique hotel experience, the architect had suggested a design in which the entrance remained close to the sidewalk. "It's all about clean lines, Liam," the architect had said. "It has a fresh, New York feel." He'd compared the design to the one he created for Liam's pal, Alex Markov, a club owner whose bars were the talk of the Big Apple.

He hadn't considered whether the design would make things nice and cozy for a sidewalk protest. Damn. Is this what he had to look forward to? His *clean lines* made it easy for the whack jobs to access the entrance.

Wade continued. "She has a copy of the city by-laws with her and keeps quoting government shit at me. When I told her I was calling the cops, she laughed and said, 'Go ahead, big boy. This is a peaceful protest. I know my rights.' And she's right. She's not obstructing pathways. She's not forcing leaflets on the customers. She's just…there."

Wade frowned like a cartoon bear who'd had his honey snatched away. "She's been lecturing me, telling me I should be ashamed of working for you. Told me I should get a job that doesn't steal food out of babies' mouths. *Go work for Cirque du Soleil*. She…she hurt my feelings, man."

Liam stared at the man who'd been his best

17

employee for years, brought low by a single woman. As Wade's face turned seven shades of red, Liam decided he needed to take another look at this hellion on the sidewalk. He approached the window again, planted his hands on the ledge, narrowed his eyes at her, and glared.

At first he'd only observed the picket sign and its inflammatory message. Now as he looked at the woman carrying it, surprise made him want to draw closer. He'd expected to see some aging hippie in Birkenstocks. What he saw instead made him want to dust off his old, trusty pick-up lines.

He couldn't make out every detail, but he saw the important things: a severe, red ponytail and the kind of curves that would make Rubens reach for his paintbrush. He stared at her face as she chanted to anyone passing by. Her eyebrows were drawn together in a face made deep pink with ire. Hell, even from four floors up, he could see the tops of her ears flush. She looked like a sexy elf, the kind they drew in Japanese cartoon porn.

And the elf woman was pissed. At him.

He looked away from the harridan and turned to Wade. "Who the hell is she?"

"She won't tell me her name. She says she'll only speak to you."

Liam let out a scornful laugh and paced back to his desk, throwing himself into his chair. He bit his fingernail, an old habit that tended to manifest when he was nervous. Although why this elf woman should make him nervous was beyond him.

"Tell her I don't negotiate with terrorists, then get rid of her. On any other day, I wouldn't care.

But on my grand opening? This doesn't look good."

"But…"

"No buts, Wade. For Christ's sake, she's just an itty bitty girl. You've handled the rowdy sons of mob bosses."

"I know, but there's something about her. I can't put my finger on it, but she…sorta makes me wanna hug her." Staring at the floor, still red in the face, Wade summoned the elevator, got in, and left.

Hug her? What the fuck? Liam spent the next few moments staring at the elevator and rubbing his chest, mystified. It was like he'd hired a professional hitman only to find out he had a soft spot for puppies.

Liam went back to the window and stared at the elf again. A strange pitching sensation assaulted him, one that had nothing to do with his grand opening. He couldn't put his finger on it either.

But, unlike Wade, it didn't put him in a hugging mood.

***

Kate spied the security goon as he came back outside again. He'd spoken to Doyle. About her.

Good. He knew she was here. He might even be watching her right now. Well, she'd put on a good show for him.

Clenching her fingers around her placard, she called to the security guard. "Back for more, big boy?"

He grunted. "You need to leave, lady. Now."

"Why? Because your *boss* says so?" She raised

her voice so tourists by the black marble entryway could hear her. "Is the great and powerful Liam Doyle afraid to come tell me off himself? I'm not going anywhere until I talk to that crook."

"My boss isn't a crook. Ask anyone who works for him."

"Yeah, and my tail is purple." She turned away from the man and called out to a woman approaching the front door. "Excuse me, ma'am. Did you know that compulsive gambling causes emotional distress to countless people and tears families apart? Children are sitting at home, right now, crying for their addict parents to come home."

The woman turned to her husband, her voice a nervous quaver. "Derek, maybe we should go to the Bellagio instead. They have a fountain in front, not a crazy lady. She might *do* something when we come out." They turned on their heels and headed back to the Strip.

Kate sucked in a breath, too excited to be offended. Okay, she hadn't turned them off gambling, she wasn't expecting to, but she'd turned them away from Doyle's establishment. Score one for the crazy lady. Maybe she had a new career unfolding on the pavement outside Vice: professional rabble-rouser.

The security guard turned pale. "Oh, lady. You need to stop."

She lowered her placard for a moment and came up to the monster of a man, though careful to remain on the sidewalk. She eyed his name tag and smiled. "Wade. You seem like a nice person. Do you gamble?"

"Nah. I like my money in my pocket."

"Then you understand. My friend's husband has lost thousands of dollars in Doyle's casinos. Money that should have gone to supporting their children. She had to leave him because it was getting so bad." She patted down the lapel of his suit. "So please believe me when I say I'm not going anywhere. Not until I talk to Liam Doyle." She batted her eyelashes at him, not above using whatever feminine charms she might possess. "Now, are you going to arrange a little meet-and-greet, or am I going to keep embarrassing him on opening day?"

"Uh…"

"As I expected." She marched back to her spot on the walkway, raised her sign, and called out to passers-by. "Gambling destroys families! Vegas doesn't need another casino! Shame on you, Liam Doyle!"

* * *

Liam loosened his tie as he once again returned to the window and appraised his red-haired enemy. She hadn't gone away all day, had remained for hours with her tatty sign, repeating the same childish chants, hassling his new customers as they tried to enter Vice.

She'd put up enough of a stink that his marketing team had been forced to improvise. Rather than hold the ribbon-cutting outside, they'd ushered VIPs and customers toward the expansive main lobby. There, speaking from the mezzanine, rather than the attractive dais outside, Liam had welcomed

21

his first visitors to great applause. He'd even cracked a joke about his lone protestor and had been rewarded with sympathetic laughter.

Despite the general excitement and press about the grand opening, it hadn't gone as well as he'd envisioned. That pissed him off. He hated when people screwed with his plans, hated losing control.

And she was still there. Even though he'd personally spoken to the police, they wouldn't do anything to remove the pesky woman. They confirmed she'd broken no laws, and with worse crimes happening all up and down the Strip, the police department had been unwilling to spare a couple of officers to cart her round ass away. Christ. The experience made him miss the days when the police were in the pocket of men like him. After bribing the right people, he might have actually gotten some service.

Liam stared out his office window, watching Wade try once again to cajole the female picketer. She ignored him and continued to pound the sidewalk, on a mission to drive him nuts. Didn't she have a job? A life? Maybe someone paid her to harass the tourists as they attempted to have a little fun in his casino?

Maybe that was it. Ever since he broke ground on his first casino, he'd made the old boys of Vegas nervous. He knew for a fact some other casino owners resented him as an upstart. A couple had even tried to get him thrown out of Chamber of Commerce meetings because they saw him as a threat.

He'd recognized the art of the deal at a young

age, purchasing derelict buildings at a steal and revamping the sites. In attracting a younger, hipper crowd, he'd alienated some of the old guard. Perhaps one of them had decided the best way to force him off the Strip was to hire a ginger hellion with a hefty chip on her shoulder.

Naw, why would they hire just one? Tons of starving actors around to organize something more impressive than that.

"Ignore her," he almost growled to himself like a tiger prowling its cage. And yet time and again, he was drawn to his window to see if she was still there.

He trudged over to his desk, but didn't manage to do much more than shuffle the headshots of famous singers he considered booking. He hadn't yet found the right talent for Vice's soon-to-be-opened piano bar, Decadence. Even major headliners had campaigned for the spot. He didn't want a superstar, though. He preferred to keep his venues free from the circus-type atmosphere plaguing other Vegas casinos. It was better to remain a little mysterious and sophisticated, and he needed a singer who would add to that ambience.

Having a lunatic on the sidewalk did *not* lend an air of sophistication. Gritting his teeth, he tossed the photos back onto his desk and stalked back to the window.

Wearing an outfit that would have made Xavier salivate with the need to "reinvent" her, she continued to march and watch. Cropped jeans hugged her ass. A striped blouse made her resemble a candy striper. Completing an ensemble which shouldn't have looked sexy, but somehow did, was a pair of sneakers. When she turned, he spotted how the top two buttons were undone, and wondered what her cleavage would look like up close and personal.

"Jesus Christ. She's a damned nut job. Stop fantasizing about the shape of her tits, you moron."

He went back to the headshots at his desk, flipping through them with disinterest, but his thoughts soon turned to the redhead outside. He tossed the entire group of photos into a drawer with disgust.

She'd messed with his day. Now she was messing with his brain. Time to act.

He removed his tie, suit vest, and cufflinks. He then rolled up his shirt sleeves and unfastened the top two buttons on his shirt. Content that he resembled most men at the end of a hard day's work, he marched to the elevator, summoned it, and got inside.

As it dropped, he grew aware of how his heart thumped in his chest, but attributed it to heading into battle. He smiled, more than ready to spar with her.

Once outside, he put a finger to his lips when Wade spotted him. His security specialist nodded, and hustled back inside, more than ready for a break. Shoving his hands in his pockets, Liam approached her.

The first thing he noticed was how the late-day sun shone on her golden-red highlights. He'd only ever seen that color in one other place, in the sky, just as the sun dipped below the horizon. How was he supposed to maintain control when she looked like a fucking sunset?

He meandered toward her and forced a smile. "You seem to have had a busy day."

She whipped around and her eyes widened. He saw her give him a quick once-over. Did she like what she saw? Interesting. There was some perverse satisfaction in that.

"It has been busy." She narrowed her hazel eyes at him. "Do you work here?"

So, she didn't recognize him. Good. "Yes, ma'am, I do." He crossed his arms over his chest and nodded, noting how her gaze dropped to his exposed forearms. Her lips parted. Clearly, working out had its merits. "And word inside is you've upset the big boss."

Her nostrils flared as she dragged her gaze away from his arms. "About time." She put her sign down and picked up her purse. "Do you know Liam Doyle?"

"I've heard one or two things about him."

She stepped closer and her lips did the most amazing thing, curling into a flirtatious semi-smile. "I don't suppose you'd be willing to share them with me? The other guy kept on sucking up about him as if he was wearing a wire." She paused. "You're not wearing a wire, are you?"

He laughed out loud. He couldn't help it. This was way too much fun. He sidled close to her, leaned in conspiratorially, and put a hand on her elbow. Her very soft elbow. "I'm not wearing a wire. But are you sure you want to know the truth about Doyle? I don't know if you can handle it."

She gawked at him and then at his lips. Her voice came out in a whisper. "Try me."

He murmured in her ear, taking note of her lilac scent. "Well, I hear at midnight he sprouts black wings and horns. And he's always searching for innocent maidens to add to his coven." He bit on his bottom lip, suddenly wishing he was gnawing on hers.

At first, her eyelids did this fluttery thing that made his imported pants spring to life. But then she blinked and began to laugh. "And here I thought I was dealing with a mere businessman. I didn't realize Doyle was cousins with Lucifer."

"What's your name?"

She regarded him from out of the side of her eye, her mouth still bearing the same flirty grin. "What's yours?"

"Consider me a friend who wants to give you some advice."

The smile disappeared from her face. "And what would that be?"

"Don't mess with Liam Doyle. He doesn't take to it kindly."

The coquettish shine in her eyes hardened. "Is that a threat?"

"No, sugar. That's not my style."

"What exactly do you do here? Are you in security?"

"Never mind that." He waved his hand. "Look, you've had your fun. Why don't you run along home now?"

She reached for her sign and tucked it under her arm. "I will go where I damn well please. And you

can tell your friend Mr. Doyle to expect me
tomorrow. Maybe next time he'll be brave enough
to confront me himself." She turned on her heel and
walked down the manicured pathway leading to the
taxi bay.

Liam stared at her ass as she walked away.
Brave?

Game on, sugar. He'd show her brave.

***

As promised, she returned the next day, bright
and early. At first Liam ignored her, but by mid-
day, he finally leaned on his windowsill and
allowed himself to take her in. Trying to dispel the
annoying case of lust that had plagued him ever
since talking to her, he pried his gaze away and
looked at the people around her.

She had attracted a little crowd of gawkers today.
Word must have spread about the asylum escapee
holding vigil outside Vice. Some of the bystanders
had their camera phones out. Wonderful. She could
end up going viral. A few patrons had already
begun to complain. It wouldn't be long before she
started driving them away.

Reporters from the local news stations had begun
asking questions too. That was perhaps the worst
thing possible. He'd done his best to deflect
attention away from the red-haired elf and toward
the delights of Vice, but he hated that she'd
hijacked some of his press. He watched as yet
another press vehicle pulled into his lot. Shit. Was
that one of the hounds from that crap Vegas

morning radio show? He did not subscribe to the "any publicity is good publicity" school of thought. Before long, he'd have Kardashians begging invites from him.

All this because of one woman. One.

He needed to get rid of her, but Wade had proven unwilling to do the job. Dammit. Wade might patrol the casino like a bloodthirsty gladiator, putting the fear of God into all would-be cheats and hustlers, but it seemed he had a soft spot for the ladies. Or this lady at any rate. After spending the better part of his day talking to her yesterday, and dealing with her again today, Wade was practically friends with her.

It was about time he handled this situation himself, and this time he wouldn't withhold his identity. She wanted to talk to Liam Doyle? She was about to get her wish.

If his business and his life had taught him anything, it was everyone had a price. You could buy anything with cold-hard cash. Even absolution.

He could tell she'd been attracted to him yesterday, even though their conversation had ended on a sour note. He'd seen her pupils and the way she wet her lips while flirting with him. If he had to, he'd use that attraction to his advantage.

Hell, he might even enjoy it.

He called Wade on the phone and told him to bring the redhead inside. As soon as he made the summons, all his blood seemed to rush to his crotch.

Well, damn.

When did his crotch develop a taste for confrontation?

Chapter Two

The doorman smiled at Kate, greeting her as she walked in with Wade. "Welcome to Vice."

"Um, thanks."

You don't have to be nice to these people, she told herself. *If you let down your guard, they'll have you drunk at the roulette table before you know it.*

Even still, when the guard held open the door for her, she thanked him. It was just in her nature. Yes, she might have channeled her inner badass for a while, but she'd always been a mild-mannered woman, the kind who said "excuse me" when she bumped into people. Life may have dealt her some shitty cards, but she'd always believed in being polite.

Shitty cards. Even her inner dialogue seemed rife with gambling metaphors. Just another reason New Horizons remained so important to her. She'd often felt used and undervalued, but the group had taught her that her father's gambling addiction was not her fault. She'd learned those lessons so well she'd been given her own group to lead.

29

New Horizons wasn't run by doctors or psychologists. It had begun as a grassroots collective who shared tragic circumstances. As her mentor had once explained, all one really needed to help others was empathy. For people such as herself, Kate had loads of empathy and advice.

Even if she had trouble putting it into practice herself.

However, since she'd turned her anger toward the unlikely target of Liam Doyle, she felt she had a new purpose in life. A way to make amends. She might not be able to fix her own life, but she could help Lisa and others like her. At the very least, it was a way to strike back at the addiction that had razed her family.

As she walked with Wade, she wondered about the man who'd talked to her at the end of the day yesterday. The amazingly-edible man who'd made her doubt her own senses. He'd warned her off in a deep voice that had scared her a little, but made her want to draw nearer. That man was the closest thing she'd ever seen to a living, breathing orgasm. She wondered what he did in the casino. Would she see him inside?

It was best to forget him. She didn't care for men who had the whole pompous, Alpha male thing down to a fine art anyway. The sort who looked as if they'd turn you over their knee before relinquishing the slightest bit of control.

She followed the security guard into the casino, shaking her head and trying not to gawk. However, it was hard not to. She'd been in a lot of casinos, but only the old ones on Fremont Street. Her dad had dragged her along many times when she was a kid, desperate for a fix and unable to wait for her mom to come home. He'd tuck her into a chair at the slot next to him and proceed to ignore her for hours while she sucked back second-hand smoke.

She'd seen things no kid should see, and had spent every waking moment since trying not to fix her gaze on the inside of a casino. No easy task in Las Vegas.

Vice seemed nothing like her memories of those old, smoke-filled casinos. Oh, there was smoke. It wafted over their heads like a second hazy ceiling. Allergic to the smell, she coughed into her hands a couple of times, but it did little to dispel the feeling she was slowly choking.

Ignoring the painful prickle in her throat, she looked around the immense room. Black-tinted windows and an absence of clocks gave a sense of time standing still. Soft LED light displays flashed everywhere, bright but never gaudy, guiding the unfortunate to their next sin. Well-dressed men and women flirted over their fancy cocktails.

She wasn't sure what was prettier, the people or the drinks. Wonderful aromas teased her from various corners of the cavernous space, temporarily dispelling the smell of smoke, and she spied the names of some of the city's best restaurants over various doors.

Plush chairs and couches littered the rooms, tempting people to sit and spend money on more things they couldn't afford. Expensive artwork hung on every wall, and gorgeous bronze sculptures of nude goddesses were perched on several pedestals in the lobby. She eyed one of the sculptures, raising her brows at the artfully-upturned nipples of Venus.

It was beautiful in a decadent sort of way. She struggled to keep up with the security guard, almost losing her way around a couple of corners. Clearly designed to make one meander, a gambler could spend hours in the facility and never see it all.

Despite the sense of titillation it created, it remained her version of hell.

It felt like hours before they made it to a private elevator. She snatched a grateful breath as they escaped the smoke. The guard swiped a couple of cards to give him clearance, and pressed the number 4 button.

Kate didn't say anything, suddenly feeling out of her league, and she just stared at the polished elevator door. As the automated voice announced each floor with the alluring finesse of a phone-sex operator, Kate felt perspiration gather on her upper lip. With a discreet hand, she wiped it off.

It was no secret Liam Doyle was a very rich man. Richer than she could ever hope to be. Little was known about his early life, but he was regarded as a *wunderkind*, the Mark Zuckerberg of gaming. Not that she made a point of reading about him, his name was just that hard to avoid.

He probably came from money and had everything handed to him on a silver platter. No doubt his attitude matched his trust fund. He probably sprinkled caviar on his corn flakes. And here she was, the first person in her working-class family to go to college. What on earth would she say to the wily entrepreneur? *Uh, hey, Mr. Casino*

Owner. How about closing up shop?

Yeah, that would go over well.

No, she would simply impart to him, in a reasonable manner, how establishments such as his exploited the weaknesses of others. As a leading member of the gaming community in the gambling capital of the world, he had a responsibility to those left behind. People like Lisa. People like herself. What was he doing for them?

When the elevator opened, she expected her escort to show her into a stuffy waiting room and leave her there alone to sweat for a few hours. However, the door opened into an open-concept office that seemed to take up a whole floor. With its professional kitchen area, fireplace, and cozy leather couches, it resembled a grandiose loft more than an office. Did Doyle live here too?

Beyond the large office, she spied a few closed doors, no doubt leading to the private chambers where he seduced young maidens. She stifled a snort as she imagined cold, stone torture chambers behind those doors, with racks and whips and other such implements.

For God's sake, you sound delirious now.

Wade showed her to one of the couches and motioned for her to sit. Eyeing the expensive Italian leather, she chose to stand. Warriors of old preferred to hold the high ground, and so would she.

"Fine," Wade grunted. "I'll get Mr. Doyle. Please wait here." She watched as he escaped behind a door, shutting it behind him. He came back a moment later, threw her a look, and left in the elevator.

As the long seconds ticked away, Kate shuffled on her feet. She tried not to look around, tried not to notice the gleaming patina on the stainless steel appliances and the massive antique desk, but his obvious riches were hard to ignore. Was that an original Picasso on the wall?

She smoothed down her tunic and toed a smudge off one of her Keds. She turned to one of the picture windows. "Don't be nervous," she said to herself. "So he has money. So what? He's just a man, not a fricking Pharaoh."

Footsteps sounded behind her. "You're right. If you want a Pharaoh, you can try the Luxor down the road, but I'm pretty sure they don't have one either. And if they do, he's just an actor."

His deep voice stirred something inside her. She chalked it up to righteous indignation and spun on her feet to face him, ready to wage war.

No. It couldn't be. Not *him*.

She stared at Doyle, mouth open, to make sure she could trust her eyes. But yes, everything was the same. Silky brown hair, cut short. Blue eyes like those of a Husky. Tall, with substantial muscles hiding under his designer suit.

Dragging her gaze away from his arms, she forced herself to make eye contact again. His features stymied her with their rakish perfection. With the hint of a beard dotting his sculpted jawline and the shimmer of amusement in his eyes, he resembled a soap opera villain: the kind who let vulnerable women dangle in his clutches.

The kind who played games.

She'd have to be careful. She could tell he was a

man who was accustomed to getting what he wanted. *Well, not this time, bucko.*

"You," she said on a breath.

"Me." His enticing blue eyes traveled up and down the length of her, one eyebrow raised in frank admiration. "You obviously didn't do your homework."

Outrage surged through her system. "Why didn't you tell me who you were yesterday? Why did you let me embarrass myself like that?"

The smirk disappeared, to be replaced by a mild expression of boredom. "There's no need to be embarrassed. I always try to size up the competition."

Doyle walked toward her, his large hand extended. The light in his eyes now hinted not so much at merriment as it did danger. She caught a whiff of her favorite men's cologne by Michael Kors. She'd bought it for an old boyfriend once, but it smelled way better on Liam, as if it were an extension of his persona.

His entire ensemble, designer suit, pressed pants, and navy blue paisley tie, reeked of power and privilege that drew her like a moth to a flame. Damn, she'd always been a sucker for a man in a good suit. *Get a hold of yourself, Kate. He's hot, but so is the Devil.*

He kept his hand out. "Please allow me to introduce myself properly. I'm Liam Doyle." His gaze drifted toward her neckline and back up again. "I think you've heard of me."

Wishing she didn't have to, she took his hand. Electricity shot through her and that damned perspiration appeared on her upper lip again. His grip was that of a man who took what he wanted, when he wanted.

She held her head high. "Kate Callender."

He held her hand for a moment, his gaze locked on hers. He then gestured toward the counter, where a teak tray was laden with biscuits and what smelled like expensive coffee. No Folgers crystals for this guy. "Coffee?"

"No, thank you."

"Tea?"

"No."

"So we're done with the niceties, then?"

"I didn't come here for niceties."

"Then you've come to the right place." Liam sat on one of the couches, motioning for her to do the same. She continued to stand. Something in his wolf-like gaze hardened even further. "Ms. Callender, why are you picketing my casino?"

His direct question set her even more on edge. She cleared her throat. "I have a right to protest what I see as wrong."

His grim smile might have made a grown man sweat, but she didn't look away. "Let me put this another way. Las Vegas is home to numerous casinos. Why mine?"

"If I'm trying to make a point, it only stands to reason I'd pick the most popular casino. I suppose I should congratulate you. Only open for two days, and Vice is already a hit. You must be so proud."

"Yes. Despite having my grand opening spoiled."

"Oh." She inclined her head in mock sympathy.

"I'm *so* not sorry."

He peered at her, narrowing his eyes. "Are you a Bible-thumper?"

"No."

"Campaigning politician?

Despite her unease, she laughed. "Do I *look* like Hilary Clinton?"

He looked her up and down, as if her vocation were scrawled somewhere on her and he simply needed to find it. "Aspiring actress? This is probably a publicity stunt to get you viral on YouTube? Trying to get an audition here as a showgirl? Sorry, I don't use them. The whole concept is dated and demeaning to my female clientele."

Okay, he got some points for that statement. "I'm not a dancer. I'm a singer."

It was his turn to laugh. Despite the bitter tone, his deep timber called to her. "Same difference." He stood. "I'm not auditioning you, Ms. Callender, as fun as it would be to get you on the casting couch." And there he lost those points again. "Have a nice day."

"Wait! I'm not trying to get an audition. You need to listen to me." In a nervous reaction, she fingered the pearl choker at her neck, the one thing she had left of her mother. The one thing her father hadn't pawned.

Doyle turned back to her, one brow raised. "No, I don't." He eyed how she gripped her choker. "So you can take your fake pearl necklace and your sneakers and your attitude and go home."

Her attitude? "No. You let me up here. I'm not

leaving until you hear me out." She let go of the choker and let her hands fall to her sides. "And my pearls aren't fake."

"Why are you here, Ms. Callender? Did you lose money at one of my casinos on your last night out with the girls?"

She didn't want to dignify that with a response, but a smug statement like that couldn't go unchallenged. "I'm not a gambler."

He leaned against the armrest of the cushy couch and surveyed her through hooded eyes. "Ah, and now we come to the crux of the matter. So, you're a do-gooder. Let me guess. Gam-Anon?"

"New Horizons."

"Never heard of them."

"That doesn't mean we don't exist. And unfortunately, there are lots of us. Far too many. What does that tell you, Mr. Doyle?"

Liam's lips twitched into a smile that appeared slightly more friendly than his poker face, as if he enjoyed their banter. He loosened his tie, but his focused gaze continued to grate on her nerves. She stared at the strip of indigo silk at his throat, and was struck by a bizarre and unbidden image.

Her, on his bed. Her hands bound with his expensive tie.

The strange pounding in her head must have been her racing heart. *Where did that come from? Focus, Kate, focus.*

"I'm not just here because it's something I believe in. I'm here because my group gets bigger every goddamn week," she said, concentrating on the task at hand, rather than Liam Doyle's bed.

38

Lisa's sad face appeared in her mind, as well as those of her children, the ones who'd spent the last two nights crying for their daddy. Kate blinked away the tears which threatened and aimed her burning gaze at Doyle. "I don't respect your work, Mr. Doyle. And I don't respect you."

From the furrow of his brow, Kate thought she'd struck a nerve. His tanned skin seemed paler. After a moment, he said, "So you're trying to take down my casino with a one-woman picket line? No offense, but I've seen better protests at a garage sale."

"I'm trying to create awareness." Kate stood, having already had enough of their uncomfortable conversation. "I'm not a fool. My intention is not to shut down Las Vegas, or your casino. That'll never happen. But if I can make a small dent in the wallet of the Strip's wealthiest hustler during his opening week, then maybe people will take notice. Have you never thought about the addictions riding your customers? Have you ever spent time chatting with the compulsive gamblers downstairs? Because I bet you'd hear a lot of stories. And believe me, the worst ones are the ones they don't tell." She paused for breath. "My friend's husband is probably down there right now, feeding your slot machines instead of his kids."

"Hold on. Don't pin that on me."

"Oh? Who *do* I pin it on?"

"Look, if you want a donation, I already make plenty. Believe me, I make regular donations to people like Gam-Anon. You know, *legitimate* charities."

"I'm not here for money, but clearly you are." The words spilled out of her, kick-started by adrenaline. "You're a wealthy man. Did you have to open casinos? Were they such a passion for you? Couldn't you have opened, I don't know, a supermarket chain instead? Or was that not sexy enough for the great Liam Doyle?"

His lips compressed. Had her comment hit home? Good.

"You have no right…"

"I have *every* right." Her face was burning now. "If I can save even a few lost souls from places like this, then I'll sleep a whole lot easier."

She had to get out before she started crying. She wanted to leave with her head held high. Leave him thinking. She turned and headed for the elevator, but he grabbed her hand before she could get away.

"Wait."

Kate yanked her hand out of his grip. "How do you even sleep, Mr. Doyle?"

His eyes bored into her. "Like a rock. But that crown of thorns must keep you up at night."

She tried to appear like she was still in control, but that had hurt. "You just keep telling yourself that."

Kate marched to the elevator and punched the button. As the door opened, she threw a look back at him.

"By the way, I *will* be back. I'll show you how many lives have been devastated by your casinos." She walked into the lift, even though she felt like running. She didn't look back.

Liam called out to her. "Watch your step, Ms.

40

Callender. I don't forgive and forget."

She channeled her last ounce of bravado before the doors shut. "You really should see someone for that. I hear being an asshole can be terminal."

Once the elevator began its descent, Kate leaned against the back of the small space and closed her eyes, winded by her hostile exchange with Doyle. She didn't open them again until the door opened.

***

That night, Liam did sleep well—until about three a.m., when he woke with a pounding headache.

He stumbled out of bed, eager for a glass of water. He attributed the headache to any number of things. Despite little hiccups, the grand opening at Vice had gone smoothly. More bothersome was a recent rash of thefts at Sin, his first casino, ones that appeared to be an inside job. He treated his staff well, and nothing irked him quite as much as betrayal from those in his inner circle.

Been there, done that, didn't want to do it again. Thank God he could rely on his security team.

Then there was the problem getting permits for his next venture. Why city officials wanted to save that crumbling old government office off Fremont Street was beyond him. There was no way the derelict shell that used to house the old works department could be considered of historical significance.

On top of that was his issue with Bridget, his ex-girlfriend, and the way she continued to keep him away from the one person who meant anything to him, Michelle. Luckily, he had his new hotshot lawyer on the case, and it would soon be resolved to his satisfaction. Michelle would be back under his roof in no time, and not a moment too soon.

Christ, he missed her.

He rubbed his face. Yes, each of these issues had kept him up on previous nights. However, even as he padded through his condo on yet another night-time quest for water, he knew this time the ache in his brain had a different origin.

One with knockout curves and auburn hair.

Why on Earth should he be so affected by Kate Callender, the singer on a crusade?

I don't respect your work, Mr. Doyle. And I don't respect you.

Bull's-eye.

He'd been called a lot of things during his career, and knew full well many resented his meteoric rise in Vegas society, but no one had ever put so fine a point on it. He supposed it stung because in a town where there were no limitations, he'd always conducted business above board. Yes, he owned casinos. Yes, tons of folks out there had issues with gambling. Still, he didn't force those people into his clubs, didn't coerce them to spend their hard-earned dollars there. He simply provided venues for entertainment.

In fact, just as a good bartender kept an eye out for drunks, his employees were trained to watch out for customers who might also have had enough. He didn't like the idea of taking someone's last dollar. Ethics aside, it was bad for business. Kate Callender might see him as a mustache-twirling villain, holding bags of other people's money, but he knew the truth.

Vice, along with his other casinos, was merely a business venture, and he'd wager most of his customers knew when to call it quits. As for those who didn't? Well, that was why he sent a lot of money in Gam-Anon's direction.

So why did none of that seem to matter when faced with that silly woman's stinging barbs?

He poured himself a glass of water and chugged it, then set the glass in the sink and stared at it.

Damn. What did he care if she despised him? More important people already did. Kate Callender was no one to him and never would be. Just a momentary inconvenience, she would soon pass out of his life and he needn't think of her again.

Still, his mind wandered as he pictured her. Upon reflection, she hadn't been quite the ethereal creature he thought he'd spied from the fourth floor. She had flaws: a bountiful figure, a generous nose, and ears that, while sort of endearing in an annoying way, stuck out a bit. It was possible her eyes might even be somewhat asymmetrical, one a tiny bit smaller than the other. He'd noticed it when she glared at him.

However, on her, somehow it all worked. Like Cleopatra, she might not be the most beautiful woman in the world, but she wore her looks well.

They made a man curious.

He wanted to drag the ponytail elastic out of her hair and watch the red strands tumble around her shoulders. He could admit he felt a weird compulsion to touch her again to see if her skin was as soft as he remembered. And those hazel eyes that flashed in anger? He wondered what else could make them sparkle.

He was most intrigued by the flirt he'd seen in her eyes when he'd first approached her outside, and was intoxicated by the idea of seeing it again. He drummed his fingers on the counter, realizing he wanted to see much more than that. He wanted to see how her face would transform after he spread those voluptuous legs.

"Shit," he muttered to himself. "Okay, on some fucked up level you find her hot. So what? The woman wants to bury you. Forget her."

Determined to do just that, Liam fired up his laptop and set it on the counter. Plunking himself down on one of his bar stools, he decided to clear a few emails in an attempt to ignore his hard-on. Within minutes, his phone buzzed with an incoming text.

Bridget: We need to talk. Can I come to your office tomorrow?

Liam: Talk to my lawyer.

Bridget: Please.

Liam: I'm busy.

Bridget: I just want five minutes. No lawyers. Just us.

A pause.

I'll bring Michelle. You two can catch up.

He stared at the screen and willed himself not to get excited, not after his hopes had been dashed so many times.

Bridget: Liam? Are you there?

Liam: I'm here. Why should I trust you?

Bridget: Do you honestly think I'd fuck with you like that?

Liam: You have before.

Another pause.

Bridget: I'm sorry for what I did. You have to know that. Will you hate me forever?

Biting back anger, he lifted his thumbs from the key pad before he keyed something he would regret later. She thought a few clumsy apologies could do the trick?

He'd never forgive her.

And once his attorney, Nando Perreira of the famed Perreira, Michaels and Johnson was done with her, she'd understand exactly how unforgiving he could be.

Liam: You swear you'll bring Michelle? You've

reneged before.

Bridget: I swear.

He didn't believe her. It was just like Bridget to keep their daughter away from him. Scratch that— *her* daughter. She'd made it very clear Michelle wasn't his. She used her own child as a pawn and it sickened him, but it didn't lessen his need to see the little sprite.

He couldn't take that chance.

Liam: I have an opening at 4 p.m.

Bridget: Perfect. We'll see you then. Good night, Liam. Thank you.

Liam didn't reply. He had no words to describe his feelings, just a sick lump of dread in his gut.

Chapter Three

With barely a slurp of her beloved morning coffee, Kate hurried over to Lisa's mom's house. Lisa had had a bad night. After trolling the Strip looking for her wayward husband to ensure he wasn't dead in a back alley, she hadn't gotten much rest. Kate had insisted she stay home and get some sleep.

Lisa's mom worked the early shift in a fast-food taco joint just off the Strip, and couldn't take her grandkids to school that day, so Kate had volunteered to walk them to their bus stop. Luckily, she lived very close to their neighborhood and could powerwalk to the house.

A bleary-eyed Lisa met her at the door, holding two backpacks. Dark circles set in a wan face rimmed her pretty eyes. She offered Lisa a hug, and couldn't help but notice how her normally-lush figure seemed more fragile today. "Lisa, please tell me you're eating."

Lisa stared into the distance a moment, as if eating were a novelty. "Uh, yeah. I had a bit of

47

dinner last night."

"Which was?"

She blushed. "Half a Toaster Strudel."

Kate wished Donny were there so she could smack him in the head and knock some sense into him. She checked her watch. "How much time before the school bus comes?"

"Thirty minutes or so."

She put her hands on Lisa's shoulders and marched her back into the house. "All right, young lady." She guided her to the kitchen and made her sit in one of the chairs at the table. "Have Georgie and Sarah eaten?"

"I made them their favorite today. They're just brushing their teeth now."

Kate felt the need to stare her pal down. Leave it to Lisa to make sure her kids were washed and well-fed, while neglecting herself in the process. Once again, memories of her mother washed over her. Elspeth Callender had always taken pains to ensure Kate had what she needed growing up, while always denying herself. Kate fingered the pearl choker at her neck and silently vowed she wouldn't let Lisa go down the same path. She let out a deep breath. "Okay. You sit there and I'll throw a proper breakfast together for you. And I want you to promise you'll eat every bite before you go to bed."

Lisa managed a small smile. "I promise. Thanks."

Kate smiled. "No problemo."

The little kitchen was soon humming with the sounds of coffee brewing and toast popping. Keeping an eye on the clock, Kate plated her less-then-gourmet meal of whole-grain toast, poached eggs, and apple slices. She poured some coffee into a mug and added an extra teaspoon of sugar, because Lisa deserved a bit of sweetness too.

"Aren't you joining me?" asked Lisa.

"Nah. You go ahead."

"Still doing the gluten-free, carb-free, taste-free thing?"

"Just trying to get healthy. Although, between you and me, I'd trade my arugula salads for a peanut butter milkshake any day."

She laid the meal before her friend, but Lisa only picked at the food. "How did it go when you told your dad you weren't going to support his gambling anymore?" she asked. "I mean, did he say anything at all? Because Donny's response has me mystified. I need to know exactly what you did so I can do it too."

Kate tried not to look like a deer caught in the headlights. "Well..." she began in a tentative voice.

Luckily the kids chose that moment to descend from the upstairs bathroom. Kate breathed a sigh of relief. Sarah, a willowy eight-year-old, walked over and hugged Kate, saying nothing.

Kate kissed the top of her head. "Hey, kiddo. Ready for school?"

Sarah nodded and walked over to her mom, taking advantage of one more morning cuddle.

As something in her heart pinched, Kate plastered on her brightest smile and turned to the younger brother, Georgie. "You are definitely taller than yesterday, George, my man."

At six, Georgie contemplated this news with a

tilt of his head. He stood closer to Kate, measuring himself against her with his hand. "No, Auntie Kate. Look, my hand is still in the same place."

She threw up her hands in mock surprise. "Well, you look taller to me!" She rustled his hair. "Let's get you two to the bus stop."

Georgie tugged on her pant leg and whispered, "Do you know when Daddy's coming back?"

Kate crouched and whispered back. "Tell you what. When I find out, you'll be the first to know."

The little boy accepted her answer, but the two women shared a worried glance.

Georgie raised his voice. "Grandma says Daddy is a rat bastard."

In spite of trying to act like a proper role model, Kate snorted a laugh.

"Georgie," cried Sarah, as she slid off her mom's lap and picked up her backpack. "Those are bad words."

The little boy shrugged. "Grandma says them all the time. Why can't I say them?"

Lisa helped Kate bundle the pair toward the door. "Just don't say them at school, okay?" She kissed them both and wished them a good day. She then hugged Kate again. "Are you sure you don't mind picking them up later?"

"Nope. These are the joys of being unemployed. I can do whatever I want." She grinned. "Besides, didn't you know I'm a woman on a mission?"

"Oh, right." Lisa elbowed her in jest. "Your single-handed quest to take down Liam Doyle and his multi-million dollar empire."

"Hey, don't laugh. Yesterday I got an audience

with his Lordship."

Lisa did a double take. "Seriously?" She leaned in closer. "Is he really as sexy as they say he is?"

Kate bit her tongue, unwilling to admit the truth out loud. "He's okay, I guess. If you like his type."

"And what type is that?"

"Tall, dark, and predatory." She pulled herself up to her full height. "But that's neither here nor there. He's probably laughing behind my back, but I'll make him see his business for what it is. And if I can make Liam Doyle realize it, others will too."

"I admire you so much. You're a revolutionary, my friend."

Kate laughed. "I don't know about that. More like a single crazy person with a lot of free time on their hands. And besides, most revolutionaries usually end up with a bullet to the brain. I think I'd prefer a happier ending."

Lisa shrugged. "Well, you know you don't have to be a single crazy person out there. What's a revolutionary leader without a few die-hard followers?"

On that note, Kate led the kids outside and headed to the bus stop.

***

A few minutes later, Kate waved at the bus as it carried off her charges. She stood there for some time observing how the exhaust fumes drifted upward, polluting an already-polluted environment, reminding her of the smoke at Vice.

She roused herself into action and wandered

down the street toward the strip mall at the end. Bypassing her favorite coffee shop, she made a beeline for the Citibank branch. She willed herself not to check her mother's old bank account at the ATM, the one they'd never closed. She could just do her own banking like a normal person, instead of worrying what mischief her father was getting into.

Hating herself for even thinking about him, she fed the machine her bank card and punched in her PIN number. She checked out her balance and breathed a sigh of relief. For someone who didn't have a job, she still had money to her name—for now. Mr. Calvert might have fired her, but her royalties hadn't run out yet.

Thank God for her frugal nature. Sure, she coveted the Louboutins and Jimmy Choos like any red-blooded woman. She just didn't allow herself to indulge. After witnessing her father's descent over the years, she preferred to keep a tight lid on her funds.

She moved a few dollars around, transferring funds into her bill-paying account, printed the applicable receipts, and stared at them.

Old guilt tightened its stranglehold on her. She took out her mom's old bank card, inserted it, and checked the account her parents had shared. She printed the list of recent activity, all of which were debit transactions from the local casinos. Fifty dollars at Caesar's. Fifty at the Bellagio. Fifty at the Flamingo. Oh, and to make things even better, one hundred dollars at Vegas's newest attraction, Vice.

The list went on and on. The last deposit had been hers, two weeks back. She'd transferred over two thousand dollars, hoping he would use it for food or rent, and not poker chips.

Well, she'd always been a dreamer.

"Just take out the card and walk away," she urged herself. "Don't give him any more. He has to hit rock bottom."

A memory from her teen years flashed before her eyes. Her dad, coming home from work, pale and shocked. She'd run to him to ask what was wrong.

"Oh, Katie-bug," he'd cried. "Someone stole my wallet on the bus!"

"Oh, Dad, no. Are you sure?"

"Yeah. My credit cards, everything. I had it in my pocket. Someone must have reached in when I wasn't looking." He'd blanched. "Katie, my pay was in there. Five hundred cash, gone."

Her dad, a mechanic, worked for an old-timer who still paid his employees with cash—a major temptation for someone who gambled.

"I can't tell your mother. She'll be so disappointed in me. I was supposed to pay the bills this month." He'd looked at her, as if seized by a wonderful idea. "Katie, you have a bit of money saved up from your job, right?"

She did. She ran the local church choir and was given a small amount for her troubles. Not much, but it felt like untold riches to a kid.

"Loan me the money, sweetheart. I'll pay it back, I swear. Then we don't have to bother your mom with this business."

He'd walked her right to the nearest bank and watched as his child withdrew her own money for him. Before handing it over, she'd asked, "Dad, are you going to gamble with this?"

He'd had the gall to look affronted. "I can't believe my own daughter would ask me that. Didn't I raise you better?"

She'd handed it over and waited for the thanks that never came. And despite his many assurances, she'd never seen the money again.

She'd been enabling him, in one way or another, ever since. After her mom died, she worried about her dad's ability to take care of himself. For the past few years, she regularly put money in his account, convinced he was starving somewhere. Every time she checked the balance, the money was gone, used for bets.

And every week she spouted garbage to her New Horizons friends about cutting gamblers off, letting them hit rock bottom for their own good, and she hadn't let her father do the same yet.

She felt sure the word *coward* or *hypocrite* was tattooed over her face. How could she allow this pattern to continue? He'd disappointed her so many times, yet a small part of her waited for him to prove her wrong, to show her he was worthy of her love and trust.

Would it ever come?

She played with her finances a bit more, shaving off a bit more from her piddly savings. A lump formed in her throat as she deposited one hundred dollars into her father's account. It wasn't much. Maybe this time he'd put it to good use. Maybe. Her eyes stung as she yanked the bank card out of the machine.

Clutching her purse and blinking back tears, she

fled the bank.

***

Liam passed Kate on the way to his car the next morning. Headed to a meeting at City Hall, he was already in a bad mood, expecting push back from the city building department about his permit and worrying about his meeting with Bridget after that. Having to see Kate Callender's new sign just put the icing on an unpalatable cake.

DON'T LET LIAM DOYLE CONTROL YOUR POCKETBOOK!'

She made a big show of curtseying like a simpering courtier as he passed her on the walkway.

"How are you, Milord? Does the emperor need new clothes?"

"Funny. No, unlike you, I have places to go and people to see."

"Oh, I'm seeing lots of people right here. And guess what? They seem to like talking to me. I think I'm making some progress."

"How awesome you have a hobby." He ambled closer. "Tell me, Ms. Callender. Do all your goals involve sabotaging those of others?"

"Only this one," she said, smiling, her hazel eyes practically twinkling with mirth. "And something tells me, at the end of the day, you'll still be sitting pretty."

He couldn't resist grinning, just a little. "You think I'm cute, don't you?"

The twinkle in her eyes turned hard as she pointed to where one of his assistants waited with the Escalade. "I think you'd be cuter all the way over there in your penis-mobile. Tell me, is everything in your life so damned big?"

She reddened as soon as she realized how her question could be misinterpreted. Liam tried not to laugh. He leaned in and whispered, "Wouldn't you like to know?"

She looked away. "Not in the least."

He decided to let her off the hook. "As for the Escalade, it's just the work car. Would you believe my other car is a ten-year-old pickup?"

"Believe me when I say I couldn't care less."

This time he did laugh. She had spunk, he'd give her that. If she didn't irritate him so much, he might even like her. He waved as he left for his car. "Have a rewarding day, Ms. Callender."

"Oh, I will. Maybe not as monetarily rewarding as yours, but I'll be fine."

Liam couldn't resist one last jab. "Maybe?"

The look on her face made getting the last word in worth it. Stifling a grin, he got into the car and told the driver where to head. And then, because his dick demanded it, he stole another glance at her.

She wiggled her fingers at him in a way that set him even more on edge. As they drove off, he pictured taking those pretty hands and pinning them over her head as he found a home between her legs.

His hands grew clammy. He realized with startling clarity that the image would become reality. He knew it.

God help him. He *wanted* it.

***

Hours later, Liam watched from the fourth floor as Kate and her associates marched in front of the entrance to Vice. When he'd returned from City Hall, she'd accosted him again, promising him reinforcements were coming. Part of him had thought she meant the imaginary kind. Unicorns and fairies and centaurs. But true to her word, about fifteen people had shown up.

Her distinctly-human pals all had placards, and none appeared to be particularly loony. One man was even dressed in scrubs. Had she bribed a doctor to support her cause, or just rented a costume?

Curious in a way he knew he'd regret later, he left his office and headed outside once more, Wade following behind at a discreet distance. Something she'd said before niggled the back of his brain. She'd asked if he'd ever had a conversation with the people in his casinos, and he realized aside from focus groups and the odd drunk reveler, he hadn't really spent much time talking to his customers.

He wasn't a fool. He understood the severity of gambling addiction. He just didn't see much evidence of it in his casinos. The customers he'd spoken to had always seemed in control of their finances and appeared to know their limits. In fact, he was willing to bet the majority of his clientele were just out for a night of fun.

He was willing to play the odds and prove it to Kate Callender. He approached her little protest, and those around her didn't seem to know whether to get quiet or chant louder.

Kate hadn't seen him arrive. He tapped her on the shoulder. When she turned, he didn't give her a chance to talk. It was his turn now.

"Come with me."

She dropped her placard. "I'm busy, in case you hadn't noticed." Busy or not, she left with him, pulled by the elbow through the casino doors.

"Ten minutes, that's all I ask. Then you can go back to fighting the good fight." When he realized he was still holding her elbow, he let go and felt heat rush to his face. He turned to the gaming floor. "Let me tell you what I see, Ms. Callender. I see hundreds of happy people out there. Yes, they're spending money, but look at the smiles. They're glad to be here. It's a bit of fantasy, a dream. I provide that and when they're done, they go back to their humdrum lives with some exciting memories to share with their friends."

She sniffed. "Well, aren't you the philanthropist?" She turned to face the floor. "Let me tell you what *I* see, Mr. Doyle. See that man? The one with the red hair on the Mt. Olympus slot machine?"

"Yes."

"Don't you think there's anything odd about the look on his face? Anything strange about his posture?"

Liam studied the man. He noticed the man's glassy gaze, how he stared at the slot machine lights, but didn't seem to be taking them in. His shoulders might have been balls of nerves, he held his arms at such a tense angle. "What? He's concentrating."

"You're right, he is. He's concentrating on how to win, and can't think of anything else. See the way his jaw is set, the way his fingers are locked on the machine? He's desperate. He's compulsive, and has probably just lost his last dollar. So are you going to do the right thing and send him home now? A good bartender wouldn't let a drunk continue drinking."

Exactly the philosophy he imparted to his staff. Despite ensuring his employees followed it, he still felt defensive. Had they done enough? She didn't seem to think so. "My security staff knows to watch out for troublemakers."

"Oh, but he won't cause trouble. He's the perfect customer. He'll smile and pretend everything's okay, and then maybe tomorrow he'll stumble home, when he realizes he's pissed himself because he didn't want to leave his spot to go to the bathroom, because he's certain it's about to pay out. Maybe then he'll realize he's in debt as well."

"You paint a bleak picture."

"I didn't paint it, Mr. Doyle. People like you did." She looked him right in the eye, her mouth tight.

"Well, let me draw your attention to the ladies lining up to cash in their chips at the wicket." He pointed out a happy group of women in their thirties. "Look at them. This is probably the first trip any of them have had in years. Maybe they're on a getaway, maybe they're taking a break from their boring husbands or boring jobs. Whatever it is, they're practically bubbling over with excitement." He turned her attention to another couple. "And those two? They just came out of one of the theatres, having spent the last few hours watching a show, not gambling. Not everyone who orders a glass of wine at a bar is a drunk, Ms. Callender."

His tirade through, all he could do was stare at her. So many emotions lanced through him that moment, ones he didn't typically permit himself to feel. The tightness in her eyes soon softened into suspicious interest, but she quickly took the opportunity to escape, rushing back out the front entrance.

Cursing, Liam turned and watched the red-haired man at the slot machine. Okay, maybe Kate's depiction of compulsive gambling didn't apply to everyone in his clubs, but she wasn't wrong about the look of hopelessness on the man's face. Liam motioned for Wade to come over.

"Yes, boss?"

"See the man with the red hair? He's been here too long. Put him in a cab, charge it to the company account, and make sure he gets home."

"You got it."

Liam headed for his private elevator, still cursing to himself. Not because he'd lost a customer. No, because before Kate had fled, he'd seen her eyes water with angry tears.

And now he truly felt like shit.

So far, opening week for Vice was going down in his personal history as the worst one ever.

***

Near the end of the day, Liam was once again drawn to his window. Once again, Kate trod the pavement with her comrades-at-arms, waving at the customers headed inside the casino and shouting do-gooder vitriol.

Only now, a part of him cheered her on. He couldn't help it. He'd always loved an underdog. Hell, he could almost understand what Wade meant when he said he wanted to hug her. Almost.

Fuck. When did he become sympathetic to her cause? When she'd shone a light on the compulsive gambler in his casino. Now he couldn't stop thinking about her, about her motives and what inspired them. He needed to know.

He'd never been ignorant about the world of gambling. One couldn't live in Vegas and remain innocent. God knew how many of the homeless folks out on the Strip had begun their downward spirals in a casino. He knew it, better than most.

But in every walk of life, there were people who couldn't hack it. Didn't matter where you went, the same story played out everywhere in different ways. Some people climbed, others crashed. He'd risen above his own trials and had survived.

So what was it about gambling that filled Kate with such ire?

Why did he even care? He had too much on his plate for these games. It was time to wave goodbye to the protestor, and in order to do so, he needed to convince her and her friends to leave. She could deal with the bee in her bonnet in front of someone else's casino.

He paged Wade to come to his office. He didn't waste any time once he came out of the elevator. "I want to talk to her again. Bring her to me."

Wade raised an eyebrow. "Sure. If I can. She was pretty ornery after you talked to her earlier."

So their conversation had affected her too. Interesting. "She'll come."

The other man considered. "I don't think she'd stop for a fast-moving train. Hours on her feet out there, and she won't even come into the casino to take a piss. She doesn't even eat. I saw her pass around cookies to her pals, but she hasn't touched them."

Liam shook his head. He had to hand it to Kate Callender. The woman was driven, the sort of person he'd hire under different circumstances. "I want to talk to her. Now. Throw her over your shoulder if you have to."

"Whatever you say, Liam."

He checked the clock as Wade left. Three-forty. Bridget and Michelle were due in twenty minutes, but he'd make time for Ms. Callender. He needed to make her understand his point of view.

Christ, since when did he *need* her understanding? He was Liam Doyle, a man known for striking a good deal. In his experience, everyone caved once they thought they had a bargain. He'd swayed some of Vegas's biggest players. He could sway Kate Callender. He just needed to turn on the charm and make the price appear attractive.

She must be ready to burst after marching all day. Perfect. He'd let her use his private washroom, let her get cozy, and then move in for the kill.

When his pulse started to race, Liam began to wonder about his motives for seeing her. He suspected it had less to do with casinos, and more to do with hunger.

His inconvenient hunger for her.

***

When Wade told Kate that Doyle would see her again, she tried to ignore her sense of shock and turned to her fellow protestors. "Rod, could you take over for me?"

"Sure. How long will you be gone?"

"I have no idea." Bemused, she followed Doyle's lackey into the casino.

So the lord of the manor wanted to see her again. She must remember to doff her hat.

"How are you today, Wade?" She tried not to swallow a cloud of smoke from some woman who was doing her best to resemble Lindsay Lohan. Wait, *was* that Lindsay Lohan?

"Fine." She thought she caught him blushing. "Thanks for the cookies earlier. Oatmeal's my favorite." He frowned. "Don't tell Liam, okay?"

She grinned and locked up her lips with her fingers as she followed the big man to Doyle's office.

Liam sat at his massive desk like a king. When he stood to greet her, she saw he wore yet another suit cut perfectly to fit his body. He must have a personal tailor on call. The expensive black cloth seemed to caress every part of him. Underneath, he wore a checked shirt and another navy tie, one that made his blue eyes look even more fiery. The ensemble, if traded for food, could probably feed an entire homeless shelter.

But he looked good. So good, she'd swear a squadron of butterflies just launched an assault on her belly. She chalked it up to needing to pee and shifted on her feet, conscious of Wade leaving in the elevator. "Mr. Doyle."

He moved toward her, stopping mere inches away, and offered her a slow grin. "I've decided we're ready for first names. Call me Liam."

"How fortunate that I have you deciding these things." She took a step back. Not that it helped the crazy fluttering inside her. "I don't really think first names are wise. You know, with me trying to discredit you and all."

"Oh, come on, Kate. You've been picketing my casino for a few days now. You're here so much I feel as if I should put you on payroll, even if you are trying to make me lose money. Don't you think I've earned the right to call you by your first name?"

Avoiding his question, she looked around and noticed some coloring books and strawberry pastries on the kitchen counter. Next to them was a *Dora the Explorer* DVD. "Um, wow. I wouldn't have guessed your tastes run to the girly."

He looked at the counter-top items. "They're not for me. I'm having visitors shortly."

"So why am I here?"

He gestured to the couches and sat. She remained standing, hoping it would bug him, but he merely shrugged. "It's time we got frank, Katie."

"Please don't call me that. I prefer Kate."

"Of course, you do. It's much more sensible. So it's settled, I can call you Kate."

64

Momentarily bested, she crossed her arms over her chest, noting how his gaze followed, and how her nipples hardened in response. "What do you want, Doyle?"

"To know your price."

"What price?"

"Really? You wanna play games with me?"

"You're one to talk about games. Besides, I'm not playing any.. I just don't understand your question."

"Ms. Callender, everyone has a price. Now, I've been very patient, but I want to know what it's going to cost me to remove you from my casino. The sooner you tell me, the sooner we can finish this."

Did he seriously think she could be bought? "I don't have a price. I'm not doing this so you'll pay me off."

"I don't believe you. People don't do anything unless they think there's a payoff somewhere down the line."

Something in his face paled. What did he mean? Granted, with his money, he'd probably met some mercenary characters. Still, it made her a little sad to see poor little rich boy act so jaded about the world. "I'm not sure how to make it clearer, Liam, but I'm not even slightly interested in your money."

They stared at each other, and she could tell he was analyzing her as much as she did him. Once again, his gaze dipped down to her breast line and back up again. "You just called me Liam. Careful. Next thing you know you'll be under my sheets."

A tingle of raw sensuality worked its way up her

spine. His amazing scent filled her nostrils as her mind wandered. Dammit. She had fantasized about them together in a few moments of weakness the night before. She shifted on her feet again, suddenly desperate for a toilet. He'd turned her insides into a roiling cauldron of something very bad for her peace of mind. "It just slipped out, Mr. Doyle."

He chuckled. "Something else is going to slip out if you don't get to a bathroom. It seems you've had no breaks since you got here this morning."

"Stalking me now, are you?"

"And if I have been watching you? What would you say to that?"

His tone had changed, the playful lilt gone. The whisper that remained spoke of seduction, of repressed carnality and greed. He may have meant to tease her with his words, but hearing them with such voracity made it hard not to react. Her throat seemed suddenly dry, and she realized something about this man. With him, there were only three options: fight, flight, or submit.

She prayed she still had some fight left in her.

"Never fear, sugar," Liam said with a shrug, his voice once again lightening with mischief. "I just wish my own team worked so hard." He motioned to a set of doors. "Be my guest."

Shoot. She shouldn't have had that extra-large coffee on the way to the protest, but she'd needed the pick-me-up after her failure to do the right thing at the bank. But to use Liam Doyle's private bathroom? "I don't know."

"It's cleaned daily, Kate. I haven't even used that one yet. No evil Liam cooties in there." He eyed the clock on the wall. "Look, I don't mean to rush you, but like I said, I have visitors coming, and if you're not planning on answering my question, we might as well call it a day."

"Okay, fine." Muttering her thanks, she shuffled to the washroom and closed the door behind her, almost slamming it with relief. She made sure to lock it as well. What if he had a hidden camera in here? What if Liam Doyle was a crazed serial killer who lured unsuspecting women into his bathroom of death? Not finding any lethal traps lying about, she adjusted her clothing and attended to business.

After washing her hands, she couldn't help but notice all the personal items in the room. For an office bathroom, he sure kept it well-stocked. "Geez, does the dude *live* here?"

Next to the black marble vanity stood a storage cabinet with clear doors. Through the doors, she spied plush washcloths, several spare sticks of deodorant, body wash, and shampoo. Oh, and a bottle of the Kors cologne she loved. Unable to resist, she opened the door and pulled out the cologne bottle, bringing it to her nose.

Liam's scent, so up-close-and-personal, made her weak in the knees. Head spinning, she shoved it back into the cabinet and closed the door.

Taking a few extra minutes to compose herself, she planned her next move. He wanted to buy her off, but when she'd joined New Horizons, it was because of a higher calling. Mere money, even piles of it, wouldn't sway her from trying to help people like herself. She needed to convince him a payoff wasn't possible in a way that showed him why what he was doing was wrong.

Just as she had her speech prepared in her head, she opened the bathroom door, and heard voices in the outer room.

"Oh, damn." She'd taken too long and now she had to excuse herself in front of his visitors. He probably had the freaking Queen out there. Or her naughtiest relative, anyway.

She took a tentative step into the hallway, but what she heard made her stop in her tracks.

"You swore you'd bring her this time." Liam's tone was heart-broken, guarded.

A woman responded. "I lied. I had to. You wouldn't see me otherwise."

Heavy steps sounded from the room as Liam paced. "And you ask why I haven't forgiven you. Why I'm skeptical. There's always an excuse with you, Bridget. Always some reason why I can't see her. You're keeping Michelle away from me. It's emotional blackmail."

"Liam, don't be like that," the woman replied in a hurt voice. "I'd never do that to you."

"You've been doing it for six months," he said in a deceptively quiet voice, the kind that dripped danger. "I haven't seen her in six whole months. I used to see her every fucking day. How do you expect me to feel?"

Oh, shit. Kate didn't know what she'd gotten into here, but she needed to get out. She'd stumbled into a very private moment, and she didn't think Liam would thank her for listening, even though she hadn't meant to.

And yet, for some reason, the pain in his voice

made her want to stay. Who was this woman, Bridget? She couldn't remember reading anything about his marital status.

"Liam," Bridget answered. "What do you expect me to do? Your fancy lawyers hound me. They say my own flesh and blood would be better off with you."

"She would be."

"It's time for you to move on. Andy and I are trying to make a go of things. He wants to be there for me and for Michelle. He knows he sucked as a father, but he's back on track now. He's given up that woman, and he's sorry. I know you're hurt, but we don't need you interfering, trying to play Dad with our daughter!"

"She was my daughter too!"

"No, Liam. She never was, and you know it. Look, I appreciate you being there for us when Andy was away, and I appreciate you stepping in as a father figure for Michelle. I know you love her, but if you do, you have to give up this insane demand for sole custody. Andy's her real dad, and he's getting tired of hearing her ask about you. You need to let us be a family."

"So I don't get to see her ever again?"

"No. You don't. I'm sorry, but that's how it has to be." She sighed, but then her voice changed and Kate heard a soft cry. "Please, Liam. Please stop punishing me."

Swallowing her queasiness, Kate figured she'd better get out before she heard anything else. She'd already heard too much. She didn't want him to think she was eavesdropping on purpose. Quietly, she turned the corner and entered the main room.

Bridget's head popped up in surprise. "Who the hell are you? Another lawyer?"

Liam looked at Kate and his pale face turned red. "Um, no. This is Kate Callender. A…friend." He shook his head, as if mystified at his own hasty description of her.

Kate didn't have a chance to react. She was too busy staring at the floor so she wouldn't embarrass Bridget as she wiped her tears away. She seemed genuinely upset, and as much as her tears worked on Kate's natural sympathies, she couldn't forget Liam was standing just a few feet away, hunkered like a wounded animal, struggling with his own demons. She didn't know which of them was the true injured party, both oozed uneasy vulnerability. What on Earth had happened between them?

Kate gritted her teeth and headed for the elevator. "I was just leaving." She looked back at Liam. "I'm sorry I interrupted your visit. It wasn't intentional."

"Kate, wait. We weren't done." The tired tone in his voice made her want to offer him emotional triage. Great. If there was anything Kate loved, it was a man with heavy baggage. Not that she was interested in him or the size of his suitcase.

"You might as well stay," said Bridget. "Liam and I are finished, anyway." She turned to him. "Please stop sending Michelle gifts and please call off your hounds. You need to stop trying to control this situation. It's not yours to control. If you ever loved Michelle, you'll let her have her real father back."

Liam didn't say a word. He just stared at the floor as if he wanted to burn a hole in it.

Bridget passed Kate, picked up her purse from a side table, and pushed the elevator button. She continued to avoid Liam's gaze as she waited for the door to close.

Kate stared at her shoes, and then at Liam. He was white, no, grey, in the face. "Liam. I'm sorry."

"Don't be. It's not your fault." He lifted his head, beaten and exhausted.

Stop punishing me. Bridget's words haunted her. Kate couldn't deny there was a part of her that wondered if Liam had a punishing side to his character. Surely he'd trampled a few people on his rise to the top. He'd warned her himself he didn't forgive and forget.

She needed to make her exit now, before she made him feel any more awkward, and before he made her feel more…whatever that turmoil in her stomach was. It was bad enough she'd seen him at such a private moment, she didn't need to make things more complicated. She pressed the button to summon the elevator.

In the uncomfortable seconds that followed, Liam walked over to the kitchen counter and fingered the little girl's coloring book. He began to tear the pages out of the book, one by one. Each rip made him look darker, more despondent, more desperate. By the time he'd torn ten pages out, his lips had pressed so tight they were almost blue.

She wanted to hate him, but right now she couldn't.

The elevator door opened.

Kate froze. *Get in. Get in. Don't come back.*

The door closed again.

All of a sudden, Liam Doyle wasn't a big, bad casino owner. He was just a man who hurt. And it was in her nature to try and take the hurt away.

Moving quietly, she made her way over to the counter and stood next to him. His cologne wafted over her again, making her want to close her eyes and dream. She touched a hand to his sleeve and then pried the desecrated book out of his hands. He started, as if shocked she was still there.

"Do you want to talk?"

He frowned, his mouth opened once or twice, but no words came out. She knew how she must appear. A few minutes ago, she'd been the harridan he'd been trying to bribe away from his property. Now, she probably sounded like bloody Mary Poppins. She should offer up a goddamn spoonful of sugar while she was at it.

When he didn't answer, she pointed to the strawberry pastries. "Are those from the restaurant downstairs?"

A fraction of his professionalism returned. "Chef Jean-Claude made them special for me."

"They're beautiful. I bet a box of six costs as much as my rent."

He looked at her for a tense moment and then cracked a sad smile. "Would you like one?"

"No. I mean, I'd love one. I could probably swallow them all whole, but I'm gluten-free and trying hard to be sugar-free."

One side of his mouth twitched, and a dimple showed under his stubble. Those Husky dog eyes still seemed so sad, though. "Why am I not surprised? Well, does your gluten-free, sugar-free diet mean you can't have coffee?"

"Probably, but a girl's gotta have some pleasure."

"Have a seat, then. I'll make some." Once again, he gestured to the cushy couches, but this time added, "Please."

She could have made a crack about how his servants should be making his coffee, but she didn't. This time, she just offered him a smile, and sat down.

Chapter Four

Liam glanced a couple of times at Kate as he prepared the coffee. She ran her fingers over the couch's leather upholstery as if she'd never sat on Italian leather before. Maybe she hadn't. It would explain why she was perched at the edge of the couch, as if afraid to mar it with her presence.

"How do you take it?" he asked, pouring a black one for himself.

"Fully loaded, please."

He cocked an eyebrow. "What was that about sugar-free?"

"What? I'm not a martyr. Besides, coffee with no sugar is a deal breaker. Of course, if you have any Stevia root in those cupboards, I'd take that instead." She raised her head and watched him work. "So, I take it Bridget's your ex?"

He brought the two mugs over, setting them on the pastry tray. "Yeah. We were together for a couple of years."

"Married?"

"No. Thank God for small mercies."

She picked up her mug and took a demure sip. He imagined the hot, sweet liquid warming a path down her throat. Despite the emotional upheaval of the past ten minutes, he imagined dragging his tongue over her. *Jesus Christ. Get your shit together.* She licked her lips, snapping him out of his funk.

Her staring at him made him feel uncomfortable but consoled at the same time. He didn't think anyone had ever inspired that feeling before. She seemed to consider her next words carefully. "Tell me about her. Were you happy together?"

He ran a hand through his hair, experiencing a familiar sense of unease. "We didn't have a typical relationship. We'd been friends for some time, ran in the same circles. When her husband took off with another woman, I was there for her. After a while, it just seemed convenient to sleep together."

"So she wasn't your grand passion then?"

He grinned. "No. I guess I always knew she wasn't over Andy, but I fooled myself into believing their relationship was done. He'd married her and then decided he wasn't quite finished sowing his wild oats. Even started divorce proceedings. He left her just as she realized she was pregnant."

"Charming."

"Yeah, I thought so too. Anyway, Bridget accepted my help, and it seemed to make sense that friends could be lovers. I convinced myself I cared more than I did, and she swore she wanted nothing more to do with him."

"It didn't bother you she was pregnant with

another man's child?"

"At first, I just thought I could give her some support. Once she started showing, I got excited. I told myself we could be a family. Looking back, I realize a part of me really wanted to be a dad. I never had much of a family life, you see. I guess I craved stability, or at least liked the idea of giving it to someone else."

As soon as he spied the look of empathy in her eyes, he forgot about the hostile circumstances in which they met. He was just appreciative having her there, showing some kindness.

"I treated Michelle like my own. Bridget was grateful, but gratitude isn't the same as love." He scratched his chin. "For a while, we had fun playing family. But as much as I loved that little girl, her mom and I couldn't fake it very long. The chemistry just wasn't there. We argued over stupid things. Made a lot of mistakes. But I held on for Michelle. Trust me. Staying for the kid never makes it better."

She sighed, as if she understood completely. "What happened?"

Liam sucked in a breath. "My job kept us apart. I work a lot of nights, and after a while I realized I was staying longer and longer at the office. I was right in the middle of making plans for this place and life was hectic. When I did give myself a day off, she purposely kept away, as if to punish me.

"Then one day she went out with friends and left her cell phone behind. It rang, and I answered, thinking it might be her calling home. It was Andy. I saw his name on the display. As soon as he realized it wasn't her on the phone, he hung up."

He stared at his coffee mug, wishing he could drown in its dark depths. "I accused her of seeing him behind my back. She didn't even deny it. Andy had said he still loved her, that he was sorry, and that he wanted to be a father to his child."

Kate's face turned down. "That must have been horrible for you."

"It was a fucking nightmare," he admitted in a quiet voice. "I love that little girl with all my heart. But at the end of the day, Michelle's not my biological daughter, even if I was there when she was born."

She shook her head, but said nothing.

"I don't even have words to describe what I went through. I've been in a very dark place since then. The only thing that keeps me sane is my work." And no matter how much his doctor suggested he reduce his hours, working less meant more time to think about what he'd lost.

"And now you want custody?" She spoke in quiet, tentative tones.

"Can you blame me?"

"Not really, but sole custody? They are her parents."

"I don't trust them, either of them. I don't trust Andy not to hurt Michelle later on. That bastard turned his back on his daughter when she needed him most, and if he thinks I'll just step aside so he can do it again, he can go fuck himself."

Kate frowned, and he could see his words struck a nerve. "But…"

"There are no buts. As far as I'm concerned, she's my little girl. She always will be. I know having a casino owner as a dad isn't exactly ideal, but I did my best. Even had a nursery set up in my last office so I could be with her while I was at work sometimes. I changed her diapers. I took her to the park on weekends. I bottle-fed her and held her in my arms. I did more for her than her own flesh and blood father ever did. Ever will. I love her. I can't just turn that off."

He gazed into Kate's eyes. Sympathy shone there, clear as day. Not that he wanted her sympathy, but it felt good to unburden himself. There was no judgment in Kate's eyes, no comments that she thought him a gullible fool. Just warmth, something he didn't feel too often these days.

The pastries sat untouched before them, and they both stared at the tray. Liam had ordered them because strawberries were Michelle's favorite. Were they still? How the hell would he know? He suddenly felt like tossing them across the room.

"Of course you can't turn it off," Kate said. "But you have to understand you'll need to cut Michelle out of your life. For your own sanity."

"To hell with sanity. I'm not cutting her out of my life. I've got the best law firm in the business backing me. They'll help me get Michelle back."

"But she's not yours. You said it yourself, and Bridget seems remorseful."

"I don't care. I was a part of her life for three years. Michelle is mine, and her idiot sperm donor father isn't standing in my way. They think I'll walk away from her? I will *never* abandon her." He knew what that was like. No way he'd do that to his little girl.

"You wouldn't be abandoning her. You'd be just…moving on."

He felt his blood pressure ratchet up a notch. "I have no wish to 'move on.'"

"I don't know if that's helping the situation. It sounds, well, controlling."

"Since when is being in control a bad thing?"

"There's a difference between being in control and being *controlling*."

"I don't care. If that makes me a sore loser, so be it."

"But Liam, this battle is poisonous. It'll hurt Michelle in the long run, and it'll devastate everyone else involved." Her soft voice sounded more logical than his own conscience had ever been. "I know it must hurt to turn away, but don't you think it's best?"

Frustration sizzled like acid in his gut and he directed his annoyance squarely at Kate. "You don't understand. I don't care if the legal battle kills me. I just want what's best for her. I can give her a better life than they can. I don't want her to grow up and wonder why I left. Can't you see that?"

"Oh, Liam. This is not right. You have to end this, for your own sake. You have to let her go. I know it will hurt, but if you don't hit rock bottom, you won't move forward."

"I won't lose my daughter!"

"She's not your daughter!"

Their raised voices echoed throughout the room, but the ensuing silence felt louder.

"Who asked you?" he said quietly, but with

vehemence. "I think you should go."

"I think so too." Still looking concerned, she stood and gathered her purse. Plain, sensible, just like her. Well, he was tired of being sensible. Sensible had lost him everything.

Without another word, she headed to the elevator and pushed the button. She slipped inside, then turned to face him, as if wanting to say something.

He watched as the door closed on Kate. And then, finally giving in to his anger, he gathered up the tray of pastries and hurled them at the wall.

As he watched the trail of expensive strawberry chunks slide down the wall, he felt his chest rise and fall with a few shaky breaths. He'd lost his cool, and all because a stranger called him out for ignoring the pitiful truth in his life. He had no daughter. He might as well have been Michelle's former babysitter. He had no claim to her.

Kate Callender had seen right through him. Unimpressed by his wealth and influence, she'd seen him for the mess he truly was.

He'd resented her for her insight.

Now, feeling just as sick for the way he treated her, Liam turned away from the sticky berry muck. What was he supposed to do? Apologize for jumping down Kate's throat? No, he didn't owe her any explanations, certainly not regarding his personal life. He'd worked hard to keep his relationships out of the papers, and just as hard to keep photographers away from Michelle. Kate had no right to question him.

If anything, she'd done him a favor. Now he truly saw her for the busybody she was. In fact, next time she so much as put a foot on his property, he would throw her over his shoulder and remove her himself.

Consoled by this steely determination, he didn't walk over to the window to see if Kate had left yet, even though a frustrating part of him remained curious. Rather, he grabbed a wet cloth from his kitchen and began to clean the mess. He could have called housekeeping, but didn't want to explain why he had fruit and whipped cream on his wall. Not that he made a habit of explaining his messes.

Once he'd finished, he planted himself at his desk, and returned a dozen work-related calls, all the while doing his best to forget a particular pair of reproving, yet sympathetic, hazel eyes.

***

After having pulled a late night at Vice, sleeping in his casino office, Liam arose for an early start. He'd taken time to sit in on some auditions by a couple of acts hoping for a spot at the casino's piano bar, Decadence. He had managers on staff who were responsible for booking talent, but when it came to hiring new acts, he liked being in the thick of things. After all, every artist under his roof was a representation of him and of his casinos. He wanted to know each act on his payroll would do him justice.

And it was a good thing too. His bar manager had wanted to hire one of the acts, but Liam had found the woman's Judy Garland act cheesy. In fact, he'd vetoed all the acts. His manager had turned to him afterward, his face lined with frustration.

Too bad. His club, his rules.

Thank Christ he had insisted on his office being such a homey environment. With the sort of work he did, he often pulled these kinds of all-nighters. There were days he didn't leave his casinos at all. At times like this, he might not see his condo for a week. It helped him keep his mind off his former family life. As he got settled at his desk, he rolled his shoulders and tried to stretch out the nagging pull of sore muscles.

He'd dreamed of her last night, of Kate. Had dreamed of finger-combing her fiery mane of hair, right before he drove into her tight heat.

Fuck.

He stretched out his arms and cracked his knuckles in a feeble attempt to banish the red-headed demon from his visions. But in the end he gave in to nagging temptation and wandered over to the window that faced the entrance.

No picket line. No Kate.

Okay. This should be no problem. He was bigger than this…this cock-driven moment of feeblemindedness.

As he attended his meetings that day, he ignored the burn in his stomach. When he once again looked back out the same window hours later, he congratulated himself on finally being rid of the pesky protestor.

***

Late that afternoon, as he drafted a few emails with his assistant, Pearl, he stood as far away as possible from the window.

"Liam?" she prodded. "How do you want to respond to the email about the building permit for the old works building?"

Pearl's voice barely cut through his consciousness and he didn't think to answer her.

"Liam?"

He snapped out of his funk for a second. "Which email?"

"The one I sent you yesterday."

Damn. He'd barely looked at it. "Just…tell him I want a definitive answer. We've wasted enough time on this issue."

Despite his strong words, he knew his tone came out quiet and distracted, and not in a good way. He knew this shit with the building permit office could have been resolved sooner if he'd pushed it more. He should have pushed it more. He wanted to start working on his next property.

Didn't he?

For some reason, he just wasn't excited about the new project. His enthusiasm for building had waned, truth be told. Was he losing his fire, his drive?

Or was his fire simply smoking in another direction?

Pearl, a kind-hearted older woman, approached him from the side and put a hand on his sleeve. "Are you okay, Liam?"

"Yeah, thanks."

"Nando Perreira left two messages this

morning."

"I know."

She gave his arm a rub, but he gently pulled away. Professional to a fault, Pearl didn't usually allow her inner nurturer to manifest, but when it did, it made him uncomfortable. He hadn't had much mothering growing up and still didn't quite know what to do with it.

His stepmom Shauna had guaranteed that. She'd made sure he never understood what it felt like to have the support of a good woman in his life. She was most likely the reason he'd fouled up every relationship he'd had. She'd turned him into an unforgiving bastard who hated to lose, who had to be in control, and every time something shitty happened to him, he heard her voice.

You're not my son. I'll never think of you as my son. You mean nothing to me.

Squeezing those memories out of his brain, he looked at Pearl. He took in the sympathetic slant of her eyes, knowing she felt the same way Kate did, that he should just let Michelle go. He'd shared the details of his custody suit with Pearl some time ago, and she'd also stated, albeit more diplomatically than Kate, that he should relinquish his claim.

Why was he the only one who seemed to understand he wanted to do right by the little girl?

Kate's voice sounded in his head. *She's not your daughter.*

He recognized the truth in her statement, and his heart broke. All his success wouldn't take this sort of hurt away either. It was the sort of pain that traditionally one could only forget with the help of copious amounts of alcohol. And even then the effect was temporary.

Pearl took a deep breath and gathered up her things. "I'll let you know when I hear about the permit."

He nodded in acknowledgment. "Thanks, Pearl."

His work day finished, he once again looked out the window overlooking the entrance.

No Kate.

By now, even Wade was on the lookout for her. He'd asked about her a couple of times already. The security guard stood sentinel outside, craning his neck, as if hoping to catch a glimpse of her on the Strip. In just a few days they'd both gotten used to her being there and felt her absence, despite the fact she'd like nothing more than to see Vice burn to the ground. It should be funny.

So why wasn't he laughing?

Temples throbbing, Liam left his office and hit the executive gym, determined to pound Kate's memory out of his head. It did no good. As much as he tore up the treadmill, he couldn't run away from her face. It seemed to follow him everywhere these days.

Feeling defeated for reasons he barely understood, he headed back to his suite. Eager to escape the working world for a few hours, he spent the night on his couch, indulging in a marathon of *The Walking Dead*.

But even the zombie apocalypse couldn't dislodge the remembrance of red locks pulled back in a tight ponytail, or of the disappointment in her eyes.

Maybe they needed some more face time. Maybe he needed to explain.

But Kate was a no-show the next day as well. And the next, and the next. A week went by without Liam glimpsing her or her placard from the fourth floor.

The sore loser in him wanted a redo of their conversations. The sore loser in him wanted her back so he could erase her disappointment in him with a long, slow kiss. The sore loser in him needed to give her the most rollicking orgasm of her life, and drive her as crazy as she'd driven him.

He had to find her.

***

"I swear, I don't know whether to hug Darren or to hit him." The background hum in the room seemed to pause for a moment. "Kate? Are you in there?"

Her head snapped up. Damn! She'd lost focus. She'd never done that in group before, but it seemed she could barely concentrate the past few days. "I'm sorry, Audrey. I'm a little distracted. What were you saying?"

Audrey grinned and picked up a chocolate chip cookie. "It's okay. I get it. Sometimes I want to tune out too."

Kate felt the burn of guilt fester in the pit of her stomach. At least group hadn't started yet and she and Audrey had just been having a one-on-one conversation. It would have been embarrassing to lose focus during the session. Some leader she was.

And it was all Liam Doyle's fault. Because of his personal situation, because of his anger toward her for telling him the truth, she hadn't been able to think of much else. Clearly she'd become deranged. How else could she explain why she should be so affected by someone she didn't even like or respect, or even know for that matter? Unless there was a part of her that wanted to know him better...

"Oh, crap."

"Come again?"

Kate fumbled for a response. "It's nothing." Feeling hot in the face, she motioned to the others in the group. "Hey, everyone. It's time to get started."

Before she could say anything, Rod piped up. "So why did we stop picketing Vice? I thought we'd made a real impact on some of those visitors last time."

"Yeah. Why the ceasefire, fearless leader?" asked Patti.

All heads turned toward Kate. "Um. I've been thinking about it, and I just don't know if it's the most effective course of action."

"What do you mean?" asked Rod. "Even Liam Doyle noticed you. You spoke with the man. We need to keep up our momentum."

"Yes, but..."

"No buts, Kate," pressed Rod. "This is important. Why the backpedaling? It's not like you."

She stared at him, completely at a loss. She had no logical answer, only feelings running rampant in her core. She felt sorry for Liam Doyle. There, she'd acknowledged it to herself. He was going through a personal hell, and she supposed she just didn't want to rub salt in the wound.

So maybe it made her look like a weakling, but she hadn't been able to step foot near Vice all week. In fact, she'd avoided the Strip altogether, spending her evenings with Lisa and the kids instead.

Somehow, her badass side had shriveled up and died. Oh well, it wasn't a mantle she wore easily. Besides, she felt like a hypocrite. She'd deposited another hundred dollars into her dad's account again today, even though it was royalty money she couldn't afford to lose.

Before she could respond to Rod, she heard a knock on the door of the meeting room. Being closest to the door, Rod got up and opened it, sticking his head out. He pulled it back in and turned around. "Kate, there's a man here asking for you."

Her pulse jumped and skittered. *Liam? Oh, Christ. Don't be so silly*. What did she expect? That he'd pull up in a pumpkin carriage, offering her glass footwear?

She got up and went to the door. She stepped outside, moving her legs in small, tentative motions. Her movements came to an abrupt stop when she saw who stood in the hallway. Her breath came to a stop as well.

She must have paled because Rod touched her arm. "Hey, you okay? Do you want me to stay with you?"

She forced down the lump in her throat. "No, thanks. But could you take over the group for a bit?"

He looked at her and her visitor. "Okay. But if you need me, just knock." He disappeared into the meeting room and shut the door behind him.

Louis Callender extended his arms and smiled. "My Katie. It's been a long time."

She avoided her father's touch and stepped back, not wanting to be anywhere close to him. "What do you want, Dad?"

The corners of his mouth fell down and he let his arms drop. Anyone who didn't know him well would think he was devastated by her cold demeanor. She didn't care. Her father was many things, first and foremost a consummate actor. He had to be in order to swindle everyone he knew. "Why do you assume I want something, Katie-bug?"

"Don't call me that," she snapped, fighting her swelling anger. "And I know you want something because it's the only time you ever show your face. How did you find me, anyway?"

He looked around the New Horizons hallway with a hint of contempt, as if he were standing in the middle of his own intervention. "You're always *here*. Does it actually do you any good?"

"More than you ever did."

He ran a hand through his still-thick, auburn hair. She had to hand it to her dad. He certainly looked the part of a con man. Despite his age, he appeared ten years younger. He'd been blessed with terrific genes. The crinkly eyes and handsome face no doubt served him well when he looked for wealthy girlfriends to finance his habits. "I can't believe my only daughter would talk to me like that. Didn't I raise you better?"

"You didn't raise me at all. Now what do you want?"

He stared at her for a long time, assessing her mood, planning his attack like a military tactician. "It hurts me that we can't get along, sweetheart."

"It's hard to get along with someone who only shows up every couple of years begging for handouts."

"Katie…"

"Are you here to seek help for your addiction?"

"Don't talk to me like I'm some sort of crack head. I don't need help." He paced the hall for a couple of tense moments. "Look, I made some mistakes. I borrowed some money from some very bad people recently."

"And this affects me how?"

"They want their money, sweetheart. These are men who won't take no for an answer. I just need a small loan." Tears filled his eyes. God, he could summon them so easily. "I'm scared, Katie. I need your help."

"I can't believe this." She put a hand over her dry mouth. "Actually, I do believe this."

"You don't wanna see anything bad happen to your old man, do you? I just need five grand, Katie-bug. That's all. And then I promise you, I'll start attending those meetings. I'll get help. You have my word."

"Five grand? What about the money I've been depositing into your account? You gamble it all away, without so much as a thank you, and now you want five *thousand* more? What makes you think I even have that much?" She realized her voice was rising with each word, so she tried to lower it.

"You have that cushy singing job. I know Calvert pays you well."

"I don't have that job anymore, and you don't know a thing about me."

He took a step toward her, his tone now menacing and desperate. "I'm just asking for a loan. Raise the money. Ask your friends. Maybe they can help you. I'll take anything. These guys...that whole busted kneecap thing isn't just a cliché to them, you understand? Think you can get off your frickin' high horse long enough to help me?" He raised a hand as if to strike her.

A lightning-hot wound lanced through her already scarred heart. Without a word, she knocked on the door to the meeting room. Rod was there in an instant.

"I'm done out here." Her friend put an arm around her shoulder and led her back inside.

Her father called out as the door was shut. "They'll hurt me, Katie! It'll be on your head!"

Kate let Rod handle the rest of the meeting while she sat by the refreshments table and held the same cup of coffee for an hour.

As she listened to the droning sounds of the meeting around her, she feared she was finally plummeting toward rock bottom.

And it scared the crap out of her.

Chapter Five

Rod took her back to her apartment that evening. She normally would have taken the bus, but tonight she didn't want to set out on her own. She didn't put it past her dad to try again.

Rod stopped in front of her white stucco building on West Flamingo. "You sure you don't want to talk about your visitor? You keep telling us we shouldn't keep things bottled inside."

She looked around. There was no one in sight. "No, I'm okay. Thanks. You go. I know your shift at the hospital already started." With a hug, she got out of the car and waved as he drove off.

Her unit was a cozy walk-up on the second floor and she couldn't wait to get inside and have a long bath. When she reached her landing, she looked around, feeling a prickle of unease. She looked around, but the street was quiet. In her cul-de-sac, one could almost forget the Vegas Strip was a short drive away. She fumbled for her keys, only to drop them. Cursing, she bent over to retrieve them, thinking that this was usually the point in a movie where the serial killer leaped out.

She stuck her key in the lock and breathed a sigh of relief, glad not to have had another confrontation with her father.

Once inside, she flicked on the living room light, illuminating the coral painted walls. Home.

Now she could lose her shit big time.

"No," she told herself. "Hold it together. You're better than this."

She dropped her purse and picked up the TV remote, hoping she'd find a trashy program featuring characters more messed up than she was. After a few minutes of scrolling through the guide, she turned it off, disappointed. She put down the remote, remembered her father's words, and tried not to cry.

Just as her hands began to shake, there was a loud knock on her door. She jumped, steadied herself and shuffled to the door. Pulling aside the little flap from the peephole, she looked outside.

Liam Doyle stood at her door.

"What the…?"

Her hands shook even harder now. She fumbled with the lock, as if she'd forgotten how it worked, before she managed to open it.

The pair stared at each other, neither one speaking. No sign of designer suits today. Instead, he wore faded jeans that hugged his lower half, a black t-shirt that emphasized his cut frame, and scuffed cowboy boots.

She'd considered him devastating in a custom-made suit, but this outfit made him look like a bad boy gone country. She struggled to find her voice.

"What are you doing here?"

"Well, hello to you too, sugar. Can I come in?"

"Okay." She stepped aside to let him in, noting how he seemed to fill the doorway as he passed. Still clinging to the door, she stared at his figure, entranced. He looked like another man altogether today, but still dead sexy. She blinked and tried to clear her head. "How did you find me?"

"Your number is listed, you know."

She shut the door and leaned on it, hands behind her back so he wouldn't see her tremble. "Why are you here, Liam?"

"I get questions instead of a 'Hello, how are you?'"

"Hello, how are you? Why the fuck are you here?"

He stood very still, and his gaze rested on her strand of pearls. He moved his hand as if to reach out for her, but let it fall to his side. "I haven't seen you at Vice. I was…concerned."

"I thought you would be relieved."

"Yeah, I know, but for some strange reason I was worried instead. So, um, why did you stop coming?"

"Does it matter?"

"Indulge my curiosity."

Those three words, echoing in her brain, made her throat thicken. *Indulge my curiosity.* Somehow, the way he'd said the words, they'd sounded dirty. Surely her frazzled mind made her imagine the heat in his eyes.

She blinked and the heat disappeared like vapor. "I'm sure you have more important things to be curious about."

He cracked a smile, the first since he'd shown up. "You know, I gotta tell you, Kate. You're a shitty hostess."

She couldn't help but grin in return. "I'm sorry. I'm not really prepared. You see, I gave the butler the night off and I forgot to defrost the canapés."

"You really do think I'm an evil, rich dickhead, don't you? That I don't have a soul?"

"Not evil. I think I glimpsed your soul when you talked about Michelle. The rich dickhead part is still true, though."

"Is that why you didn't come back? Because you felt sorry for me?

Kate said nothing.

"I don't want your pity, Kate."

"What *do* you want?"

The moments the words left her mouth, she regretted it. It was getting hard to rein in a desire that she didn't even understand. Yes, she felt concern for him, but right now, all she knew was a near-feral need. His looks and deep voice and even his arrogance turned her crank in such a way she knew from now on she'd compare every other man to him.

Still, he drove her nuts.

Liam seemed to have trouble finding his words. "I'm still trying to understand what I want. You're not making it easy for me."

Okay, so clearly she drove him around the bend a bit too. "What does that mean?"

He drew closer until their feet just about touched. He reached for her hand and she almost leaned into him. Almost, but not quite.

"Goddamn, you ask a lot of questions," he said. "It means I don't know what to make of you."

Liam's gaze dropped and traveled a hot path from her head to her toes, and her body responded to the visual caress. Already her nipples pebbled under her light shirt. To her horror, she realized she was practically leaning in for a kiss. The thought of him claiming her mouth had her weak in the knees.

Just when she suspected he wanted the same thing, he took a step back, but did not release her hand. "Look, sometimes my job requires me to act like an asshole, but I shouldn't have been one to you when you were being honest with me. I'm sorry."

Kate had no explanation for the barrage of sensations Liam caused all over her. His sensual voice made her ears perk up. His touch made her skin feel luxurious, like a warm, soapy bath. He might be less put together tonight, but he was still just as much a feast for her eyes. She wanted to run her fingers over his washboard abs and fondle each plane and hollow. His stubble seemed a little thicker, almost a beard, as if he hadn't trimmed it in a couple of days, and served to make him look more like a rugged lumberjack rather than a captain of Vegas industry.

His masculine beauty affected her the way a newly-discovered Van Gogh might affect an art collector.

She removed her hand from his and ran it shakily over her face, trying to rein herself in. "You don't owe me an apology. I butted in where I wasn't wanted. And I'm the last person who should be giving anyone advice." Oddly comforted in his presence, she let her shoulders droop and sighed.

Liam put a finger under her chin. "Hey, what's wrong? Tell me."

"You really don't want to know."

"If I didn't, I wouldn't ask. I'm a rich dickhead, remember?" He grinned and slowly removed his hand from her face.

"Okay. Fine." She paused to collect her thoughts. "I'm even worse. I'm a fraud. I lecture others about hitting rock bottom, and the truth is I've never done it myself." She looked up, expecting to see him judge her, but saw only a new heat in his blue eyes. "My dad's an addict, and I've been enabling him for years. I can't seem to stop. I'm scared to let him go cold turkey. I'm scared to stop giving him money. I'm scared. I'm just scared."

Liam gazed at her for a time, then moved his hand back to her face, sliding his fingers over her cheek. She fought the urge to close her eyes and luxuriate in his touch. After what felt like forever, he smiled.

"Just because you've had trouble following your own advice doesn't mean it's not good advice. I was thinking about what you said, that I need to hit rock bottom. I figured I'd give it a shot tonight. Care to join me?"

Her heart leaped, and she nodded.

***

Liam spied the amused look on Kate's face as

they approached his truck. He opened the door to his old F150 for her. "What?"

"Nothing. I thought you were lying about the pickup truck."

"Would I lie about this beauty?" He patted the rusty exterior. "It might look like crap, but it's still a smooth ride. Another plus is the paparazzi expect me to drive a fancy car. When I'm in this thing, they don't even see me." She slid into the passenger seat and he leaned on the door. "What do you drive?"

"I don't have my license."

"How old are you?" he teased.

"Thirty."

"Just a few years younger than me. You're getting pretty ripe, woman. Time to get that learner's permit."

She grinned but her cheeks reddened. "I don't drive because I have epilepsy."

"Oh." His face burned up as well. "Damn. I didn't mean to…"

"Don't worry about it." She slapped her thigh in anticipation. "C'mon. Get in the car. Let's go."

He wondered about her condition. Were her seizures bad? How long had she suffered from them? Did she take medication? A million questions ran through his head, none of which were his business.

"Hey," she said when he didn't move. "Rock bottom's not going to hit itself."

"Right." He shut the door and got in on the other side. As he started the engine, he noticed the way her denim-clad thighs looked next to his. Soft and round, tapering to an elegant knee. It was so tempting to reach over and run his fingers up her thigh. The thought gave him an immediate hard on, one he tried to disguise with an arm casually draped across his lap. Shit, he hadn't come all this way to ogle Kate Callender's legs or any other part of her, for that matter. He'd come to get shit-faced with someone who understood his shame.

He peeled out of her neighborhood and headed for the Las Vegas Freeway, turning away from the Strip on W. Sahara Avenue. He wanted no flashing lights tonight, no reminders of who he was or where his obligations were. He wanted to be in a place that reminded him of his roots.

Once they were well on their way, Kate turned to him. "Where are we going?"

"A place I know called Franky's."

"Franky's? Wait, I know that bar. It's a total dive."

Liam feigned horror. "Which makes it the best bar in town, even if it wasn't run by my friend. Anyway, if it's such a dive, how do you know it?"

"Like any professional singer, I've done my share of waitressing. One of my friends waitressed at Franky's. I popped in once or twice."

"I still can't believe you're a singer. So, do you wear a metal breastplate and horns on your head?"

She giggled. "No, I don't sing opera. I sing torch songs. Piano-bar stuff."

"Is that so?" Well, well. He still needed a crooner for Decadence. Maybe he could get her to sing for him. Too bad Franky didn't offer karaoke so he could see what kind of skills she had. He'd never really been of the belief that the universe provided, but something had provided Kate.

"Any chance I've heard you somewhere?" he asked.

"Maybe. My one and only claim to fame is being the voice of Calvert's Used Automobiles."

"No shit? Those ads are so bad they're good. You have a sexy singing voice, Kate."

The roses on her cheeks made her few freckles pop. "Well, thanks, but you might not be hearing much of it in the future. I quit."

"How come?"

"Let's just say Mr. Calvert has busy hands and leave it at that."

He turned, keeping his hands on the wheel, his eyes wide as he was hit with a strange combination of shock and anger. "Are you serious?"

"Yup. I'm officially out of a job." She then threw him a smile. "Where do you think I got all this free time to bug you?"

"Ah, hell. Did you at least kick the bastard in the nuts?

"Actually, yeah."

"Good. If you hadn't, I would have offered up the services of some guys I know who'd be happy to do it for you." No lie about it. Suddenly, he felt a strong desire to pummel that lemon-peddling shit Calvert.

She cocked an eyebrow. "No need for violence on my account. And anyway, I'm pretty capable in the nut-kicking department."

"Well, tonight's on me. I hope you can hold your liquor."

"Do you always solve your problems with alcohol? You know that won't work, right?"

"I know, but I'd like to forget one or two things for a while."

"And how are we getting home afterward, Mr. Forgetful?"

Their banter made him smile. "Well, if we're *really* successful at forgetting, I'll call my driver. Franky won't mind stowing my truck in his garage overnight. God knows no one will steal it. Don't worry, I won't abandon you."

He could tell from her pensive expression she recalled their last conversation, all of it. "I could always take a bus," she said. "I have before."

"Not on my watch." The idea of Kate waiting at a Vegas bus stop late at night was about the least appealing vision he could conjure up. It gave him a weird, nauseating stab in the gut, like it would end up as an episode of *CSI* someday.

It was time he admitted to himself that this woman fascinated him in a way he didn't quite understand. From the moment she'd first set foot on the pavement near Vice, he hadn't been able to wrestle her out of his head. Part of the reason he'd shown up at her door was the hope that spending an evening with Kate would allow him to see the real her. And that in getting to know her, he'd find something he disliked, and give himself a reason to stay away.

It wasn't working. He did like her. A lot.

He wished he didn't. He didn't have time in his life for romance, or whatever foul desire plagued him. Romance, right. His inflated cock was *all* about romance right now. No doubt his cock wanted to order her some flowers and recite her some poetry too.

No, he just wanted to sleep with her, and the slight hitch in her breath when she looked at him told him she wanted the same thing.

He stifled a laugh. As if she'd have him. He was pretty sure she still thought he had horns hidden under his hair somewhere.

They pulled in at Franky's and parked near the back, right next to Franky's Harley. While Kate gathered up her purse, he got out and opened her door for her. She put a foot on the ground and grasped his outstretched hand, eyes shimmering with a hint of disbelief. "No one opens doors for women anymore, do they?"

"I just did."

"Noted." She slid out of the car, her face still pink. "Crowd looks a little rough tonight. You sure about this?"

A couple of familiar bikers stood outside the front door, taking drags on their cigarettes. "I happen to like things a little rough." He smiled and put a hand on the small of her back as he led her toward the entrance. She continued to tense as they reached the door, so he put her out of her misery. He called to the bikers. "Beck. Nolan. How's it going?"

Nolan, a leather-clad bear of a man, smiled from behind his full beard . "Doyle, man. How's the new place?"

"Awesome. You gonna ditch Franky one of these nights and come see it?"

The two of them laughed, as if leaving Franky's was a physical impossibility. "Only if you promise to save me one of those pretty pink cocktails with the umbrellas," Nolan crowed.

"People pay fifteen bucks for those pretty pink cocktails. Gotta give the customers what they want." He turned to Kate. "Kate, these are my buddies, Nolan and Beck."

Kate didn't seem to know how to react. "Um, nice to meet you?"

Beck, a handsome shit-disturber, reached for her hand and kissed it, lingering a little too long for Liam's liking. "Honey, the pleasure's all mine." He grinned like he wanted to eat her up. "Doyle, where have you been hiding this sweet thing?"

Her giggle came out like a snort. "He hasn't hidden me anywhere, but he probably wishes he could. I've been causing him trouble." She turned and smiled at him, more comfortable with the situation now. "Isn't that right, Liam?"

"Honey, whatever trouble you're selling, I'm buying," said Beck.

"Dream on," Liam responded, getting a little annoyed by the man's transparent interest. "You don't have enough money for this kind of trouble."

Liam marched her into the bar before Beck could make another play. He should have guessed that guy would try it on with her. He did with every other woman. Well, Kate deserved better than to be pawed over by a guy who needed a secretary to keep his girlfriends organized and away from each other.

He looked at her as he led her to the bar, curious

about her reaction to Beck. She seemed to be hiding a grin. "Your friends are nice."

"Oh, yeah. Real nice." He rolled his eyes. "They even sing in the church choir. Come on. What's your poison, gorgeous?"

"Gorgeous?" She laughed.

"You could try to look flattered."

Still grinning, she scratched her head, a schoolgirl unsure of how to take a compliment. "Right. Beer's fine."

"A girl after my own heart." He looked for Franky, but his buddy was probably stuck in the back room. In his absence, he ordered two Stellas from the bartender in charge, then led her to a quiet booth in back. She slid into one side of the booth.

He thought about sitting opposite her. He really did. But there was something about the way the bar lights hit the auburn strands in her hair that made him want to sit next to her. So he did, much to her surprise.

"What?" He tried to act as if it was no big deal. "The music's loud. We won't hear each other talk."

She seemed to accept his excuse and smiled.

Liam realized seeing her smile felt good. Better than he'd expected. It made him strangely protective as well, especially when he remembered her epilepsy. "Are you okay with the flashing lights in here, you know, with your condition?"

"Yeah. Strobe lights don't bother me. I take medication. Drinking alcohol is more of a trigger, but I just won't get carried away." She took a ladylike sip and looked around the bar, her head bobbing to the music in the background. The usual band was in the house, knocking off an acoustic cover of "Welcome to the Jungle."

They didn't talk for a couple of minutes, but Liam caught her staring at him once or twice. Hell, she caught him doing the same thing. They both blushed like kids each time it happened.

He couldn't remember the last time a woman had made him blush. Had he ever?

They laughed it off, and he asked her about her singing career. Pretty soon, they were talking comfortably, and somehow ended up on the topic of dating experiences gone wrong. He had to admit it pleased him to hear she was single. Before long, they were clinking bottles like old friends and teasing each other with good-natured pokes and jostles.

An hour later, she changed the subject. "So, aren't we supposed to be hitting rock bottom? I don't think it's meant to be this much fun."

"Yeah," he agreed, dropping back to reality. "I guess I'm avoiding it."

"So what does that mean to you? What's your rock bottom? Calling off your lawyer?"

Shit. He wasn't sure he was ready for that yet. All of a sudden, he didn't want to focus on his own issues. "We'll get to that. Tell me about your father first."

Her smile ran from her face. "Do I have to?"

Liam looked her straight in the eye. "Rock bottom, remember? I'll share mine if you share yours, group leader." She still seemed hesitant so he prompted her. "Your dad gambles?"

She let out a long sigh. "Yeah. The only times

I've seen him the past few years were when he showed up to ask for money."

"So he's not in your life at all?"

"I don't think he ever was, not even when I lived under his roof. He's obsessed. If he were here, he'd bet on which of us would finish our beers first. He's sick and has no desire to get better."

"You told me your friend's husband gambles too."

"That's how Lisa and I met, at New Horizons. She was one of my first attendees. Donny is almost as bad as my dad. Neither of them will have a happy ending."

"Thus, your protest." He took a swig of beer, careful not to turn this into a blame game.

"Look," she said, puffing out her cheeks. "I'm sorry I hassled you at your grand opening, but you have to understand where I'm coming from. A compulsive gambler is like a drug addict. They can't stop. They don't know how. So it's up to those of us left behind to try to make sense of it all." Kate picked at a nick in the table, tracing it with her fingertip, lost in thought.

Liam waited for her to continue.

"My dad doesn't want to change. He doesn't think there's anything wrong with him. He thinks the rest of the world is askew. I can't change him or the past, but maybe I can affect some small change in the world where he lives." She stared at him, her brow furrowed with worry. "You seem like a decent person, Liam, but I won't sit here and lie to you. I won't pretend I like your line of work, because I don't. I can't. I've been hurt by it too many times."

And here he wondered if she might sleep with him? He probably had a better chance with Beck outside. "And yet you give your dad more money so he never hits rock bottom?"

Her lip trembled in a way that made him want to put his arm around her. And, though he hated to admit it, it also made his pants feel tight. "I know, and that's why I'm a fraud," she said. "I shouldn't be leading those meetings. My friends would be so disappointed if they knew the truth."

He put down his beer and reached for her hand, wanting to make her feel better. Damn, her skin was soft. Surely it was no different than another woman's, but for some reason it felt like velvet in his hands. "Last I checked, you weren't nominated for a sainthood, so don't worry if the halo doesn't fit. Maybe you should stop worrying about helping your friends, and concentrate on helping yourself."

"I don't know how."

"Yes, you do, Kate. You've always known. Stop giving your father money. He has to hit his lowest point before he can get better."

"The problem is, I'm afraid his rock bottom will only come with him at a cemetery. He should have hit his lowest point years ago."

He brushed a hand against her cheek. "Why do you say that?"

She looked at him, her eyes now brimming with tears. "My mother died because of him. If he didn't hit rock bottom over that, he won't change just because I cut him off."

He caught one of her tears as it trailed her cheek. "How did she die?"

"She killed herself."

Fuck. Maybe the beer had rendered him overly sympathetic, but out of nowhere waves of sorrow began to wash over Liam, making him feel as if he were drowning in a vast ocean. "Oh, Jesus, Kate. I'm so sorry." He gathered her into his arms and held her. She didn't fight back and laid her head against his chest. It felt right there. He ran a hand over her soft hair, gathering her ponytail into his hand and fingering the silky mane.

"It happened ten years ago, but it feels like last week. She'd put up with my dad's gambling since I was a kid, had begged him to stop until she was hoarse. When I was at college, he lost everything, cleared out my mom's accounts, threw it all away. She'd begged so many bank managers for leniency, had borrowed so much money from family members and friends. The shame was just too much. She took a bunch of painkillers one night, and left a note saying she wanted it all to go away."

Kate's shoulders trembled in his arms. "And you know what he said to me when he found out? He said, 'Katie-bug, I can't believe she'd do such a thing after all the good years I gave her.'"

Liam said nothing. What could you say to that?

"I still feel sick when I think about it. Right after he said it, I must have spent the next hour crouched over the toilet. I puked my guts up every night for a week afterward. And my dad just kept on betting. He didn't even come to the funeral. It made my skin crawl, to see him so diseased."

"I don't blame you."

"I just couldn't look him in the face anymore.

My mom supported him their whole married life. She dug him out of every hole. And when he'd finally broken her, he still didn't snap out of it. I don't want my friend Lisa to end up the same way."

"I'm sure she won't. She has you."

"My mom had me too." She let out a bitter laugh and swallowed back a huge gulp of beer. "What good am I? Lisa says she admires me, but she has no idea I still enable my dad."

He grasped her by the shoulders. "Then justify Lisa's faith in you. Right here. Right now."

She blinked away a few more tears. She reached inside her handbag and produced a bank card and a small pair of craft scissors. "This card is how I leave him money. Will you cut up the card for me?"

"No. But I'll hold it while you cut it up."

She gazed at him, unsure. Liam offered her an encouraging grin and held the card out for her.

"Go on, Kate."

With a nod, she positioned the scissors and cut straight through the plastic. Half of the card dropped on the table with an anti-climactic tap. Liam picked it up and she did it again to both halves.

She looked up at him as she put the scissors back in her bag, pale, but clearly relieved. Like the weight of the world, or at least a good-sized chunk of it, had been taken of her shoulders.

"I'm proud of you."

"I've been carrying those damn scissors around for months, trying to get up the courage." She let out a quiet but shaky laugh. "I don't think I could have done it without your help."

His chest swelled with pride at that. He couldn't have felt better if he'd discovered fire. "This calls for another beer."

She smiled. "I'd like that. But you'd better make mine a cranberry juice. I've had enough excitement for one evening."

As he motioned for the waitress, his gaze still locked on Kate, he was determined to give her a lot more excitement. Just not the card-cutting kind.

***

Kate stood in the ladies' bathroom at Franky's while Liam took care of their order. As much as possible, she cleaned up her mascara smudges with a wet tissue. She still had the chopped-up bits of bank card in her jeans pocket. Before she lost her nerve, she walked into one of the stalls, dug them out and dropped the plastic chunks into the toilet, flushing for good measure.

No way she could fish them out in a moment of weakness now.

Only she didn't feel weak anymore. She felt like freaking Wonder Woman. Liam Doyle had helped her surmount her greatest fear. That had to go in the dictionary under the definition of ironic. In cutting up her card, her plastic crutch, she felt as if her last connection to her dad had been severed, and the ever-present ball of tension in her shoulders seemed to have rolled away.

As sad as it sounded, she needed to eliminate that bond. Their relationship was toxic, and until he accepted help, there was nothing she could do for him. It was time to start taking her own advice.

She reapplied a bit of lip gloss and pinched her cheeks to give them some color. It seemed important to look good for Liam now. It was bad enough he looked as edible as a country-western sex god with his muscles, jeans, and boots. She didn't need to look like a pasty, snotty kid next to him. Grinning at her reflection in the mirror for encouragement, she left the restroom.

The shouts in the bar area caught her attention before she even got back to their booth. The band had stopped playing and everyone's attention had gathered around two men. She craned her neck to look.

Liam had another man pressed up against the bar.

"Oh, my God." She raced forward, pushing past a couple of bikers.

"What did you say to me?" Liam's face was inches away from the other man's.

"You heard me. Call off your boy Perreira. You're fucking stalking me and my family. It's bad enough I can't go anywhere in my own house without hearing your name. Now I have to get threats from your legal team? Fuck you, Doyle. I don't care if you can afford the best lawyer in town. You. Don't. Get. Michelle."

So this was Andy. She wanted to dislike him on Liam's behalf, but she supposed she could see why he had a hold on Bridget. He was handsome, although lankier than Liam. She had to admit there was something about him that set her on edge. Perhaps it was the self-entitled air that surrounded him like a halo of smoke around a Vegas gambler.

Sure, she could understand why he'd resent Liam, but shouldn't he also be somewhat appreciative? Liam had taken care of his family for three years. You'd think the man could muster up a little humility.

On the other hand, she hadn't been harassed by lawyers for who knows how long.

"We'll see about that," said Liam. "You said yourself, Michelle loves me, not you. She'd be happier with me, you piece of shit. You abandoned her."

Andy pushed Liam back. "Get the fuck off me, Doyle. I made my mistakes. I owned up to them. Bridget forgave me."

"Well, I didn't. And Bridget doesn't know which way is up. Don't play good daddy with me. I know you're scum."

"You're pissed because Michelle's my kid, not yours. And now the great Liam Doyle wants to get one of his prized possessions back."

"She's not a possession." He curled his fist in the other man's shirt.

"Could have fooled me, the way you're after her. You got a special trophy case for her to live in?"

Kate sidled up to him and put a hand on his back. She felt his muscles tense, ready to lunge. "Liam, don't rise to it."

His eyes stayed locked on Andy. "He doesn't deserve her."

"I know. Come on. Let's go sit down."

Kate gently pried Liam off Andy. The crowd dispersed and the band resumed playing.

Andy straightened his collar and sneered. "Call off Perreira. And if I ever catch you trying to contact my wife or kid again, I'll have you arrested." He grunted. "You know, all this attention to another man's daughter makes me think you might be a pervert. Some sort of sicko who gets off on children."

Before she could stop him, Liam turned and let his fist fly. The resounding crack was one Kate would never forget. Andy fell back against the bar, cradling a bleeding nose.

"I'll sue your fucking ass," he shouted in a nasal voice. "I've got witnesses!"

A few of the men drew near, Beck and Nolan and a big man from behind the bar she assumed to be Franky. Beck ambled forward and put a hand on Liam's shoulder. "I wouldn't be so sure of that, friend," he said. "It's pretty dark in here. Hard to see."

"Yeah," echoed Nolan. "Hell, I've had so many beers tonight, I'm not even sure where I am."

Franky helped Andy to his feet, but not out of kindness. "Get the fuck out of my bar, dipshit. I don't like people who upset my regulars." He wiped a glass with a tea towel, but his gesture indicated he'd rather wipe the floor with Andy.

Andy let out a laugh laced with spite and glared at Liam. "Guess you own this place too, huh?" Muttering to himself, he staggered out of the bar.

Kate ushered Liam back to their table. He still resembled a serpent waiting to strike, his shoulders and arms tight, and muscles coiled.

He turned to her as they sat down. "You don't

113

believe that garbage he was spewing, do you? Please tell me you don't believe it."

The crack in his voice moved her more than she'd expected. "Of course not. He's angry and just wanted to hurt you. How did he even find you?"

He shook his head, staring at the table. "Bridget must have told him I come here. When I spotted him, I lost it." He looked at her, his brows pulled together, his mouth tight. "I lost it, Kate. They've made it clear I'm not part of the family. Michelle's not mine, but it's so hard to see her saddled with that asshole. What do I do?"

She placed her hand on his leg. She longed to stroke his thigh, but she kept her hand still. What would Liam want with a nutty protester who'd been trying to shut him down a week ago? They were just nursing old wounds and trying to find a little bit of support in each other.

"You let them go, Liam. Just like I had to let my father go. Right here. Right now. For three years, you did right by that little girl, but for your own peace of mind, you need to say goodbye. Call off your lawyer."

"She won't remember me."

"But you'll remember, and you'll know you always acted in her best interests."

"It doesn't feel that way. I feel like I need to protect her from him. Do more for her."

"A wise man once told me I needed to take care of myself too." She squeezed his leg, unable to resist the pull any longer. He covered her hand with his. "Take care of yourself. Give yourself what you need now."

Liam gazed at her, his eyes bright. His expression, full of surprise and sudden heat, made her squirm in her seat. He leaned in and his masculine scent flooded her nostrils. He smelled so good, looked so good, and she wanted him more than she wanted anything else.

When he spoke, his voice low and his mouth near her ear, he shattered what was left of her resistance. "I need you, Kate. Fuck, I need you right now."

"Oh…"

She barely got the exclamation out before he pulled her to him. God help her, she let herself be wrapped up in his arms and indulged in a moment she knew would inspire future, copious bouts of self-pleasure.

He pulled her against his wall of a chest, and she let out a squeak. His lips smashed against hers and she struggled to catch her breath under his unexpected but welcomed invasion. Their lips parted and his tongue slipped between hers, soft and strong all in one tasty package. She opened to him, panting, wanting more, wanting his touch all over her body.

She wanted him to kiss and lick and tease her. She craved the feel of his silky tongue on her neck, on her breasts, and sliding between her swollen pussy lips. She wanted Liam Doyle to swallow her whole, ride her on a wave of orgasmic delight, and then do it all over again.

Cradling her head, he took her mouth in an even more demanding fashion. Minutes passed. She assumed it was minutes, but it might have been hours. When he finally released her, his pupils were large, black circles rimmed in blue heat. He stroked her bottom lip with his thumb, no doubt appraising his handiwork. Her lips felt twice their size from his fervent caresses, and never better. She'd gladly endure puffy, bruised lips to feel those kisses again.

He looked deeply into her eyes, as if trying to glean whether she would accept more from him. "Kate," he whispered. "I'm going to take you home now and I'm going to fuck you. Do you have a problem with that?"

Her eyelids fluttering, Kate shook her head.

"Say the words so it's clear."

She had words? She couldn't seem to remember any right now.

Okay, Kate. Get it together. A very hot man just told you he wanted to do very naughty things to you. You need this.

"I don't have a problem with that."

He didn't smile but his face seemed to relax. He grabbed her hand and led her out of the booth. "That's my girl."

My girl? Kate barely registered anything as Liam waved goodbye to Franky and his biker pals. She just kept focused on the bar door, the portal that would lead her to a night of untold pleasure. Following him like a hungry puppy, she didn't say a word as he bundled her into the Ford and drove away.

Only a week ago she'd been protesting Liam's casino hotel, and now she was about to sleep with the man. Certainly he was just doing this to get out his frustration, to work off his testosterone after confronting Andy. If he'd been out with any other woman, the outcome would be the same. Surely she was going along with it because she had her own demons to dispel. And, although her exploits were hardly legendary, she knew enough to know that nothing vanquished demons like a night of rollicking sin.

She didn't bloody well care. It wasn't as if he'd asked to marry her. Like he'd said, they needed to take care of themselves right now, and she couldn't think of a better way than where this night was headed.

After the way he'd kissed her, like a man tasting water after a walk in the desert, she was pretty sure he would assume control tonight. Not that she had a problem with that.

Yes, she would let Liam Doyle dominate the hell out of her. She just knew she'd wear a huge smile for hours after that.

She could hate herself for it in the morning.

Chapter Six

Liam drove to her apartment rather than his condo or Vice. Despite the hungry pumping of his heart, going to Kate's place would give her an out in case they came to their senses.

He didn't want to come to his senses.

Driven by a primal need to orchestrate what happened next, he fought the urge to grab her and throw her on the nearest surface. Not easy to do, considering he wanted to fuck Kate until she screamed his name. He needed to lose himself in her and forget the ghosts in his life, the ones that haunted him in spite of his successes.

As he tore up the freeway, he recognized what was really behind his needs. Andy had said Liam was pissed at losing Michelle, his possession. As much as he railed at the idea, he wondered now if there might be a kernel of truth in the statement.

He'd never been a gracious loser. When you'd lost so much, it was hard to smile as life sodomized you again and again.

Part of the reason he had trouble letting go of

Michelle was because others had let go of him without a thought for his feelings. Without one word of comfort.

Now he wanted to seek a different kind of comfort with Kate. What was so wrong about that? They both needed the release. They'd both planned on turning a page tonight. She'd already begun to dominate his every thought. Now he'd have a chance to dominate her for a while.

They arrived at her building and parked in back. Kate frowned at her purse, searching for her keys.

"Hey." Liam ran a hand up her arm, hoping to calm her as much as himself. "You can always say no."

"I don't want to say no," she answered in a hushed voice, and handed him the keys.

He didn't say another word as they got out of the car. They walked hand in hand as he led her up the staircase. He opened the door and locked it again behind them once they were inside.

He hadn't taken note of her décor before. Her walls were coral, bright and cheerful. The focal point of the living room was an overstuffed chintz couch with big flowers. Shelves were crammed with books and decorative frames which housed photos of an older woman with auburn hair. Kate's mom? He could ask later. He liked the atmosphere she'd created in these humble quarters. The place seemed warm and homey, much like her.

He looked toward Kate. Her ponytail rested on her shoulder and she played with the end. She was nervous. The knowledge excited him as much as it disappointed him. She seemed to look around everywhere but at him.

"Um, would you like a drink? Coffee? Or I think I have some iced tea in the fridge." She shifted her weight from foot to foot, like a gazelle getting ready to bolt.

He approached her, feeling as ravenous as a tiger, and allowed himself to linger on the cleavage that had intrigued him for days. "No drinks."

She twisted the tip of her ponytail. "Right down to business, huh?"

He stood in front of her and breathed her in. Damn, she smelled good. It made him want to traipse barefoot through a fucking meadow. "I want to do something. I've wanted to do it since I met you."

She frowned.

"Trust me, Kate. I won't hurt you." He reached around her head and gently tugged the elastic from her hair. He watched as its red radiance tumbled over her shoulders. So beautiful. He fingered the soft strands. "Damn, woman. You don't know how much I've wanted to lose myself in all this hair."

She narrowed her eyes, clearly not believing him.

"It's true," he said. "Just thinking of you on a bed, your hair spread out on a pillow, makes me so hard."

Her blush made him even bolder.

He lowered his hand, rounding it over her hip, reaching toward her ass. Jesus, her curves felt so good. They seemed designed for his touch alone, and he longed to explore her more fully. To see what she hid under her sensible blouses. She gasped as he touched her, stiffened in his arms, but then relaxed into his caress. Just that little smidgeon of surrender had him biting his lip and straining in his jeans. "When I get your jeans off, gorgeous, am I going to find some more pretty red hair?"

In a moment of lustful madness, he grazed the area between her legs with one finger. Her knees gave in to a quick buckle. "I don't want to give too much away. Maybe you should find out."

He grinned, tightening his grip with his other hand, holding her up. With one, slow caress, he removed his hand from between her legs. "I can't wait to see you. All of you." He turned her around, and marched her into the bedroom. Her every movement, every breath, spoke of desire and white-hot fire.

She wanted him too.

Damn, he was going to enjoy this way too much for his own good.

***

What am I doing? This is Liam Doyle of Doyle Gaming. You hate him.

Only she didn't.

Yes, she was uncomfortable with everything he stood for, and didn't understand how he could go to work every day and not feel an ounce of regret. But she didn't hate Liam the man. In fact, she realized she quite liked him. Wanted to please him. And there was no denying how much he attracted her. Like a gawker at a roadside crash, she couldn't look away.

Surely the sentiment was bad. She didn't understand the pull he had on her, like a vicious undertow, dragging her into frightening new depths. But in this moment, as he began to undress her, she was more than willing to drown.

His hands traveled slowly over her frame, stroking and teasing as he slid them under her shirt. Each focused glide of his hands was proof of his sexual prowess. How many women had he undressed in the same, torturous manner? Each confident touch let her know that he must have had his share of women.

Once her shirt was off, he cupped her breasts over her most worn bra. Her nipples came to stiff points under his palms, the thin layer of silk barely a barrier. Why hadn't she thought to change her underwear? Probably because she'd never dreamed she'd actually jump into bed with the owner of the casino she'd been picketing a week ago.

How could she do this and look herself in the face tomorrow?

"You're so quiet," he whispered, scratching his thumbnail over her one nipple. "Second thoughts?"

Second thoughts? Hell, she barely had first thoughts. She should probably turn him away in the loudest, clearest voice she could muster. But she didn't want to.

Tonight, he was her own personal vice.

"No."

As soon as the word had escaped between her lips, an image of Lisa's kids sprang to mind. Were Georgie and Sarah miserable because their dad was caught up in a gambling spiral? Probably. In letting

Liam take her to bed, surely she was betraying them. Betraying herself?

He leaned in and licked at her neck, a sweet temptation that destroyed her resolve. Her normal breathing escalated into pants, and Liam stepped back and looked her over from head to toe.

"Undress for me."

Oh, nuts. What did he want, a striptease? She was pretty sure she'd look like a lame goose if she tried to shimmy like a pole dancer. "What do you mean?"

"I think it's clear, sugar. I want to watch you take your clothes off." His mouth set in a tight line, he sat on the bed. Liam Doyle on *her* bed. She bet if she looked outside, she'd also find the sun and moon colliding. He leaned back on his arms and waited.

Okay. How hard could it be, disrobing before a man who looked like he belonged on the cover of *Esquire Magazine*? He'd already started her off by removing her shirt.

Wishing she were more graceful, she toed off her Keds, doing her best not to avert her eyes. She supposed she should be returning his sultry gaze, but was pretty sure she resembled someone about to throw up.

"Kate," he interjected. "I already think you're stunning with your clothes on. Trust me, the view will only get better." He glanced at her hips. "Take off your jeans."

Channeling the badass warrior woman who had protested at Vice, she unzipped her jeans and slid them off, then removed her bra and slid her cotton panties down and stepped out of them, all without thinking of repercussions, or guilt, or gambling.

Tonight, he was just a man and she was just a woman. And they both needed this.

For that reason, she did what her body was aching for her to do. She caressed her breast, plucking at her nipple.

"Fuck," he muttered, palming his cock over his jeans. "Keep doing that."

She drew closer to his prone body, standing between his spread legs, and touched both her breasts. Repeating a move she'd once seen in a cheesy porn movie, she licked her fingers and circled them around her nipples. He stared, glassy with hunger, and went for his belt buckle. Okay, maybe porn stars knew a thing or two.

It seemed strange to be completely nude before his still-clothed form, but when Liam released his cock, she stopped caring. She couldn't tear her gaze away from his exposed member. It throbbed for her, and she dropped to her knees. Laying her hands on his thighs, she lowered her head and took him in her mouth.

He tasted good, salty, clean, and strangely sweet. He moaned as her lips tightened, and he grew harder inside her mouth, twitching with need. Kate lapped at a drop of precum. His flavor coated her tongue, whetting her appetite for him, making her want more. She rubbed his thighs, stroking tense muscles, and took him to the back of her throat.

He let out a string of curses that almost made her laugh. Thinking Liam Doyle was enjoying her blowjob was enough to make her giddy. She continued to lick happily, but then he grabbed her shoulders and eased her up.

"I can't take it," he said. "To see you on your knees, naked, sucking me off…Jesus, I'll come like a teenaged boy during his first porn."

"But…"

"No, sugar." He got up and laid her down on the bed, then slid down her body. "You come first." His blue eyes glittered, hypnotic gems, as he spread her legs.

She couldn't look away as he met her pussy for the first time. He traced her lips with his thumbs, sending delicious jolts through her system, and exposed her clit. To tease her, he tugged at her red pubic hairs, and winked. And right before she lost herself completely and begged him to take her, he lowered his head and…

She threw her head back on the bed as his tongue swirled. *Oh God, I did need this!* He administered the sweetest of torments, slow licks that made her doubt her sanity. So good, so good.

He groaned, as if relishing each fresh taste of her juices. Each small sound ratcheted up her lust, driving her closer to pleasure's pinnacle. Two fingers, then three, slid inside her and he gauged her response. With each small twist of his wrist as he massaged her, she grew wetter and her body seemed to lighten and float. She just needed a pinprick to set her off, and she'd careen into the sky.

"You're delicious." He stopped a moment to kiss the inside of her thigh, then suckled her clit.

"Oh, Jesus!" The shrieking voice, as unfamiliar as it seemed, was hers. She came, and Liam continued sucking until he'd wrung the last shudder from her body. Shock and fucking awe.

Even as her legs crumpled and her knees folded inward, he held her open and continued to lap. Her body flailed as new spasms shot through her. When they did subside, she wriggled under him, enjoying the warmth and wetness he'd created. He finally moved from between her legs and sat next to her, smiling wickedly at his handiwork.

"Oh my God. I can't believe what you did to me," she said on a breath. "You, of all people."

The corners of his mouth began to droop. He wiped his wet lips with the back of his hand and looked away.

Shit. She sat up, blinking over burning eyes. "I'm sorry, Liam. That came out the wrong way."

He tucked his still-hard dick back into his jeans and stared at her, his face suffused with a strange mix of hunger and disappointment. For a second, she glimpsed a frightening gleam in his eyes. The embodiment of Bridget's words: a punisher. A man who held grudges and never forgot. His cold, blue eyes now held a feral glint, and made him appear capable of anything. All traces of congenial Liam disappeared, and only a hard shell seemed to remain.

This angry Liam scared her.

From this man, she expected some sort of retaliation. She could feel her muscles tense in anticipation.

However, as quickly as she spied the fury in his gaze, it disappeared. Those Husky eyes softened, becoming more like that of a scorned puppy.

After the longest, most awkward moment of her life, he reached over and tucked a strand of hair behind her ear. He let his fingers graze her in the gentlest of gestures, and considered her face. Under his quiet scrutiny, she sighed, her body wanting to relax into him.

He got up from the bed, reached for her shirt, and placed it over her head, feeding her arms through the sleeves as if she were a doll. And she let him dress her. She fucking let him.

He took a step back. "Good-night, Kate."

As he walked out of her bedroom, she finally rallied herself. "Wait."

His back was to her, his shoulders rounded and tense. He looked over his shoulder, but not at her. "Make no mistake. I want you, but not like this. Not when you hate yourself for being with me." He glanced at her. "I'm not a villain, Kate. Once you figure that out, maybe we can talk."

She didn't move, and listened as he walked out, closing the door behind him. She stayed frozen to her spot, listening to his fading footsteps on the metal staircase outside until she couldn't hear them anymore.

And then she tried to devise a way to deliver a swift kick to her own ass.

***

One hour and a demolished pint of mint chocolate chip ice cream later, Kate stared at the TV, clothed in her favorite terrycloth robe. Normally, sliding into the fluffy garment would elicit a sigh of relief from her. Tonight, the fabric grated. After all, she'd felt Liam's hands and tongue on her body. Nothing else would ever feel as good. Not silk or expensive lotions. Hell, not even a bath in chocolate sauce.

"Don't be ridiculous," she muttered. "It was just an emotionless one-night stand that got all fucked up."

Only her emotions were currently riding at an all-time low. Her emotions felt like dust that had been scattered in the wind.

She'd hurt him.

As if. He'd probably already forgotten her. In fact, he'd probably headed right back to one of his casinos and picked up one of the honeys that no doubt constantly batted their eyes at him. Touching her? That was skill, not passion. It likely meant nothing to him. Playing an instrument, nothing more. This was Liam Doyle, after all. What had she expected? Pledges of love and romance?

Perhaps not, but she'd been up for a good, solid hammering, something she hadn't had in a while.

Someone on the TV spoke and she looked up. She grimaced at the eHarmony commercial, as if it had been put up just to taunt her.

"Shit." She dropped her spoon in the empty tub. "Shit, shit, shit."

She'd had Liam, a veritable sex god, disrobing her in her apartment, and she'd messed it up. A jury of horny women would surely hang her for such an offense.

And she'd insulted him, all because of her stupid values. Last time she checked, values didn't keep her warm at night. Values didn't snuggle on the couch with her. Values didn't want to fuck her into next week, but Liam had offered. She knew he would have delivered too. The miserable voice inside her head told her she'd lost out on the best night of her life.

The worst part was knowing she'd wounded him. All he'd wanted was a bit of solace at a bad moment in his life, and she'd managed to rub salt in his wounds and make him feel like a worm. She didn't think she could hate herself more, and didn't understand why it should bother her so much.

As soon as the eHarmony spokesman reaffirmed that he had the perfect match for her, she decided to call it a night. Dumping the remains of her gluttony in the sink, she made her way to the bathroom, then wandered back toward the kitchen to make sure her freezer door was closed tightly. Damn door had a tendency to pop open.

It was then she noticed the open living room window. But the A/C was on, and she wouldn't have left the window open. As the sinking feeling hit her soul, she turned and saw a figure in the room.

He was no more than a dark shadow. But he was real, and he was big, and he was in her living room.

He moved in front of her, his body a wall of black clothing. Before she could scream, he pinned her to the kitchen wall and grabbed her jaw.

"Well, well." His voice was like gravel and cigarettes. "Louis Callender's kid. I can see the resemblance."

"Who the hell are you?" Kate managed to say.

"Sorry, Red. I ask the questions here and you'd better answer. " He looked her up and down, his iron grip locked on her face. "Now, be a good girl and hand over the money."

"What are you talking about?"

"You are Louis's kid?"

"His name is on my birth certificate, if that's what you mean."

The man eased his grip and caressed her cheek, making her want to vomit. "Well, Red, your daddy borrowed a lot of money from me. And it's time to pay it back. With interest."

She would not cry. She would not cry, as terrified as this shit made her. "So talk to my father. It's his problem, not mine."

The man angled his head. "Oh, I did talk to him, sweet cheeks. And he pointed me in your direction. I know old Louis doesn't have a pot to piss in, but he said you've helped him before. So it's your problem now, darlin'."

"What makes you think I have that kind of money just lying around?"

The man's measured movements made her think of a komodo dragon in a nature show. His beady eyes and thick limbs even resembled the predatory reptile. He slithered his hand from her cheek down to her neck, his touch light but ready to strike. "You'll just need to find it somewhere. Five grand. If you don't come up with it, I might be forced to cash in another way."

She wanted to scream, but the sound stuck in her throat. "Please…"

He leaned in and breathed on her. "You know,

you are very pretty." He moved one large hand down her torso and loosened the tie on her robe, pulling until the two flaps opened. He gawked at her chest. "*Very* pretty. That's why I won't break anything tonight, but you might have a few bruises when I'm done. Something to remember me by."

She tried again to scream, but only succeeded in squeaking. She threw up her hands to protect herself. It was no good. Within seconds, his hands were on her shoulders and he'd shoved her against the wall. Reeling from the impact, she barely had time to recover before he hauled back and let his fist fly toward her face. Hard bone cracked and shards of lightning flashed in front of her. She fell to the floor.

Somehow in her fall she'd finally managed a scream, but it sounded so far away.

Somewhere in the foggy distance she thought she heard a man's shout and someone banging down her door. In the eternity it took for her to raise her head, she saw her assailant race to the open window, hauling his body through to the fire escape. And then, a loud noise from the front door.

"Kate!"

Cradling her already swollen eye, she managed to prop herself up on her elbow to see better, sure she'd drifted into unconsciousness and a new dream world. There in her living room again, fists clenched, was Liam. With his lips stretched thin and his jaw ticking, he looked ready to murder her attacker. He sprinted to the fire escape window and lunged out the window in an attempt to grab the man. However, she could already hear him pounding down the fire escape steps.

"Fuck!" Liam shouted. "Get back here, you fucked up piece of shit!" She flinched when she heard another bang, but realized it was just Liam slamming his hand against the wall.

Shock and pain made her arms give out and she fell back to the floor. As agony claimed her body yet again, she closed her eyes. Within seconds, Liam's arms supported her, gently sliding under her and picking her up. He carried her to her bedroom and laid her on her bed, cursing the entire way. When he set her down, he brought the flaps of her robe together and tied it, preserving her modesty.

Even in her haze, that one small action made her heart skip a beat.

She didn't know why Liam had come back, but she was glad he was there. Too stunned by events, she didn't have the wherewithal to question his sudden reappearance. She just lay back and closed her eyes as the mattress rushed up to cushion her.

The bed dipped under his weight as he sat next to her. "Who the hell was that nasty fuck?" He touched a hand to her hair.

Kate didn't say a word, she just enjoyed his gentle touch. Way better than a bath in chocolate sauce, or so she imagined.

"Don't faint now."

His clear, forceful tone brought her back to reality. "I won't. I just had no idea getting popped in the eye would hurt so much." She cracked open her good eye. "I guess this'll be my first shiner."

The paleness of Liam's face made her wonder if he might lose consciousness instead. "Who was that man?"

"A loan shark, I think. My dad borrowed money from him. A lot."

"And now he's come after you?"

"Seems that way."

More swearing. He stood and ran his hands through his hair.

"Don't go," she said softly. Not again.

"I'm not going anywhere." Liam's voice rose. "What if he comes back? We need to call the police." He pulled his cellphone out.

She touched his hand and his head snapped up, his gaze locked on her. "Please, Liam. Just give me a chance to breathe first."

He frowned, but put the phone away. "Okay, breathe." He touched a hand to her brow, checking out her eye, grazing her skin softly so as not to hurt her. "I don't suppose you have any frozen steaks in your freezer?"

"Is that all you can think about? Food?" Wanting to cry, she'd made a joke instead. Maybe humor, as feeble as her attempt might be, would ward off the tears.

He glared at her, as if angry she could kid under the circumstances, but then his mouth relaxed. "You're a piece of work, you know that?"

"I wouldn't argue the point tonight."

He brushed a hand over her head and sighed. "I'm going to raid your freezer for a bag of...gluten-free peas or whatever. Are you okay for a minute?"

The waterworks threatened like a tsunami gathering momentum, but she blinked them away.

"I'm sure I'll even be okay for two or three."

With a look that suggested his desire to turn her over his knee, Liam stood and made his way into her kitchen. She couldn't help but look at his ass, but then remembered she was on the verge of having a nervous breakdown and shouldn't be noticing men's rounded tushes at all. Especially not his.

The pain in her head launched another assault on her, making her see stars. Or were they dancing pumpkin carriages? She wasn't sure. She just wanted to close her eyes, take a lot of medication, and forget the world for a few hours. Groaning, she held her head and turned into the pillow.

As much as she'd always dreamed of being able to put her one jujitsu lesson to work, tonight was proof she'd never have a career in martial arts.

She heard Liam's footsteps return and opened her eyes. Her pain must be written all over her face because he began cursing again. The man knew a few colorful words, probably from hanging around his casinos. He came bearing a bag of frozen peas, a glass of water, Tylenol, and what looked like a clean, wet tea towel.

He put the items on her bedside table and helped her sit up. "Here. Let me clean you up."

She reached for the tea towel. "I can do it."

The laser-like focus of his eyes resembled a lead dog sprinting forward on the Iditarod. "Kate Callender, you will sit still and let me help you. Understand?"

She nodded, unsure if she was grateful or pissed off for his macho attitude. Grateful might be the better plan, given his current frame of mind. She could easily see how Liam had become such a powerful businessman. As thoughtful as he could be, he made it very clear when he wouldn't take no for an answer.

He opened the Tylenol bottle and popped a couple into her hand. As she swallowed the pills, he held the glass to her lips. Again, she wanted to argue and say she could manage a drink on her own, but she was embarrassed to admit she sort of liked this dynamic.

He continued to stare at her lips as she drank, but he might have been staring at a puzzle whose last piece he couldn't locate. After a few sips, he removed the glass and turned away.

"Now," he said, grabbing the tea towel. "Let me see if I can clean that cut. You'll probably have a black eye from this. If I ever see that bastard again..."

He didn't say what he would do, but from the darkness in his eyes she knew it wouldn't be good. She had no idea why Liam would be so upset about her being hurt. Sure, most guys would hate to see a woman battered, but there was something in his face that told of more than just general concern. Still, they barely knew each other, and just when they'd begun to get along, she'd managed to piss him off again. Although the set to his jaw certainly hinted at a possibility of him caring. Maybe a little.

No, that punch must have made her loopy. He was only being nice.

So why had he come back?

He wrapped his hand in the wet towel and

applied a soft pressure to the cuts on her brow. Shit, it hurt. Despite trying to appear strong, she let out a slight moan. As soon as she winced, he pulled his hand back. He sighed and continued gently, cleaning the blood from her brow. His fresh breath fanned over her, minty, despite drinking beer earlier, and his amazing cologne combined to enhance his already-intoxicating aura of manliness. She felt a little light-headed. Had he found the old prescription for Tylenol 3 in her medicine cabinet and fed her that, rather than the regular stuff?

"There," he said. "I think the worst of it's gone." He placed the towel on her bedside table, then ran his thumb over her forehead. The touch sent ripples of warmth through her, and she fought the urge to grab his hand and make him touch her properly.

They stared at each other for an awkward amount of time, and then Liam produced the bag of peas. "Lie down," he urged. "I have to call the police. And I want my doctor to take a look at you."

"It's really not necessary."

"Don't even think of arguing with me." He put the peas on her face. "Lie down and close your eyes."

Even though she felt she should protest further, she did as he asked. The cold vegetables numbed the tender areas around her eye. When she felt him move, she cracked open one eye. Liam had left the room, but she could still see him as he stood just outside her bedroom. Facing away from her, he pulled out his cell phone. Broad shoulders gave way to a long, lean back, tapering down to a slim waist. He had the sort of body meant for embracing a woman. She knew this, and she hadn't even seen him naked, even though he'd seen her. He was the sort of man who could make a woman feel secure, cherished.

Even as those silly thoughts invaded her brain, the dancing pumpkin carriages rolled before her eyes again. She closed both her eyes and grabbed the hand of the imaginary footman. She boarded one of the carriages, waved at her invisible admirers like the princess of Crazytown, and drifted off into unconsciousness.

Chapter Seven

Near daybreak, Liam showed Dr. Chan to the door, thanking him for his assistance. Kate had put some proper clothes on, thank God, because if he had to see her on the couch in that fuzzy robe, it would do him in.

To think that bastard had seen her the same way, and hurt her…

Now dressed in khaki shorts and a pink t-shirt, she seemed no less vulnerable. Staring out the window, curled up with her knees tucked up under her, she reminded him of a little girl. Her hair was still down from when he'd removed her elastic.

She made for a sweet image, except for the circles of fatigue under her eyes and the darkening shiner.

No wonder she was tired. He'd accompanied her to the police station, where she'd pored through countless mug shots and ID'd her attacker, a local loan shark named Hugo Vaughan. He'd managed to stay under the radar for years, but was known to police for roughing up his customers and getting a little too friendly with the ladies.

Liam had confirmed the picture of Vaughan resembled the man he'd chased out of the apartment, although the loser had a shorter haircut than the one he sported in his mugshot. He'd held Kate's hand while she'd recounted the incident several times and answered their questions, all of which just seemed to make her retreat into herself.

Afterward, he'd brought her back to her apartment and had his physician give her a once-over. Nothing serious, thank God, but disturbing all the same.

Now it was time for him to go and leave her alone. Only he couldn't seem to make his feet head out the door. He'd already walked away once, and that had made his stomach turn over with queasiness.

After his time with her earlier, after seeing how her orgasm transformed his world, he couldn't turn his back on her now. He still wanted her, even though she wasn't sure what she wanted.

Kate glanced at the clock. "Liam, thank you. For everything. It's way past late. You should go home. You've done enough."

Had he? It didn't feel that way. He never should have left her alone. He should have stayed, pride be damned. "How are you feeling?"

"Numb."

He joined her on the couch, taking a moment to look around her living room, noting the lack of secure locks and cracked old window frames. "We need to get you to a more secure location."

She let out a giggle. "You sound like the dude on

Hawaii 5-0." She ran a finger over one of the red blooms on the chintz couch fabric.

"I'm serious, Kate. You're not safe here."

Once again, quiet fell over the room, long as a church service on Christmas Eve. Twice she was about to speak, but each time she said nothing. She simply took turns staring at her lap and staring at him, and he'd never felt more anxious.

What the hell was happening here? This woman was destroying all his resolve. After her slip of the tongue, he'd decided to walk out the door and not turn back. Give her time to decide what she wanted. But he'd only managed to pace up and down her street for the better part of an hour, wondering if he could fix things between them. Sure, he'd come on really strong, but they'd both been caught up in the moment. He'd walk away, forgetting that he felt at home with her.

Home.

Hell, any sense of home he'd ever known had been skewed, but in being with Kate, in breathing the air around her, he'd finally felt it.

He acknowledged he could have, should have, handled things better, but his desire had overwhelmed him. The moment he'd declared his intentions, he'd abandoned common sense, and became oblivious to the gentle rules of courtship. He'd only known red hot need. He'd returned, hoping to make things better, only to find that bastard Vaughan in Kate's unit. He'd wanted to tear the big ape to pieces. But right now it was more important to help her.

"Kate, you told the police your dad owes that

man five thousand dollars."

"Yeah."

"I'll give you the money."

"No, you won't. It's my problem, not yours. And it's not your fault my family tree is diseased."

"It's a drop in the bucket for me. I want to."

"I said no." She narrowed her good eye and her warm hazel gaze frosted over, hardening her face.

"But I want—"

"You want, *you* want! Is that how you operate? By browbeating people to accept what you want? Well, I don't work for you and I don't have to listen to you. And I certainly don't want you to give me money to pay off a crook."

"And if that shit tries to hurt you again?"

"Look, Liam. I appreciate the gesture, but all my life I've failed in distancing myself from my father's addiction. I've fucked everything up and I need to be strong now. He'll come up with the money. He always does. He may be down right now, but before you know it, he'll be flashing the cash around again. I've seen it all before. That man tonight was not the first person to demand money from me."

Liam had to close his gaping mouth. "You've had creditors come after you before?"

"It's not a big deal. They've shown up at my door many times. This was the first one to hit me, but others have made threats. They come to nothing. This guy will disappear like the rest once my father pays him back."

"And if he doesn't?" He knew he sounded angry but he couldn't help it.

She didn't reply.

"Kate, talk to me."

She stared into the distance, as if recalling unhappy memories. When she spoke again, her voice was almost a whisper. "I don't like going there. All my life, I've known my dad was no better than a thief and a cheat. But he's never left me holding the ball. Sure, he's played the blame game and begged for cash, but he'd never put me in real jeopardy." Now she really did look like a little girl, one who still believed her dad would keep her safe, if only in this one, small way.

It made Liam sick to think about that kind of pain. "He put you in jeopardy tonight."

"I've dealt with disappointment before," she replied, still in that sad, quiet voice. "I'll deal with it again."

He reached for her hand, but the phone rang and stopped him short. She vaulted off the couch like a gymnast.

Thank God someone chose to call, because he was on the verge of doing something stupid, like claiming her lips again. He could just envision his tongue coaxing her mouth open once more, tasting her. Dismissing his ridiculous fantasy, he watched as she answered the phone.

"Hello?" She paused and frowned. "Hello?" Liam could almost see the chills skittering down Kate's spine now.

"Who's there?" she cried, and then dropped the phone.

Liam jumped to his feet and grabbed the handset. He shouted at the person on the other end. "You even think of terrorizing her again, Vaughan, and I'll have you killed, you hear me, you sadistic asshole?"

As he slammed the phone back into its cradle he heard a man's dark laughter. He turned to Kate, shocked his reaction would be so violent. It made no sense. They barely knew each other. But the shattered expression on her face was one he didn't want to see ever again. For the first time that horrendous evening, she began to cry. Seeing those tears made his stomach pitch.

"I hate him," she said on a breath.

"He's a crazy fuck."

"No, not him. My father. I hate him."

His chest rattled with a strange pain. Her words broke his heart. And before he stopped himself to analyze exactly how much it bothered him to see her cry, he gathered her into his arms. At first, she stiffened as if to protest, but within seconds she let out a deep sigh and relaxed against him. Arms wrapped around her, he buried his face in the crook of her neck.

Home.

Her body yielded under his hands and he resisted the urge to explore her curves. God help him, he'd already memorized her shape, but he wanted to learn it anew. He spread his fingers, loving the roundness of her hips and soft dip at her waist. She dressed like the girl-next-door, but he realized he'd gladly spend a great deal of money to dress her in a flowing gown or silky lingerie, something to compliment her offbeat beauty. She deserved it.

"I hate him so much," she whispered against his

collarbone.

Her words brought him out of his reverie. That was it. "Kate, you're staying at Vice. I'll put you up in a suite there."

"Vice?" She pushed away, horrified. "I can't stay there!"

He wanted to shake her and hug her at the same time. He settled for putting his hands on her shoulders so she had to look him in the eyes. "Look, I know how you feel about my casinos, but there you'll have my security keeping an eye out for you. You'd be safer there than to stay here and take your chances with Scarface."

"If I stayed at Vice, I'd be a total hypocrite. How can you suggest it?"

He let out a sigh. "Just think of it as a fancy hotel. I know it's not ideal, but we are very good at being discreet. You'd be safe there, and you'll have everything you'd need. I can arrange a car to take you to your meetings or wherever you need to go." He smiled. "And you already know my security team. Some of them are pretty fond of you."

She held his gaze, ignoring the joke, shaking her head. "Why would you help me? I mean, after the way you left…after what I said earlier?"

"I know what you meant, and I can't blame you for saying it. And I'm helping you because you listened to me when I needed it. Although I hate to admit it, you gave me some good advice about Michelle. I don't know if I'm ready to call off Nando Perreira, but you've helped me…reconsider the situation." He wet his lips, remembering how easily her knees had buckled. She'd been so responsive to him. He'd seen the beauty of her orgasm, needed to see it and inspire it again. He gave her shoulder another slow squeeze, almost a sensual rub, and smiled, wanting to lighten the mood for her. "Now do you need help packing a bag? I may not have too many talents but packing a bag is one of them."

Her good eye widened and her eyebrow arched with amusement. "It's safe to say you have a few talents."

She was flirting. That was a good sign, a very good one. "I appreciate that. Let me help you."

"I think I can manage, thanks." She ran a hand over her head. "I still don't know about taking this…this little mini-break at your casino."

"This isn't a mini-break. Think of it as a safe house. Someone hurt you. I'm just putting you up for a few nights, not asking you to job shadow the blackjack dealers."

"I can find a motel."

His face scrunched up. "Yeah, I don't think so."

"Well, I'll pay my way. Every cent. It'll take me the next ten years but…."

Liam rolled his eyes. "Sure, whatever. Now while you get ready, I'll call the hotel to make arrangements." He shooed her into the bedroom. "Go on. If you don't, I'll be forced to take charge. And if I do your packing, you'll end up wearing orange shirts with purple pants."

She scooted to the bedroom, trying to hide the smile on her face. A smile. And he'd put it there with his dumb attempts at humor. Damn. Seeing that Cheshire cat grin on her face was a thrill he couldn't ignore. It worked on him in strange, powerful ways.

She stopped at the bedroom door and looked back at him. "I'm going to regret this, aren't I?"

"Don't be melodramatic. It's a hotel, not a trip on the *Titanic*. No one needs to know. After a few nights, the cops will locate Vaughan and you'll be safe. And then your life can go back to normal."

She frowned, as if unsure of what "normal" meant any more. To be honest, he wasn't sure either.

***

Kate walked into her new room, the suite in Vice that was destined to be her home for a couple of nights. Hopefully it wouldn't take longer than that for the police to find her attacker. Dismissing the shiver of fear that coursed through her at the thought, she looked around the suite.

It was unlike any place she'd ever lived. Thanks to her father's issues, the family living arrangements had always been modest at best. Penthouse 5D at Vice possessed a sophisticated opulence she'd only glimpsed in style magazines. No wonder Liam's clients seemed happy to while away their days at his lavish establishment. It would be difficult to leave such glamor.

Almost everything in the unit was silver or black, with splashes of scarlet here and there. Against a backdrop of white walls gleamed stainless appliances. Streamlined black leather couches seemed an extension of the dark hardwood floors.

And around the rooms, beautifully-coordinated red cushions, flowers and prints offered a hint of sumptuous color.

No velvet paintings of Elvis in this joint.

"I'll put your bags in the bedroom," said Liam, hoisting them through yet another designer-styled portal. She knew he employed bellhops, but Liam had insisted on carrying her things himself and hadn't let her lift a finger since they left her apartment.

It felt good, she couldn't deny it.

He dropped her bags onto a fluffy, crimson confection she assumed to be a bed. At least, she thought it was one, even though it was larger and more luxurious than any she'd ever slept in. Suddenly, her basic Malm from Ikea didn't seem all that cozy.

Liam turned, smiling, hands on hips, as if he'd built the room himself last night. "Well? Do you like the place?"

"What's not to like? It looks as if it should come with its own masseuse and sommelier."

"Actually, I do have staff who..."

"Liam, why have you put me in this room? You know I can't afford this. I'd be comfortable with something more low-rent." She ran a finger along the pristine surface of a cherry wood dresser, and then considered the dust on her furniture at home.

"Just enjoy it."

"I hope you didn't have to bump one of your VIPs for me. This looks like a love den for heads of state and their mistresses."

"You really don't know how to accept a gift, do

you?" He shook his head at her snarky humor but his eyes gleamed with appreciation at the same time. "Just smile and say thank you."

"But…"

"Kate." His hands clenched in a way that made her want to experience his tight grip again and again.

"Thank you," she said, holding up her hands in mock surrender. "I promise not to touch anything breakable."

Liam moved about the bedroom area, muttering something about making sure the room was set up as he'd requested. She'd heard him order all kinds of extras over the phone, ones she could never hope to afford: free movies on demand, large toiletry bottles instead of those puny sample sizes, and a full-sized fridge stocked with everything from vintage wines to exotic fruits she'd only ever glimpsed at the market. For all she knew, he might have tucked a Lamborghini under the bed.

She touched the soft duvet cover, checked out the label, and gasped at the astronomical thread count. "This is too much."

He walked over and pried the duvet edge out of her fingers. "You've had a shitty time. Just relax for a few days. Is it such a sin?"

"Ha. That could be the new slogan for Vice."

"You're right. Want a job on my marketing team?" His confident bad boy grin was back and put a wobble in her belly.

"Look, I know you're doing this to bribe me." She caught the look on his face and rephrased. "I don't mean bribe…I mean by getting me into your

148

casino, you'll convince me it's not such a bad place after all, and I'll give up my protest."

"You already gave it up."

"I can always start it again any time I want. I can bring you to your knees, big boy." She'd meant it as a joke, but as they stared at each other, the air grew heavy between them.

"Woman, I know you can."

His words made her want to tumble into that fluffy, red bed with him and not tumble out again for a few days. She didn't know what to say to lift the sexual tension, so she voiced the other thought plaguing her. "Do you always rescue damsels in distress?"

"Just redheaded singers who hate my guts."

"I don't hate you, Liam. In fact…"

He moved closer, making her all too aware of his size and shape and smell, all the things that made him attractive to her. Her pulse leaped and her breaths grew shallow.

"In fact, what?" His voice, so deep and quiet, coaxed a flutter of strange delight inside her.

"Just this." She put her hands on his shoulders and stood on her toes. Leaning into him, she dropped a chaste kiss onto his cheek. His stubble tickled her lips and she couldn't help the resulting fantasies that raced through her brain. She couldn't help wanting to experience the tender abrasion of his stubble on her pussy lips again.

Shocked at her thoughts and actions, she pulled away. But Liam put a hand to her back and held her firm. He wound his arms around her and cradled her head with his other hand and lowered his head. Her heart beat out of her chest, and before she knew it, she'd closed her eyes in anticipation.

A crush of sensation hit her as their mouths met. His kiss was gentle as he brushed his lips against hers. Sweet, sliding simplicity, as natural as embracing an old friend. But then his fingers curled against her body and his lips parted. His tongue darted out, and she took it in.

His hunger drove him deeper and he flicked at the inside of her mouth. Sucking her tongue, he made low, growling noises and his every touch screamed of want and fire and impatience. The kiss became one to annihilate all others from her memory.

"Dammit," he finally whispered as he snatched a breath.

Any coherent thoughts she'd had turned into a silly muddle of sex-saturated imagery. Her body, entwined with his. Pounding, driving motion that carried her to the highest heights. Finishing what they'd started earlier.

In that moment, she remembered where she was. In his casino. A place she wanted to destroy. And yet she'd agreed to stay, because she was weak and hadn't been laid in so long.

This was wrong. All of it. She had to forget it, and keep her distance from him.

He stared at her, blinked a few times, and seemed to glean her reticence. She wanted him, she knew it like she knew her own voice, but each interaction only succeeded in making her feel more guilty. She'd lived with guilt her whole life. Could they do this? Could someone like her actually take someone like him to bed and not wake up ashamed?

Damn, she sure as hell wanted to try.

But with everything that had happened that evening, neither of them seemed ready to take the plunge again. As if to confirm her suspicions, he removed his hands from her body and smiled at her. No longer a happy-go-lucky sort of smile, his expression had darkened with confident sensuality.

"Get some sleep. It's been a long night." He reached into his pocket and pressed a business card into her hand, taking time to stroke her palm. "This is my direct contact information. If you need anything, you know where to find me."

"Thank you."

He walked to the door in the outer room. As he put his hand on the doorknob, he turned and gave that take-no-prisoners grin once more. "Enjoy the suite while you can. You'll trade it in for my bed soon enough."

"Uh, that won't happen."

"Oh, it will and you know it. Enjoy your stay, sugar."

She watched him stride out of the room, unable to say anything that would make him understand why they couldn't. Before the door closed behind him, she saw him speak to the security guard posted outside.

Riddled with tension, Kate flopped onto her luxurious bed, rolled down the covers, and kicked off her shorts and underwear.

Remembering Liam's velvety voice and naughty smile, she touched herself and imagined him there. Right there. As she visualized his hard body between her legs, she came with a silent scream that did nothing to eradicate her fever for him. After removing her hand, she moaned, turned her face into the pillow, and tried to sleep.

Chapter Eight

Liam stormed into Sin, the first casino he'd built on the Strip, ready to bust some heads. He'd been called by John, the head of security there, before he even got twenty winks, let alone forty. They discovered who'd been stealing from him, and he was not impressed.

He'd dealt with theft before. It was a fact of life in the casino world. And each time they'd encountered a shark amongst the ranks, he'd been quick to act. If there was one thing he didn't tolerate, it was disloyalty. He treated his people well, and expected the same in return. No one fucked with Liam Doyle.

Wade, John's peer at Vice, accompanied him so he could offer input. He muttered as he tried to keep pace. "Liam, hold on. I can't keep up with you. It makes me look bad."

"So walk faster."

He headed toward the staff elevators behind the casino floor, ignoring the pointed looks from a couple of women in flashy dresses who looked as if they hadn't gone to bed yet either. They waved at him, clinking their wineglasses together. One of them gave him an unmistakably suggestive wink.

"Have a nice day, ladies," he said, ignoring their interest.

"Damn," Wade whispered. "You're stronger than I am, Liam. Those two are clearly looking for some action. Hell, that might have turned into a Liam sandwich."

They got to the elevator and Liam hit the button hard. "I'm not interested."

Wade raised a brow and stared at him. "It's her, isn't it? That Callender girl?"

He crossed his arms and glared at the closed door. Why was the elevator taking so long? "We're here on business, remember?"

Wade let out a hoot, clearly not believing a word he said. "I can't believe it. You're fucking Kate. Talk about screwing your rivals."

The door opened. Finally. He wished he could shut it on Wade and make him take the stairs. When his security head stifled a guffaw, Liam turned to him. "One, don't talk about her like that. She's been through a lot. Two, none of your goddamn business. If you weren't a friend, I'd fire your ass. Bad enough I have to deal with a goddamn thief right now."

"Excuse me for stating the obvious, boss." He peered at him through narrowed eyes. "Hang on. You're not fucking her, are you? *That's* why you're pissed."

"Wade," he threatened.

"No wonder you went to so much trouble to

make sure your little protestor was tucked away safe at Vice." He grinned and pinched Liam's cheek, as he would a child's. "Well, I hope you get some action soon. It's been a while."

The elevator stopped on their floor and he got out. "Are you keeping notes on me or something?"

"As head of security, I'm obliged to." Wade smirked. "Naw. I just know you." He stopped Liam by putting a hand on his shoulder and changed the subject. "Look, I know you're in a hurry to pound something, or someone, but I'm trying to make you take a second to breathe. You look ready to kill. Patrick's a kid. From what I've been told, he's been a model employee up until now. If he's been stealing from you, there's a reason. Let's just talk to him before you give him the axe."

"I didn't say I was going to axe him."

"You look like you wanna axe somebody."

Liam's lips pressed together "When did you turn into such a big softie?"

"It's part of my natural charm." He offered his boss a sly smile. "So, Kate, huh? She makes good cookies, you know."

Liam let out a grunt and proceeded to John's office. "Not now, Wade." Now he was in the mood to axe someone. A big, nosy, security guard someone.

Inside the security office, John already had Patrick Lester sitting uncomfortably at his desk. The kid stiffened as soon as he entered.

Like Wade said, Patrick was no more than a kid, maybe nineteen. But this kid had quietly pilfered funds from one of the casino counters. He worked as a ticket agent, selling tickets to some of their musical shows. He'd been caught pocketing some of the cash that crossed his desk, to the tune of a couple of thousand dollars.

He glanced at Liam and whispered, "Oh, shit. Oh, shit."

Liam shook John's hand and congratulated him on catching their thief. Not exactly Ocean's Eleven caliber, but frustrating all the same. He sat next to John while Wade leaned against the closed office door, watching.

Liam didn't know Patrick personally, but something in his frightened demeanor was awfully familiar. This wasn't a hardened criminal of the Hugo Vaughan variety. He got a sense Patrick regretted his bad judgment. Sure, he was shaking like a leaf at being caught, but there was a measure of bravery in the thrust of his shoulders, as if he'd accepted he'd have to face the music. This boy reminded him of himself as a younger man, one who made a hell of a lot of mistakes. He rested his elbows on the desk and contemplated a plan of action.

The old Liam wouldn't have even been here. He would have told his team to call the police and end the matter. But since he'd met Kate, he'd started to read between the lines. Yes, there were people in his life who'd surprised him with their callousness, but others continued to shock him with their hidden depths. Things weren't always as simple as they appeared.

He looked Patrick in the eye. "Why did you steal from me?"

"Am I going to jail?"

"That depends."

The boy took a deep breath. "I'm sorry, Mr. Doyle. My dad just lost his job and money's tight. My parents can't pay the bills. I try to help, but it's never enough, and so much passes through this place. I didn't think it would be missed. I did the wrong thing. I know I screwed up. I know you're going to fire me, but please don't send me to jail. My parents need me."

A kid trying to hold his family together, trying to make decisions in a grown-up world. Liam sympathized in more ways than one. "What did your dad do for a living?"

"He was a janitor at one of the other casinos but he got downsized. He was with them for years. Supervised his own crew."

He turned to Wade. "Don't we have an opening at Vice in Facilities?"

"Yep."

Liam stared at Patrick for a moment, then bridged his finger over his lip. "Tell your dad to come to the HR office at Vice tomorrow. I'll tell the HR manager to expect him."

The boy stared, then blinked. "What?"

"You can stay, Patrick, but I'm transferring you to a back-office job, one where you won't have to worry about temptation. We'll be keeping our eye on you, but it's still a second chance. Most people wouldn't get one. What do you say?"

"Hell yes, sir!"

They shook hands. Or, more accurately, Patrick rang his hand like a dinner bell on the ranch. "Then keep your nose clean. John here will report back to tell me how you're doing."

John, who matched Wade in bulk and height, merely nodded at Patrick, which said more than words could.

"Thank you, Mr. Doyle. I promise not to let you down." He jumped out of his chair and out of the room.

Once the kid was gone, Wade turned to Liam and grinned. "Who's the softie now? More of your new girlfriend's influence?" He and John traded laughs at the boss's expense.

Damn Neanderthals. Liam stood, letting them have their little moment. Maybe he'd screw around with their vacation time to get them back. He stifled his own chuckle at the thought.

As they left the casino, he did wonder about Kate's influence on him. Jesus, it seemed all he did was wonder about her these days. He checked his watch. It was still early. Maybe he could head back to his condo and sleep for a few hours and then hit the gym. He needed an outlet, needed to get physical with something.

Since tasting Kate yesterday, feeling the rush of her wet pussy, he'd been out of his mind— especially after seeing the look of disappointment in her eyes. Clear as day, her face had fallen because she'd realized she'd liked how he touched her. Him, the big, bad casino owner. On some level, she still saw him as the enemy and she hated herself for being tempted.

He was tempted too, and with a force that verged on the frightening. Her body had felt right under his fingertips. Her scent was burned into his brain, making him want to keep her naked and fuck her senseless. And her taste. He was still reeling from her particular sweetness. For someone who claimed not to eat sugar, she'd tasted like sugar pie, hot from the oven.

Sugar. She probably thought he used the pet name out of habit with any woman, but he'd only ever used it with her.

He shook his head and banished those images of Kate that would only come back and haunt him later.

Hating that the bothersome redhead had once again drifted into his consciousness, Liam grunted and returned to his waiting car, slamming the door behind him. Damn. Forget sleep. Maybe he'd go straight to the gym after all.

As his driver maneuvered the Escalade through Vegas traffic, Liam stared at the passing sights without really seeing them. Why was he so obsessed with this woman? So she was afraid to submit to him. There were worse things in life, like having Michelle ripped from his arms and out of his existence. Like watching his mother die when he was five years old. Like watching a heart attack kill his father nine years later, then having his stepmom turn on him when he was just a kid, like out of some fucking fairy tale. He'd wallowed in misery for a good part of his life, and was determined no one would ever do it to him again.

And yet the way Kate had looked at him after being so intimate made him feel defeated, as though she thought him no better than a wad of gum under her shoe.

Ah, hell. He needed some perspective. It just hurt because he was hard up. In his quest to get Michelle back, he'd avoided the dating scene, not that he'd felt like it anyway. Now his body was paying him back, making him lust over a woman who equated him with Satan. What was he bloody well thinking?

He was thinking, despite her bruised face and frightened demeanor, that she looked beautiful. Now that he'd had the opportunity to examine her many times, he wasn't sure how he'd ever thought her anything but beautiful. He could admit that much. With her cheeks flushed in anticipation, she'd been the most ravishing woman he'd ever seen. And she'd wanted him as much as he wanted her.

Yet her face had changed so quickly. She hated herself for staying in a casino hotel, felt she'd betrayed her morals, and she blamed him for all but forcing her into it. Well, she'd have to get over that. If the loan shark had found her home, he'd be able to find her regular haunts. At least under his roof he could have a security detail for her.

He stared out the window as his driver headed back to Vice. A drunk young woman carrying a pitcher of beer wobbled on the sidewalk nearby. She toppled, spilling the brew all over in front of a frowning, elderly tourist. Sin City at its finest.

Sometimes he was so tired of this place.

Was Kate? Surely a non-gambler couldn't enjoy living so close to the Strip. As he once again wondered about her opinions, he fought the urge to pound her out of his brain.

Shit, why am I doing this?
Because you want her.

Yes, sheltering Kate at Vice was lunacy. She might implode from indignation alone. Was he just being a Good Samaritan? He'd never pictured himself in the role. Frankly, he'd been too busy trying to stay alive during his formative years. After losing his parents, things had degenerated so badly he'd barely bounced back.

But he had. He was a fighter.

And as a fighter, he'd learned to wear a mantle of distrust around his shoulders. The philosophy served him well, in business and in life. He knew there were few people in this world he could truly count on, at least of those who weren't on his payroll. After all, he'd been betrayed by so many who were close to him. And the sense of abandonment he'd experienced after losing his parents was unparalleled.

He'd tried to be a good person and do a good thing by temporarily housing Kate. But he knew his motives ran deeper than simple philanthropy. She moved him. She excited him. And he needed to be inside her like he needed food and drink.

So what should a fighter with abandonment issues do? Well, clearly he had to persuade her to give in to her own hunger. Because now that Kate was on his turf, he wasn't letting her go.

***

By the evening of her second night at Vice, Kate was going stir-crazy. Staring at the same four walls, no matter how exquisite they were, made her break out in hives of restlessness. She needed to have a break from hotel TV programming and room service. She needed to stretch her legs.

Granted, the room service had been spectacular. Even though she'd tried to order the cheapest things on the menu, she'd been dazzled by the quality. The only room service she'd ordered before Vice was at some dingy hotel in Reno, where she'd had the processed chicken fingers with a side of nausea. But at Vice she'd had Angus burgers, freshly-squeezed juice, and a breakfast platter of bacon and eggs Benedict that had her salivating just remembering them now. Liam had taken great pains to ensure even the casual fare at Vice was worthy of Michelin stars.

Just as he'd taken great pains to make her comfortable. Every few hours, she received calls from Liam's assistant, a lady named Pearl, asking if she needed anything, and the man himself popped in frequently. He never stayed long. Each visit was fraught with tension, but he brought her lots of little treats. To say nothing of how Wade's security detail stood sentinel outside her door. She felt like freaking royalty.

Or maybe a prisoner. No, definitely royalty.

Okay, more like a pretend princess with a lop-sided crown.

As nice as everything was, she needed an hour or two of fresh air, or a reasonable facsimile. Surely a change of scenery wasn't off-limits. She'd spoken with the police again. They approved of the idea of her holing up at Liam's hotel. Of course. It saved

162

them from having to send officers to babysit her. However, they'd told her to stay put if she could. Any crook who'd break into a woman's apartment and try to rearrange her face couldn't be trusted not to do it again.

But a girl could only order pay-per-view for so long. She needed to see other people. It seemed her only option was to go for a walk within the confines of Vice, as much as the idea pained her.

"Oh, come on. It's not as if you're rolling the dice. You're just going for a walk."

She caught her reflection in the mirror and almost changed her mind. Her shiner had deepened into a hideous brown, as if covered in grotesque shadows. Thank God it hadn't puffed up too much.

Still, did she really want to promenade around Vice like that? Perhaps she could disguise the bruises. Grabbing her makeup case from her suitcase, she headed to the bathroom.

With a light touch, she applied some foundation, taking care to add a little extra on the tender spots where her skin had turned green. When she'd finished, Kate judged the final product and decided she still looked like a woman trying to mask a hideous bruise. Sighing, she picked up her purple eye shadow, the one she never used because the aubergine shade overwhelmed her fair skin. Applying some to her eye shadow brush, she proceeded to paint her other eye, very much hoping the end result would be a stylish, smoky eye on both sides of her face.

She gazed at herself in the mirror. Between her red ponytail and colored eyes, she resembled a whorish, sleep deprived Pippi Longstocking. Realizing she'd never completely camouflage the black eye, she released her hair from its ponytail, brushed it and flipped it so the fall of hair mostly covered the bruised eye. Veronica Lake, she could never hope to be, but it was good enough.

Letting her hair down reminded her of when Liam had done the same. The moment had gone down in her personal history as one of the most seductive ever. To feel his big hands in her hair, with a gentle yet demanding touch, made her wonder if he was the sort of man who liked to pull hair in bed. The sort who would turn her onto all fours, gather her hair in his palm, and pound her to heaven.

She blinked hard and tried to dislodge the aggressive yet enticing vision from her brain. "Yikes."

After taking a few cleansing but otherwise ineffective breaths, she changed into the best clothes she had brought with her. Clean jeans and a cotton top with a few sequins scattered beneath the neckline might not win her a prize at Fashion Week, but they'd do. She spritzed herself with her favorite perfume, the one that made her smell like her mom's garden, grabbed her purse, and opened the door.

Wade, now on duty, turned to greet her. He took in her outfit and hair with a raised eyebrow. "Hey, you look nice. Goin' somewhere?"

"I was hoping to escape my suite for a little while. The walls are closing in on me."

The big man smiled. "I get ya. Let me alert the

team and I'll show you around."

"No chance of me getting away on my own for a bit?"

"Not if I value my job. Liam left strict instructions to cover you at all times."

Ignoring the sudden flutter of nerves at the mention of Liam, she closed the penthouse door. "Well, I guess some company would be nice too." She deposited her key card in her wallet and heard Wade on his walkie-talkie, detailing their whereabouts to whoever was on the other end. Then he pulled out his cell phone and quickly texted someone.

"Who are you texting?"

"Liam."

Of course. "Why?"

"He wanted to know when you left your room."

"He's busy. Surely he doesn't need to know every time I pee."

Wade suppressed a grin. "Something tells me the busy man will still appreciate knowing."

Soon she was walking the casino floor, observing some of the customers with Wade in tow. It was easy to spot the gaming addicts from the various expressions on their faces—ranging from vacuous to obsessed. Each turn she took around the great room made her feel a little sadder. However, there were plenty of people there who just wanted a good time. Newly-married couples, singles on vacation. She even spotted a few who looked familiar. She suspected some of the ones wearing shades were celebrities. Liam certainly had a varied clientele. They weren't all compulsives, either.

Most just wanted to have a little fun.

For the first time in her life, she regretted taking such a hard stance on gambling. Who was she to judge everyone for the failings of a few? Addiction was inside us, and one way or another it tried to find a release. If she searched hard enough, she could probably find an addiction in everyone.

She certainly had one, a tall man with an intense gleam in his eyes.

They turned a corner and moved into an alcove with endless rows of slot machines. Kate noticed a man sitting at one, and something about his sandy hair made her look twice. She took a few more steps until she could make out his face.

Donny.

Lisa's husband sat transfixed in front of the slot, his hand hovering over the various buttons. She cleared her throat, hoping to catch his attention, but nothing short of a crumbling sinkhole under him would distract him from his game.

She moved toward him but Wade put a hand on her arm. "You know that guy?"

"He's my friend's husband. I just want to say hi."

Wade frowned and pulled out his cell, murmuring something into it. Ignoring him, she approached Donny and smiled. "Hey, Donny."

He didn't look up.

"Donny?"

"*What*?" He stared at the machine, frowning, and then pulled out his wallet to count his cash.

"Donny, look at me," she said in a louder voice. "Lisa's worried about you."

His head snapped up at the mention of his wife. Donny's lip curled, his usual greeting. He didn't like Lisa going to New Horizons and hated her association with Kate and the other members. "Shit. Did Lisa send you to spy on me?"

"No, of course not."

"Then piss off." He turned back to the machine.

"Look," Kate said, "maybe we could pop over to one of the cafes here and grab a coffee. You look like you could use one and, frankly, so could I."

"I don't want a coffee."

"Okay, a sandwich, then. Are you hungry?"

Donny growled.

"I just want to talk with you."

"Leave me the fuck alone, *bitch*."

A male voice sounded from over her shoulder. "What did you say to the lady?"

Liam was there standing next to Wade. Kate's heart skipped a beat. His anger was clear as he moved next to Donny.

"Liam, it's okay," she said.

"No, it isn't." He addressed Donny. "I asked you a question."

"And I'm not answering." He looked Liam up and down. "By the way, you can piss off too. I don't need you jokers preaching or handing out pamphlets about sin and vice. I'm in the middle of something."

Liam hauled him out of his chair and pushed him toward the doors. "Not anymore, you're not." Wade followed at the ready. Kate scurried after them.

"Hey," shouted Donny. "Take your hands off me! Who do you think you are?"

Customers lifted their heads to check out the

commotion. Well, some of them did. Others didn't bat an eye, still focused on their activities.

Liam offered him a small smile. "Oh, no one important. Just the owner." He shoved Donny toward the revolving door at the entrance. "Get out of my club and don't come back."

"B-but…" Donny stammered. "It wasn't my fault. She interrupted me." He looked at Kate as if seeing her for the first time. "Why are you here, anyway? Shouldn't you be at one of your precious New Horizons meetings, tearing families apart with your stupid New Age bullshit? Because of you, Lisa kicked me out. I'm fucking homeless because of you."

"Don't you dare," she began. "Lisa couldn't take your crap anymore."

He broke free from Liam and made a lunge for her. She froze, remembering Hugo Vaughan's attack. But Liam already had him by the scruff of the neck. "It's okay, sugar. I've got him."

"Sugar," Donny spat. "Well, isn't that just fucking heart-warming?" He glared at her. "Fucking the toast of Vegas, are you? Wonder if Lisa knows her little saint isn't quite so saintly?"

She looked away, horrified. She'd completely lost track of Lisa and the folks at New Horizons. She'd only been able to think of Liam and her own situation.

He pushed Donny through the revolving door and told Wade to put Donny in a cab, and to bill it to the casino. Donny reluctantly left, with Wade's help, shouting at her the whole way.

Liam now turned to her, grasping her hands, then

168

stroking them. He ran a hand over her loose hair. "Are you okay?"

That was when the tremors hit. She couldn't handle this…whatever was happening to her. The guilt, the desire, the feeling that she shouldn't surrender to him. It was just too much. Liam took her in his arms and held her close.

"Kate, sweetheart. You're okay. I've got you."

Damn, that scent! She just wanted to be with him again in some small way. Was that so horrible? She felt horrible for wanting it.

Even as she fought the wave of guilt that washed over her, she decided she was tired of being a victim. To her dad, to men like Hugo Vaughan, and most of all, to her own desires. She wanted Liam Doyle, had to experience him looming over her in bed, even if only once. It might be wrong, but she no longer cared.

She let out a sigh and looked at him, feeling oddly better now. His roguish face, gentle and savage all at once, gazed down at her.

"I've tried to stay away but I can't stop thinking of you," he said. And then his lips turned up into a grin. "Let me take care of you."

Her resistance shattered, she nodded. "I want you to do much more than take care of me, Liam. I want you. I want you to fuck me until I beg you to stop."

His grin became a wolfish smile. "As you wish." He grabbed her hand and led her back to the elevators.

Chapter Nine

Crazed hunger.

That was the only way Kate could describe the scene as Liam got her into her hotel suite. Not that she had time to stop and analyze their actions. This was a time for…well…vice. Dirty, nasty, fantastic sin. They both seemed to need it.

From the moment he shut the door, his lips were joined to hers. Feeding off her, drinking from her, opening her up and devouring her trembling lips. Claiming her mouth the way he would soon claim the rest of her.

His hands roved over her curves as he moved her into the suite's foyer. "Bed," he commanded. As if he needed to.

He pulled her into the bedroom. She kept her eyes closed, relying on him to guide her, overwhelmed by their heat. She knew when they'd arrived because he'd stopped moving. Like a coma patient waking, she cracked her eyes open and took him in.

Liam stood before her, yanking at his tie. Part of

her knew she ought to start removing her clothes, but she couldn't take her eyes off him as he disrobed. His navy tie flew across the room. One or two buttons popped as he pulled at his shirt. And then, as need radiated from his every feature, he worked his belt buckle.

He beckoned to her with a finger and a smile, and pushed his pants down, revealing black boxer briefs that looked as soft as a second skin. His erection strained inside them, stretching toward his waist band. She stepped toward him, already craving him, wondering how he would move inside her.

"You look like a kitten approaching her first bowl of cream," he said.

She dropped to her knees before him, not bothering to answer. She palmed his length, marveling at the bulk of him. Liam let his head fall back as she touched him, and groaned low. Those carnal tones spurred her on and she slid her fingers under his waistband, luxuriating in the feel of manly skin. His hand tangled in her hair, caressing her. But as soon as she pulled down his boxers and licked him, his grip tightened and he tugged.

She took him deep into her mouth and gave thanks for men who loved to pull hair. Right now there was almost nothing she could imagine liking more.

"Christ, Kate," he muttered, clenching his glorious ass. "You're no kitten. You're a hellcat."

Giddy from his response, she smiled. And then as he watched, she licked him from balls to tip, drinking him down. Nuzzling the skin near his sac, she breathed deeply, smelling soap and just a hint of excited sweat.

Perfection.

Sensing him so close, she latched her hands around his thighs and took him to the back of her throat. Liam groaned and reached under her arms, gently tugging. His balls tightened and his thighs flexed. She had no choice but to release him and stood up, pouting.

"I wanted you to come in my mouth," she said.

He ran his thumb over her lip and kissed her hard, biting her flesh. "Not yet. You don't even have your clothes off and I need to see you come first. All I can think of is you coming, over and over."

Liam kicked off his shoes, pants, and socks. He had the body of a god, and obviously took care of himself. His slim waist, tapered hips, and amazing pecs had her drooling. His biceps and quadriceps made her dream. And his cock, well, that lengthy miracle just made her ravenous.

He stepped around her, yanked back the comforter, and sat on the bed. He made her stand between his legs and began to work on her shirt, lifting it over her head. He brushed his large fingers over her ribs and she sucked in a breath. She'd always been nervous about exposing her curves, but Liam made her feel like a goddess.

There was nothing in his eyes that made her feel heavy or less than perfect. His hunger made her brave, it made her want to display everything to him. To show him parts of herself she'd never shown anyone before. Her tummy flexed when he touched her there, and for the first time she didn't regret her extra padding. He continued to run his hand over her skin, as if wanting to banish all her insecurities.

"You take my breath away," he said.

Emboldened by the compliment, she reached behind and unclasped her bra. His gaze dropped to her breasts and his pupils dilated. She quickly unbuttoned her jeans and stripped out of them, kicking off her shoes. Clad only in old purple leopard-print panties, she straddled him on the bed and he wrapped his arms around her.

He throbbed against her pussy as she ground against him. He took her nipple into his mouth and sucked.

Kate let out a moan and arched her back, but he held her firm. He seemed to grow even more under her, his cock touching her tummy. Wishing she'd removed her panties as well, she swiveled her hips and felt her moisture soak the thin layer of cotton. Liam tended to her breasts, reaching one hand between them while the other felt between her legs. He let go of her nipple with a pop and grinned at her.

"So wet. I fucking love it."

Perspiration began to take hold. She ran a hand through his hair. "It's what you do to me."

His grin disappeared and he looked at her through somber eyes, ones that didn't miss the intensity of the moment. He made her wet, he made her want. He drove her out of her mind, and they both knew it. It was a relief to admit it to herself, and to him.

"Yes, well," he said. "You have that effect on me too." He took his rigid cock and slid it over the crotch of her panties.

Already reaching the breaking point, she dropped her head onto his shoulder and sighed. He let out a chuckle and angled his head so he could connect with her breast again. She held on for dear life, rocking against him and watching as he ministered to her body. He seemed to understand exactly what sorts of touches she required. He licked gently at her nipples, bringing them to stiff peaks, then closed his mouth and applied more pressure, sucking until she cried out. Just when she thought this oral caress could not make her squirm more, he bit down and dragged his teeth along the distended tips.

Before long, Liam's hand snaked around her hip and down into her panties. He danced his fingers over her ass, allowing his middle finger to tease a path between her cheeks. Lower and lower he went, moving around until he'd gone so far he could play with her clit. Tapping and circling, he stimulated the little nub. Kate moaned and pressed her ass against his hand, wanting more of him. Wanting him inside as well as out.

With his free hand he made her look at him, then penetrated her with his other finger. With an aching slowness, he pressed deeper into her, scoring her insides and making her bite her tongue in mad lust.

"Fuck, you're making me insane," he said.

"Wanna feel it where it counts?" she teased.

He let out a deep breath as he finger-fucked her and then removed himself on a wave of new moisture.

"Oh," she whimpered, lamenting his loss.

"Don't worry, gorgeous. I'm not done." Liam rolled her onto her back, and she felt the warm covers cushion her. Her legs hung over the side of the bed and he knelt before her, between them. He walked his fingers up her legs, winding up to her panty elastic. As he reached her pussy, he teased her, swiping his thumbs over her swollen mound. She arched her back, her nipples reached for the sky, and he rewarded her by giving them a hard tweak.

"Do you like that, baby? Do you like how I touch you?"

Her only answer was to thrash on the bed.

"I can do you one better, Kate." He slid his hand back down her torso, claiming each inch of skin, and hooked his fingers in her panties. He slowly pulled them down her legs.

Kate raised her head to watch. No sight was quite as intoxicating as watching Liam lick her pussy. The look his face had already proven a game-changer for her.

Once he'd dropped her panties on the carpet, he spread her legs and inhaled. She hadn't waxed in some time, and hadn't even shaved because he seemed to appreciate her little thatch of auburn curls last time. He smiled and touched a reverent hand to her lower lips, stroking them gently. And with every caress, his eyes showed his consuming interest, and then narrowed with obvious pleasure.

He looked at her as if he'd never seen such a perfect woman before, and it made her feel cherished and alive.

"You have a beautiful pussy, Kate." Liam dragged a finger through her seam. "I see how it clenches and flutters whenever I touch you."

"Liam, please."

"I've been dreaming of tasting you again. Everything tastes like ashes compared to you."

Before she could respond, he lowered his head and slid his tongue inside her. He explored each sensitive nook and cranny, then spread her legs wider, keeping his strong hands clamped on her shaking thighs. She dug her hands into his thick hair, needing to hold onto something as the swirling cyclone of delight ravaged her core.

Liam flicked his tongue against her clit, his hungry noises punctuated by the odd groan. She wiggled under him, pressing him even closer, as her orgasm signaled her in the distance, warning her of its imminent arrival.

He glanced up, sensing how close she was, proving his intuition as a lover. He latched onto her, sucking and sucking, raking his fingernails over her bottom. The cyclone inside her rampaged, flattening everything around it. His tongue laid waste to her and she cried out his name. She held on like a sailor facing an oncoming storm.

As Kate imagined what it would feel like to have him thrust his cock inside her, the storm arrived. She came and her sightlines went black. All she knew were shudders and sweet agony and the sheer devastation of the cyclone razing her world.

Part of her prayed he'd stop, the pleasure was almost too painful. The other part of her exulted when he failed to do so.

176

He lapped at her, his tongue flat and greedy. And just as her body quieted, the storm reared its head once more, threatening in the distance, intent on ravaging her again.

"Liam, please stop."

He arched a brow and tormented her clit with his finger. "Really?" The bastard then grinned at her.

"Are you crazy? Of course not!"

Clearly amused by her response, he buried his face in her pussy once more, sucking her lips into his mouth.

"Oh, Jesus. Jesus, shit. *Christ*!"

He laughed against her skin. "What a sacrilegious little hellcat."

"Should I...be praying instead?"

"Oh, you might wanna pray." He rose off her and reached for his discarded pants. He pulled out his wallet with one hand, keeping his other hand on her body, stroking her thigh, tickling her pussy, sliding a finger inside her and then teasing her. He produced a condom, ripped off the wrapper with his teeth, and quickly rolled it on.

Kate eyed his impressive package and waited for the imminent onslaught. Instead, he surprised her by picking her up in his arms and carrying her over to a large dresser in the corner. He set her down before the sturdy piece of furniture and bent her over it. There was a beveled mirror attached, the kind with three panels. She looked into the mirror and saw not one, but three, Liams behind her, each of them red in the face and breathing heavily, like a bull preparing to charge.

"Hold on," he commanded.

She reached for the sides of the dresser but the surface was too wide. It was all she could do to grip the top, her fingers laid out flat.

With one determined thrust, Liam drove inside her, grunting her name. She felt herself stretch with the wonderful invasion, her nerve endings waving flags of surrender as he plumbed her pussy. He moved so easily in her, as if he belonged there. She didn't even have to try to clench as he thrust. Because of his girth, she naturally tightened around him, and he moaned in what could only be satisfaction.

"Fuck, Kate," he spat, curling over her. "Shit, woman, what you do to me."

He picked up his pace, swiveling his hips like he wanted to punish her. She clutched at the dresser top, but moved with such force she couldn't get purchase. Her hands slipped and squeaked over the polished surface, but she didn't care if she left streaks. All she could think about was how Liam filled her, moved her, consumed her with his touch. He owned her body already.

As another orgasm barreled toward her, he clutched her hair in his fist. Tugging, but not too hard, he made her look in the mirror.

"Watch while I fuck you. I want to see your face when you come all over me."

She caught his intense, fierce gaze as he voiced his demand. Three Liams stared down at her as if they wanted to devour her. His jaw, dotted with stubble, clenched. His brow was furrowed. And there was a wildness in his eyes that drew her in as much as it terrified her.

178

A man with demons. She suspected he'd only allowed her to glimpse one or two of them so far. Seeing him in this primal state, so virile yet vulnerable, made her want to please and comfort him. God help her, she wanted to know more about him, needed to know everything, and wanted to share herself with him in return.

This wasn't just a quick, careless coupling. No one night stand. Something big was happening here.

But she couldn't contemplate that now, not while he touched her with such savage grace. Caught up in his own rapture, Liam threw his head back and pounded away at her. She closed her eyes and concentrated on the delicious friction. So animalistic, yet so sweet. But just as her womb began to flutter again, he withdrew.

She opened her eyes and almost cried out from the loss. "Liam?"

"I'm right here, sugar." He grabbed at her hips, held her tight, and re-entered her with a mighty thrust that made her see stars. As she cried out her ecstasy, he withdrew and plunged back in, over and over, each thrust deeper than the one before. Still grasping her hair, he slapped her ass and everything inside her vibrated. He seemed to grow harder and heavier inside her, and her body hummed and sang and bloody well shrieked its delirium. She came again in a fireball of lust, and had to cover her mouth because of the strange sounds erupting from it.

He slammed into her one last time, shuddering and shaking, then collapsed onto her back and kissed the nape of her neck. He didn't release his hold on her hair, but loosened it, gently massaging her scalp where he'd tugged it.

"My God," she managed when she found her voice.

He chuckled behind her and nipped her shoulder. "Jesus, Kate. That was unreal."

Her heart pounded at the thought she'd satisfied him. More than satisfied, she dared to hope, when she felt how he lifted off her with another series of shudders. She couldn't move. She remained bent over the dresser, her ass in the air, her eyes closed.

Liam laughed and slapped her ass as he headed to the bathroom. "Too worn out to move?"

"Too worn out to breathe."

Soon he'd returned and stroked her bottom. "Careful, Kate. If you keep showing me that pretty ass, I might take advantage of the view." He crouched and bit her on her right cheek.

"Ow!"

Liam laughed. "I warned you." He put his hands on her shoulders and gently pulled her up into his embrace. He ran a hand over her sweaty brow and pushed aside her messy hairs. Then he just looked at her, his gaze full of an emotion she couldn't quite decipher.

They stared at each other. She began to regret not doing it in bed. In bed, it would have been natural to turn to each other and cuddle. But here, in front of a dresser? What were they supposed to do? Should she ask him to climb into bed with her? It was still early and he probably worked late. Was he anxious to leave? She didn't quite understand the post-coitus protocol in this situation. She doubted such a protocol even existed in their case.

"So," she said. She was at a loss for words, only knowing she didn't want him to go.

He brushed his fingers against her face, grazing the area under her bruise, more soft and intimate than any old touch on the cheek. One look, one caress, from this man and she was mush.

"It's okay," he said. "You don't have to say anything. Just feel." And like that, he enfolded her in a big bear hug.

Feel. Damn, it seemed all she did was feel around this man. She felt anger, guilt, raging desire. She'd never felt so much for anyone in such a short time and was pretty sure most of it was wrong.

Her eyes began to itch, but she blinked the burn away. He released her, kissed her forehead, and walked into the bathroom, returning with two complimentary bathrobes. He placed one around her shoulders and slid into the other one. She immediately lamented losing sight of that amazing body, but told herself it was better this way. Too much naked Liam made Kate a crazy girl.

He motioned to the bed, then sat. "Sit with me."

She nodded, glad he was taking the lead. She sat next to him, cross-legged. He watched her tuck her legs under her and a small smile crept onto his face.

"I like you, Kate. It's been a long time since I've smiled like this."

A thousand butterflies took flight in her belly. "I'm glad you're smiling. You deserve it." She played with the rumpled bed covers, smoothing the fabric between her fingers. "You said you were starting to reconsider suing for Michelle's custody."

His smile disappeared. "I don't know. She's so little. I just wish I could explain to her that I'm not abandoning her. She won't remember why I left. All she'll know is I'm gone."

He said the last word with such vehemence, she made a horrible realization. Someone important must have abandoned him. The idea bothered her so much she had to know if it was true. "Who abandoned you?"

His head snapped up, his expression now cold. "No one."

"I think we both know that's not true."

He shook his head, but said nothing.

"Liam, I can see you're hurting. And it's about more than just Michelle."

"You're wrong."

"There's no shame in talking about it."

"How very New Horizons of you."

"Well, the program has its merits. They helped me. Let me help you."

"Kate," he groaned, running his hand through his hair in exasperation. "We're having a nice moment here. Why ruin it with needless talk?"

Needless talk? Boy, she knew she was stubborn, but he took the cake. "Liam, you told me you were ready to hit rock bottom. You can't do it unless you open yourself up."

He glared at the sheets. "Maybe this rock bottom thing isn't such a good idea."

"Liam…"

"Look, it's not important."

"You're important."

He stood up and gathered his clothes, frowning

as if he didn't quite believe her. "I don't know why you're fishing for information. You want me to tell you I had a hard life? Fine, I had a hard life. Yeah, it's pretty sweet now, but I had to work for it. I worked my ass off for it."

"I'm not disputing that."

He looked at the bunched up suit in his hands. "I know what you think. Nice clothes. Nice career. Fancy cars. Oh, and women. Lots of women, if I so desire. And you're right. I can have all of it, if and when I want it."

Ouch. She had a sneaking suspicion he'd said that to wound her. Mission accomplished. "How very nice for you."

"It's fucking awesome." He twisted his hand in the wad of designer clothing. "So I don't need you playing shrink, getting me to admit my deepest, darkest fears, and expect some kind of breakthrough. That shit only happens on TV."

Kate was dumbstruck. What had happened? He'd turned on a dime, and all because she'd tried to help the man who'd helped her.

Yet she couldn't help feeling he was pushing her away on purpose. She'd struck a nerve, and it made him scared. So did she let him walk away, or did she continue to probe?

Well, she'd never been the sort to accept defeat. She wouldn't now.

She hauled her body out of the bed, ran to the door and blocked it.

"Get out of the way, Kate."

"No."

"I mean it."

"No. You are going to stay here and you are going to tell me what happened to you. And I don't mean the bullshit you'd find on a press release. I mean the real you." She put a hand on his chest. "The real Liam."

He stared at her, his face drawn and sad. Then he laughed in such a way her blood ran cold. Once again, he resembled the man Bridget had described, the man who got off on punishing others.

"You don't ever wanna meet the real Liam. Trust me. Now move out of the way, Kate."

"No," she said, quiet but firm. "You're trying to push me away to see if I'll come running after you. Well, here I am. Running. What happened in the bedroom felt real. It wasn't some random fuck. And I know you felt it too. When you looked at me in the mirror, I felt...centered and scared all at once. I don't understand any of it, but there it is."

He made no response, but stared at her robe.

"Dammit, Liam. I shared my soul with you! How dare you take that and try to walk away? I know you're in pain, so let me be here for you. Please."

His chest rose and fell and he gave it a vigorous rub.

"What's wrong?"

"Nothing."

"Then talk to me. I'm not going anywhere."

After what felt like an eternity, he let his hand drop. She swore she saw wild barrens in his cold eyes as they bored into her, could almost feel frostbite nipping at her fingers and toes.

He grabbed one of her hands, turned it over, and kissed her palm. "You won't like what you hear."

184

"Maybe not, but I can take it. Now sit down, Doyle, or I'll smack your sweet ass."

He cocked a brow at her, the first hint of anything less than quiet fury. He might be ready to talk, but she didn't trust that he would. Even still, he walked back into the bedroom, sat down on the bed, and patted the spot next to him. "You asked for it."

She stared at him, almost afraid of what he would say next. What had the world done to him? She was terrified to know, as much as she needed to hear it.

Her heart pounded madly as she joined him in the bedroom.

Chapter Ten

As Kate plopped down on the bed next to him, smelling of flowers, sweat, and of him, Liam fought the urge to take her once again. She made him forget himself, and at the same time she forced him to remember.

Who abandoned you? She probably had no clue she'd hit the nail on the head with that question. And dammit, she deserved an answer.

But could she handle it? All of it?

He wasn't quite sure how to explain. After all, he'd never shared the truth with anyone other than the social services worker who'd followed his case so long ago.

He'd been able to bury the pain, to ignore it, at least most of the time. But since meeting Kate, the old demons seemed to want to take another stab at him. Every time his heart galloped unsteadily, he knew suppressing those feelings wasn't working anymore.

As if to prove the point, a sharp pain stabbed at him. He sucked in a breath and fought the urge to clutch his chest. It was just stress, nothing more. Stress could be controlled.

Kate touched his face. "Liam? I'm here for you."

His eyes were burning. Shit, that was a new feeling. He really didn't want to blubber in front of Kate. He took a deep breath. "Okay. When I was a kid, I lost everything, everyone who meant anything to me. That's why I've been fighting so hard for Michelle. I didn't want her to go through the same thing."

Kate crossed her legs and her robe fell open, exposing her calves. Liam stroked them, wishing he could lose himself in her body again and forget the past for a few minutes longer.

I never wanted you. And now it's time for me to have my own family. Liam, you're just not part of it. You never were.

The voice of his stepmother made him want to spit. He must have made a face because Kate leaned in and kissed the side of his mouth, soft yet urgent, as if wanting to take his pain away.

"Tell me."

"My mom died when I was five. We were at home, having lunch. I remember she made us ham sandwiches. I have trouble picturing her face sometimes, but I can still see those damn sandwiches." He paused, unable to recall the exact shape of her eyes. "I was sitting with her at the table when she began to make strange noises." This much he did remember, as if it was yesterday. "My mom started to choke in front of me and I was too young to help her."

Kate's hand flew to her mouth. "Oh, no."

"I thought everyone would blame me. Of course, no one did. I was just a kid, but even at that age, a part of me felt responsible."

"You couldn't have helped her. You must know that."

"I do know it. My dad explained later that she'd had an aneurism. But for a long time, I told myself I should have been able to save her, only to find out there's no way I could have." He closed his eyes for a second, recalling the terror that kept him up for so many nights afterward. "An aneurism. Just the thought of it scares the shit out of me. How do you possibly fight something like that?"

"No one would have expected you to do anything."

"I know. My dad said the same thing, but he was also struggling. Her death changed him. He sort of lost interest in parenting. I got put in front of the TV a lot, read thousands of comic books. He still took me to school, helped me with my homework, but I could see his heart wasn't in it."

"He was grieving."

"Of course. And that's why I was happy when he started dating a couple of years later. Kids can be smart. They may not have all the details, but they know what's going on. And I wanted my happy-go-lucky dad back. It's funny, some kids get scared when their dads bring home a stepmom, but not me. I was excited to meet Shauna. I missed having a mom and I really hoped she'd like me."

Kate frowned. She could no doubt see where this was going.

Liam chuckled. "Oh, it wasn't obvious at first,

but like I said, kids soon figure things out. Shauna was just, well, *prickly* when I met her. Maybe it was nerves, I don't know, but she didn't give me the warm fuzzies."

"How old were you then?"

"Nine." He rolled his shoulders, trying to release the tension in his neck. "She was a beautiful woman, sophisticated and elegant. So different from how I remembered my mom. My mother was beautiful too, but in a homey way, you know? Comfortable. She wasn't concerned about the latest fashions. She was just happy being a mom and a wife."

Kate nodded her understanding.

"But Shauna wanted to be wined and dined and didn't really make an effort to hang around me. I could tell she wished my dad hadn't had a kid. And I guess he was so taken with her he didn't notice how frosty she was to me. I was sent to a lot of babysitters. I remember sitting in other people's houses, wishing I could be at dinner with them. Wishing she wanted me."

Kate reached over and caressed his thigh under his robe. Her fingers, so cool and soft, felt wonderful on his warm skin.

"Anyway, they got married. I remember overhearing a conversation as they were planning the wedding. Shauna didn't want me there. She said she didn't want any kids at the reception, but I knew it was just me she wanted out of the picture."

"Why?"

"She never said, at least not to me. Maybe she was threatened at having her predecessor's son around. Maybe she felt my presence diminished her place in the family, or that she'd never have complete influence over my father because of me. She was the sort of person who needed that, to have some kind of control over another person."

"That's awful. How could anyone behave like that to a child?"

"People do all sorts of terrible things to children. Look at Andy, leaving Michelle and her mom before she was even born."

Kate nodded.

"Anyway, my dad insisted on me coming to the wedding, but by that point, I didn't even want to be there. I was the ring bearer. I remember feeling tempted to drop the rings down the toilet."

"I can't blame you there."

"Well, I didn't. They went on a long honeymoon, and I was sent to stay with the elderly neighbor next door, an old friend of my mom's. The next couple of years were a blur of sports practices that Shauna never attended, school concerts that only my Dad came to see, you get the picture."

"Was your dad happy?"

"I think so, for the most part. And after a while, he got sick. A heart condition. He spent a bit of time in the hospital."

Kate's face darkened. "Liam…"

"He died of a heart attack when I was thirteen. And so I was left with Shauna, the woman who never wanted me in the first place."

She grabbed his hand, squeezing, her face contorted with clear pain.

His bitterness manifested in a sour smile. "To

her credit, she did house me for a year. She was never cruel, just indifferent. But to a kid that's worse. We just existed together, did our own things. But deep down, I wanted her to hug me and tell me she was glad I was in her life. I wanted her to accept me as her own."

"And you never got that."

He shook his head. "But she put a roof over my head for twelve months, even though I spent that year wondering when she'd grow tired of me. I suppose she kept me that long because she felt guilty, and I know she did love my dad. But at the end of that year, she met a man. A wealthy man. He wanted to marry her, but he didn't want another man's moping kid in his house."

Liam spotted a tear falling from Kate's eye. He wiped it away for her, hating the fact that she felt pain on his account. He leaned in and kissed the trail left from her tears.

"Anyway, it gave Shauna the push she needed. One day, she pulled me out of school and told me my bags were already in her car. She drove me to Aunt Margaret's, a distant relative of my dad's who I didn't know very well, and told me that I wouldn't see her again."

"What did you do?"

Liam bit his lip. Since the day Shauna left, he hadn't wasted a tear on her. But now they fell, and he wanted to slap at the wet tracks on his cheeks, hating this display of weakness. "I begged her to keep me. She was the only parent I had left. I promised to be good, told her I could be a good son to her. That I'd make her proud. She said, 'Liam, you were never my son. I never wanted you. Now I have a chance to build my own family and you're not part of it.'"

Kate pulled him into her arms, and he rested his head on her shoulder. "I'm so sorry."

"I felt like my world was over. I'd already felt abandoned because of my parents' deaths. But this woman, who should have been a mother to me, chose to abandon me. She told me to get the fuck out of her life and never looked back. And I was left with an old woman, who despite her good intentions, had health issues and her own concerns. She only took me in because I was blood, but we were basically strangers. We did grow closer, but it took time, and God knows I added to her stress. Then Aunt Margaret died by the time I got out of high school. Leaving me alone. Again."

She looked at him, her mouth open, unbelieving.

"When she sent me to stay with Margaret, I was so angry. Shauna had made all the decisions for me and I hated the choices she made. So I made one for myself after she left. I ran away from Margaret's house and stayed away for a month."

"Where did you go?"

Liam swallowed hard. He'd already shared more than he'd shared with anyone. Could he tell her everything?

No.

"Liam?"

"I was homeless."

Kate's mouth fell open, as if she couldn't believe the story got worse. He was right. He couldn't tell her everything. He'd only scratched the surface of his tale and she was already in bits.

"What happened?"

"Look, all you need to know is I straightened myself out. As much as I didn't want to hang around with an old lady, I realized that it was better than being on the streets. I went back to Margaret's place and things got better. Let's just say the streets of Vegas are no place for a kid."

"Liam." The word came out as a broken cry.

"Kate, I've spent the better part of my life feeling alone and unwanted. Do you understand why I don't want Michelle to feel like I walked out on her?"

She nodded. "I do. But don't you ever equate yourself with that woman. Your motives are good, and Shauna was an evil douchebag."

Despite his tears, he broke into laughter. "Thanks for saying that. Maybe it's not quite accurate, but it helps to hear."

"I hate what she did to you."

"I suppose I don't blame her. I mean, I wasn't really her kid."

She shook her head. "Anyone with half a heart would have done the right thing and kept you. It was her loss. She missed out on something special."

As she cried, he choked back his own tears and took her in his arms. She climbed onto his lap and he held her, stroking her hair and back. As much as he'd hated reliving his past, he felt better now, knowing Kate understood.

God help him, he was falling for this woman. She smashed his barriers and tore down his walls. She'd commandeered his heart with a few words of kindness, and shone light on a very dark corner of his life. He would always be grateful for it, and would gladly do the same for her.

"What happened to you, on the streets?"

He hadn't allowed those memories in for a long time. He could almost convince himself someone else lived them. "Forget I mentioned it."

"How can you say that? I won't forget it."

"It's done. I learned from it. That's all that matters."

Her sigh told him she wasn't done with the topic, but would let it go for now. Well, he'd deal with her questions as they came.

"Did you ever see Shauna again?"

"Only once," Liam said quietly. "In my early twenties. I was back on track, done with college and apprenticed at a building firm. I got a call from a lawyer one day, telling me Shauna was in poor health, cancer, and that she wanted to see me."

She looked up. "Did you go?"

"I wanted to tell him to fuck himself and to give her the same message. But I guess I was curious. What could she possibly want with me? As much as I despised her, I knew it would always bother me if I didn't go. So I swallowed my feelings and visited her." He closed his eyes for a moment as he remembered the scene. "It was strange to see her, looking so small, in a hospital gown. She'd always been a stunner before. When she saw me, she began to cry. Nothing surprised me more than to learn the ice queen had emotions after all."

"What did she say?"

"She apologized. Told me God had cursed her

for her cruelty by making her barren. She never had that family she wanted so badly. And after a few years of trying, her wealthy husband paid her off and divorced her." He took a few deep breaths. "Shauna handed me a fat envelope filled with money. Said it was her divorce settlement, that she'd never touched it. She wanted me to have it. Because she hadn't supported me in life, she wanted to die knowing she was finally supporting me."

"That's amazing."

"No, it's awful, Kate. Because you know what I did? I took it! I took her blood money and I left. I invested it, and the next year I began plans for my first casino. Shauna's money paid for my business. And I think I've been sick about it ever since."

Waves of nausea and guilt poured over him. For a moment, Liam thought he'd have to toss Kate onto the bed so he could run into the bathroom and hurl his self-loathing into the bowl. He bit back his feelings, as he'd been doing so effectively for years, and managed to keep it all down.

He must have still looked sick because Kate ran her hand up and down his back, rubbing and soothing his muscles. Perfect. The idea of her seeing him at his worst was as appealing as a vomit popsicle.

Kate massaged the top of his shoulder. "Liam, you did nothing wrong in accepting the money. She wanted to make amends, and I guess it was the only way she could do so."

"Some days I feel like my business is built on a foundation of shame."

"It's not. You built up your business. You are the

success behind it, no one else. Plenty of people in your shoes would have climbed into a hole and died. But you turned your life around, Liam Doyle. You became a success. You should be proud."

He grinned, no longer feeling like a helpless kid. "You know, the reason I decided to build casinos is because of the money they make. I wanted to know that if I ever had a family, they'd want for nothing. So I studied the competition and recognized a lot of gaps in the market. I tailored my properties to cater to those gaps. Now I can't keep people away. But does it make me happy? I don't know anymore."

She grabbed his hand and drew whorls on his palm. "Despite how I feel about casinos, I'm woman enough to admit you've created amazing hotels. The best on the Strip."

"The best on the Strip. That meant something to me a few years ago. But now? Who the hell knows? Kate, since I opened Vice, I just haven't been myself. I haven't been motivated. And I'm sick to death thinking I might end up being the failure she always knew I'd be." He rubbed his chest, trying to erase the pains that always seemed present.

"There's nothing about you that says failure to me. You are an amazing man," she said, sighing. "And I want you so much it makes me crazy."

To hear her say the words almost erased all his pain. The flood of emotion made his cock throb. He had to have her again. Now.

"Liam, you have to tell me about your time on the streets. I won't stop wondering and worrying."

Raw need suppressed his sigh of frustration. "Just let it go, Kate."

"But…"

"No buts. You know everything that's fit to print." He reached for the tie on her robe, untied it, and removed the garment. He gazed at her beautiful body, the gorgeous curves which provided him with the best solace he'd ever known. He removed his own robe. "Just let me be with you. That's all I want right now."

She stared at him, her face crinkled with uncertainty, but she lay back on the bed and held out her hand.

Liam situated himself between her comforting thighs, and together they forgot the world.

***

Liam shut the suite door after accepting the tray of room service breakfast he'd ordered. She huddled on the couch, wrapped in her robe, and grinned at him as he brought it inside. "I've never been so happy to see a tray of food," she admitted. "I'm starving because of how you've used my body all night long."

He didn't say a word, but offered her a heated look and deposited the tray on a table.

She tightened her robe and tripped over to the table, her bare feet loving the feel of the thick carpet. She moved next to him and put a hand on his shoulder. "Hungry?"

His grin didn't reach his eyes. "I guess."

"You should be. I know I worked up an appetite."

Again, he said nothing, turning instead to the

television in the corner. The morning news was on, but he stared at the report as if he wasn't absorbing a word.

Kate eyed him. He'd been strangely quiet this morning. She feared their talk had scared him off a little. He'd still been affectionate upon waking, holding her close, kissing her as if she were a fragile doll. To see him retreat now scared her more than she cared to admit, and she felt the need to coax him back out of his shell, if she could.

Their talk had scared her, as well. Her dream last night had been colored with images of abandoned children and life on the streets. What had happened to him out there? She knew the question would continue to plague her.

She lifted the lid to the tray and took in the incredible smell of bacon and eggs. Liam watched her and a dark gleam lit up his eyes, like a tiger preparing for the kill. She picked up a piece of bacon, held it to his mouth, and he bit off a piece.

"Liam," she said, wanting to make him feel better. "Are you okay?"

He continued to watch her as he swallowed his bacon.

"Aren't you going to say anything?"

"I don't feel like talking."

Just as she suspected. After his confessions, he'd clammed up again. It had felt as if they'd broken down a wall and grown closer, but this morning she awoke to find he'd erected a higher one. She might have woken up with a different man altogether. After their breakthrough and an astounding night of pleasure, it seemed guarded Liam was back in control.

Okay, maybe she should give him some space. He could share more when he was ready. But the neediness in his eyes told her he needed to express himself, more than he realized.

"I'm here for you," she said. "Last night you shared so much. I want you to know I didn't take it for granted. Just don't shut me out now."

He seemed to absorb her words at first, then his gaze dropped and he tugged at her robe tie, loosening it.

"What are you doing?"

He removed her robe and tossed it to the floor. "Stop talking, Kate." His own robe soon followed.

"Liam..."

"You want to know what I need? What I want? I want *you*, hot and wet and ready for me. And I want it now."

"I don't think we should..."

He molded his hand around her breast and kissed her hard, as if to stop her from talking. She pulled away, surprised at his change in mood, but he held her face and took her mouth once again. His tongue plunged into her mouth, tasting of bacon and lust. Even though she hadn't started out in the mood, her body responded and melted before him.

His touch intensified as his hands explored her. He tweaked her nipple hard. When she gasped, he swallowed her cry. When she moaned, he wrestled his hand between her legs and claimed her there. She didn't want to be wet for him, but she couldn't help herself and he knew it.

He had taken control of her.

Pulling back his hand, he moved her to the floor-to-ceiling window and turned her to face outward. She shied away, worried someone would see them.

"One way glass," he said as if reading her mind. "Now stay put." He positioned her arms over her head so her palms rested on the window. He moved her hips toward him so her bottom stuck out. Before she could protest, not that she wanted to, he slid inside her.

Kate cried out as he slammed into her again and again, feeling at the edge of a precipice with the Strip laid out before her. As he claimed her, as he forced them both into a state of orgasmic agony, she felt she might fall right through the window and down to the sidewalk below.

She didn't want this right now. But she did as well. Liam seemed to understand the addiction streaming through her veins, a need she couldn't articulate.

As she came with a shocked whisper, with a sense of awe, she marveled at the sway he held over her. His grunts of crazed satisfaction turned into blasphemous exclamations as he pulled out and shot on her behind.

When he finished, she looked over her shoulder, dizzy, and saw him reach for a cloth. He cleaned her up, his mouth tight, avoiding her eyes. The lines at the corners of his eyes had deepened to a sad crinkle.

"Liam," she began.

"Have your breakfast," he said, dropping a kiss on her shoulder. The bristles on his chin pricked her as his sudden coldness scored her heart. "I'm going to hit the shower."

He picked up his robe and walked into the bathroom, leaving her alone with the most expensive eggs and bacon on the Strip.

***

"Again." His demand, so hot on her ear, acted as food for her weirdly-famished body.

"I don't think I can."

One touch. One lick. "Yes, you can."

"Oh, God."

He slid between her legs, his thick erection throbbing. They'd been at it for hours, had watched night turn to day and back into night again. Since admitting his secret, Liam had been a machine. And as exhausted as she was, he'd managed to coax orgasm after orgasm out of her. She was barely doing any of the work at this point, just lying there while he teased her body into the pulsing, weeping mass of wetness he so craved.

He thrust deep into her, and her pussy welcomed him yet again, as much as her brain railed against such excess. "More. I want more."

"Liam, please, I can't."

But then he hit that spot again and she cried out, making lies of her words. She began to fall apart on an incredulous shout.

"That's it, baby." He drove her harder, taking his pleasure like a man obsessed. "Come for me. Oh fuck, that's so good, Kate!" He let out a cry of his own and collapsed on top of her.

They lay on the bed, drenched in each other's

sweat. She wasn't sure how long they remained prone, but she felt each second plod by. Each passing minute left her more and more convinced he was drowning his sorrows in sex.

Surely it couldn't be healthy.

He moved. She breathed a sigh of relief, grateful to finally have a few moments to sleep. He moved off her to discard the latest condom, and she closed her eyes. Once again, warm hands slid up her legs, parting them.

"Open up for me."

"Liam, we should talk…"

"No talk." He pulled her close and threw her legs over his shoulders. His greedy tongue put a silky period on the end of his sentence.

And once again, Kate could do nothing more but let him have her, as another terrifying orgasm swept her away.

Chapter Eleven

"Just a few drinks. I promise." Liam ran his fingers up her bare arm and appraised her look for the evening. "Christ, you look gorgeous, Kate. I can't wait to show you off." He brought her over to the full-length mirror in her suite and made her look.

She did, with hesitation, and marveled at the fantastic creature staring back. Liam's assistant had reminded him of a charity obligation and he'd somehow convinced her to go with him. She wasn't really sure what to expect at a Governor's Ball for the local chapter of the Heart Association, and certainly didn't have the wardrobe for it. However, during the last couple of days, Liam had taken care of everything, from finding her a beautiful gown in navy silk, to bringing in hair and makeup artists and jewelry.

The makeup had been so carefully applied she couldn't see her bruises. Her hair had been piled onto her head in an artful chignon. Liam seemed to like the up-do, and took advantage of the neck access it provided. He kissed the top of her spine and goose pimples exploded in a riotous dance over her skin.

Despite her response to his touch, something felt off. She felt uncomfortable in an outfit paid for by Liam, the silk grated on her skin with each soft swish. She'd never been the sort to accept expensive gifts.

To say nothing of the fact she'd rather stay in the suite and talk about what the hell was happening between them. She thought she'd made a major breakthrough with Liam a few days ago, but so much had been left unsaid as well. Yes, he'd shared a lot and it had been emotional for both of them. However, if they were to move forward in any way, didn't they need to keep talking?

She'd tried to bring up the topic again this morning, but he'd brushed it off. Rather than talk about the past, he'd rolled on top of her and begun his very persuasive seduction routine, and she'd been unable to say no. When he kissed her, when he slid his hands between her legs, she couldn't say no.

He was using sex as a distraction, that much was clear. As eager as she was in bed with him, she couldn't help feeling Liam evaded a lot of issues this way. It made her uncomfortable. It made her feel as if she'd fallen into bed with a different man, one whose appetites both excited and scared her.

"I've never been to such a fancy event," she said now.

"Stick with me. You can have as much high society life as you want." He cast an appreciative glance at the way her breasts swelled under the navy silk. "You look amazing in that color. I knew you would. We might have to take you shopping for more clothes."

"I don't want any more clothes. I have clothes at home."

He frowned at the mention of her home. "I'd like to get you some special things. You know, for nights like this."

"I think I'd feel more at ease wearing jeans at Franky's." She wiggled her toes in her new stilettos, wincing at their tight pinch.

"Me too, but I promised to make an appearance at this shindig ages ago." He spun her around to look at him and struck a cheesy pose worthy of a Sears catalogue, letting his mischievous side reappear for a split second. "So, did I clean up good?"

She smiled, surprised by how much she'd missed playful Liam. Intense Liam had his charms, but he wore her down. She touched a finger to the sleeve of his slick tuxedo, relishing the musculature underneath. "You'll do nicely." She felt more overcome by his beauty than by her own startling transformation.

All too soon he turned serious. "You sure you're okay to go out? My security team will be with us."

She couldn't exactly say no now. He'd spent a billion dollars on her dress, from the looks of it. "Sure. We've got to go out some time. Maybe when we get back we can hang out and chat? I feel like we haven't talked much the past few days. I miss it."

Liam tweaked her nose. "You're cute, but way

too serious. Just enjoy the ride, sugar." He pulled her close, eyes narrowed with desire. "When we get back, my plans don't involve chatting. They involve getting this dress off." He brushed his thumb over her rouged lower lip, looking puzzled when the lipstick didn't rub off.

"It's a stain," she explained. "The makeup artist said it wouldn't come off unless I get mauled."

As he stared at her lips, his expression grew dark once more. With so much focused attention, her body responded in kind. "Well, I'll maul you later and see if I can't nibble the stain off."

After a few rushed kisses, they gathered up their things and left, making their way to the Escalade waiting out front. As they passed through the main hall, so close to the casino, Kate realized she didn't hold her breath anymore while surrounded by the cigarette smoke. She'd become almost accustomed to it. The idea bothered her, though she said nothing to Liam.

Once outside, she took note of the spot on the sidewalk where she'd conducted her protests. It seemed like an eon ago. Where had that woman gone? She'd never been the sort of woman to play "dress up," to fritter away her evenings at society events.

Had she already forgotten who she was?

Guilt made the acids in her stomach bubble and she swallowed a sudden bad taste. She *had* forgotten. And here she stood, dressed in a lavish gown bought by the man she'd thought she hated less than two weeks ago. If someone had told her then she'd be sleeping with Liam Doyle, she would have thought them unhinged.

Maybe she was the unhinged one.

She tried to ignore the gut-wrenching *mea culpa* sounding in her brain as they drove to the Governor's Ball at the Venetian Hotel. She wondered how the fates had led her to be a guest at two casinos in the same week. After years of avoiding them like her own personal plague, she couldn't seem to avoid them now.

The atmosphere at the ball didn't help. The conference room at the Venetian was stunning, but someone, in their wisdom, had decided to make the evening's theme "Monte Carlo Night." Talk about redundant. Everywhere she looked she saw images of dice and poker chips and money signs.

It was enough to make her hurl in her new sequined clutch.

Several members of the press made a beeline for Liam the moment they entered the ballroom. He evaded them and steered Kate toward an unending table laden with all manner of sweets and fingers foods and a massive chocolate fountain. He picked up two small plates shaped like poker chips and handed one to her. She took it but put it back down on the table.

"Aren't you hungry?" Liam reached for a cracker piled high with pink caviar and playfully held it up to her. "Open up."

Despite her nerves, which ratcheted up a notch each second, she opened her mouth and accepted the cracker. She kept a bashful hand over her mouth as she chewed, and then wiped the corner of her mouth with a napkin.

He grinned as she swallowed, leaning in to whisper, "You're sexy when you eat. Now I'll be dreaming of feeding you all night long." His tongue darted out and he moistened his lips. "Or maybe I'll do something about it."

"All I did was eat a cracker."

"I know. Wait until I feed you my cock."

Kate gasped, hoping the person next to them hadn't overheard. Liam chuckled, clearly unconcerned.

"Doyle, aren't you going to get this pretty lady a drink? She looks parched."

Kate looked at the newcomer, a tall man with buzzed blond hair and sex in his smile.

Liam shook the man's hand. "If I leave her alone with you, you'll carry her away. Kate Callender, meet Alex Markov. He's a total shark, so make sure he doesn't lure you into any dark corners."

"Don't tempt me, my friend." Markov reached for her hand and kissed it. "It's a pleasure to meet you, Kate."

Under other circumstances, the pleasure might be all hers. Markov, blessed with an intimidating build, much like Liam, oozed an old-world charm despite his youthful appearance. "Likewise. How do you know each other?"

"Alex and I go way back. We apprenticed at the same building company together. He headed east. Owns a few nightclubs in New York."

"They pale in comparison to your casinos," said Markov.

Liam grinned. "You're such a bullshitter. Don't listen to a word he says, Kate. He acts all modest, but contractors cringe when they have to go into a meeting with him. He makes them shit their pants."

Markov's eyes narrowed, but other than that he seemed content with the description. "My standards are no less exacting than your own."

"True. So what brings you back from New York?"

"I've been scoping out potential sites. Thinking of doing some work here in Vegas."

Kate listened as the pair talked shop for a few minutes. So, Alex Markov knew Liam as a young man. She might have to corner him and see if she could pry some information loose.

As they chatted, Alex glanced at her direction, his lips curled in clear interest. Despite their obvious friendship and his professional regard for the other man, Liam stood close to her, hand locked about her waist, a signal to his friend she was taken. His possessiveness was sweet and made her want to curl into him.

He might have his moods, but he did seem to care for her.

As the evening wore on, he introduced her to what felt like half the attendees. She shook hands with his associates and competitors alike, noting one similarity between everyone: every single person in the ballroom was filthy rich. Once again, her nerves got the better of her, and she found herself hanging in the background each time someone cornered Liam for a conversation. She had nothing to offer as far as chit chat went anyway. No, she hadn't seen the new production of *Swan Lake* at the Nevada Ballet Theater. No, she was not related to the Callenders of Cape Cod. And no, she really didn't want to participate in the casino games in the adjoining room.

A couple of hours had dragged by, and she realized she was holding her breath a lot. The more she tried to fit in with these people, the more she stood out. And because she was there with Liam, everyone wanted to know her business. She'd never been the sort to feel ashamed of her background, but tonight she felt a little like Molly Ringwald trying to fit in with the rich kids.

Her emotions only compounded whenever Liam did anything remotely sweet or considerate. He covered her shoulders with a shawl and her palms began to sweat. He introduced her to VIPs as if she were more important than he was, and heat streaked across her chest. Each kiss from him, each slow dance, made her feel like more of a hypocrite.

Liam led her to yet another group of people whose wealth seemed to drip from their fingers and necks. A couple of the women in this glamorous huddle eyed her from top to bottom as they approached, their waxed brows arching and their lips curling. That was when the churning in her gut finally did her in. Her stomach pitched and she almost tasted the bile that crept up her throat.

Liam stopped in his tracks. "Kate, are you okay?"

"I can't do this," she whispered. "I can't be here. They don't have a clue, Liam. Can't you see it? They have no clue what it's like in the real world. I know, and you know, but they don't."

"Kate, I get it. I'd rather be throwing back a beer

210

with Beck and Nolan, but a lot of good can come from an event like this. Remember, it's for charity. That's good, right?"

She shuffled on her feet. "I suppose, but..."

"Kate, you belong here as much as anyone."

She plucked at the billowy skirt on her gown. "No, I don't. I shouldn't have let you buy me these things. I'm no better than my father, taking money from others."

The muscles in Liam's cheeks clenched. He pulled her aside. "Don't talk like that. Look, I can afford the dress and the jewelry. And if I want to spend money on you, I will. Why can't you accept that?"

"Maybe because we still barely know each other." She fingered the diamond bracelet he'd insisted on making her wear, even if it was a rental. "It feels a bit early for diamonds."

"You deserve to wear nice things." He ran a hand through his hair, messing up his slicked-back coif. "I enjoyed it."

"I told you when we met I couldn't be bought, Liam. I meant what I said."

He stared at her, and his eyebrow arched. "Exactly what do you think I'm trying to buy? Your cooperation? Your affection? Your body?"

Liam's voice had risen but he didn't seem to notice the heads turning in their direction. Heat lit up Kate's face, no doubt echoing the angry flare on his own cheeks.

"I just...I don't understand what we're doing. You and me. What's happening between us?"

"Why do you have to question it?"

"Because someone has to, and it's clearly not you."

Liam's gaze swept over her like the beam from a lighthouse, illuminating a black sea, searching her personal darkness. He grabbed her hand and pulled her out of the ballroom.

They passed people on their furious dash, but Kate saw only the back of Liam's head, and the way his muscles moved under his tuxedo jacket as he dragged her along.

She'd never been so entranced by another person.

Liam tried a couple of doors down the long conference room hallway, only to find them locked. He cursed.

"Where are we going?" she asked.

He said nothing, his face still grim. Eventually he tried a door marked "Piazza Room" and it opened. He pulled her in and closed the door, locking it behind them.

He turned on her and backed her up to the marble-top boardroom table. The edge of the table met with her bottom and she gasped.

Stepping close, invading any sense of personal space she had in the moment, he curled his fingers around her neck. "You asked what we're doing. You want to know what's happening between us? I don't fucking know. You think it doesn't scare the shit out of me too?"

"I never said you were scaring me."

His face crumpled. "Do you think I can't see it all over your face? I terrify you because I want you so much. Don't you understand what you do to me?

I ache when I'm not inside you. My hands shake when I can't touch you. And to hear you put yourself down makes my brain want to explode. You're worth a hundred of those people out there."

On his last, hushed sentence, her body tensed. Despite his frantic demeanor, he made her want him. Now. Her silky underpants felt as comfortable as a burlap thong. He moved his large hands over her shoulders and she bit her tongue, imagining his fingers parting her folds and diving deep.

His face rested so close to hers, his lips a hair's breadth away. "Surrender to me. Right here, right now. Give yourself to me."

Kate nodded, worried, but overcome by hunger. Liam picked her up and sat her on the boardroom table. He urged her to lie back and she did, watching as he unzipped his pants and found a condom. Once sheathed, his eyes glinted as he pushed up her skirt, pulled aside her underwear, and slid two fingers into her. She cried out, arching her back at his less-than-gentle yet perfect touch. His fingers moved inside her with a unique grace, marking her, stretching her, getting her ready for him.

She wanted him like this—rough and demanding.

When he was satisfied with her almost-shameful level of lubrication, he removed his hand. Positioning his cock at her entrance, he waited until their eyes met, and drove into her. Maddening thrusts made her close her eyes and bite her tongue. With each forceful thrust, he grunted, clutching at her. He spread her legs apart. Through the slit of her closed eyes, she was barely aware of her stilettos up in the air. Just the thought of someone discovering them forced her to the edge, and his movements drove her over.

"Fuck. Kate. Fuck." He spat his words in time with each pump.

Her pussy clenched, tightened, and sighed its release. As he came, she barreled over the precipice again, lost in the churning waters below. She opened her eyes and took in his messy hair and sweaty brow. His fresh dishevelment only heightened his allure. He shuddered and pulled out of her, clearly bashful about having given her such a forceful fucking. He pulled her into his embrace, and she went, her legs still wrapped around him.

He buried his face in her neck and shuddered once more. "No more questions. Just be with me, okay?"

Kate bit her trembling lip. He needed her. She needed him. Like this. Hard. Often. Victims to an unnerving passion.

She could forget her apprehensions, couldn't she?

Maybe just for a while.

Chapter Twelve

"I told you I'd get you in my bed."

Kate smirked. "Don't be so cocky, Doyle. I'm in your office, not your bed."

They got off his private elevator and Liam pressed a button to take it off service. No sooner had he set her bags down on the floor, than Liam backed her up against the nearest wall and kissed her, letting his tongue trace her lips. "Oh, you'll be in my bed soon enough."

He picked her up and threw her over his shoulder. Kate gasped and giggled at his insane enthusiasm. She'd never known a man with such stamina. Or was it their particular chemistry? Because God only knew she felt it too.

Over the past week, they'd barely spent a moment outside each other's arms. Kate wasn't the sort of person to sleep in a man's embrace, but she'd spent her nights tangled with Liam. The first thing he'd done upon waking this morning was gaze into her eyes, as if he saw great mysteries there, then reached a hand between her legs, pleased by the answers he'd found.

He'd taken her before their room-service breakfast and again afterward. They hadn't stopped. They didn't seem to know how.

Sure, it still felt strange to be part of such emotional fire, but she asked no more questions, as he'd requested,

And now, as he'd gently threatened not long ago, he'd moved her to his office suite. She hadn't argued, figuring he could now make some revenue from booking her suite.

He turned the corner and led her to a room she hadn't seen before, his bedroom. Once inside, he set her down, patting her derriere. "Here we are."

Kate took a moment to look around. This was where Liam slept when he stayed at the hotel, his home away from home. In many ways, the room was as luxurious as she would have expected, but it held a few surprises.

A tinted floor-to-ceiling window made up the wall on one side, with an ideal view of the Strip's lights. A flat-screen TV ornamented the wall opposite the bed. The door to the large walk-in closet hung open in the corner, where she spied countless pressed shirts and a rack full of navy blue ties. She giggled, realizing now she'd never seen him wear any other color. "What's with the navy ties?"

"A long time ago, my mentor in the building industry told me about the importance of a strong image. That was back before I had any kind of image. 'Wear a navy tie' he said. 'Whenever you walk into a room, people will think you own it.'

When I put on those ties, I forget the scared kid I used to be."

Kate sensed an opening and prodded for more info. "Tell me more about this mentor. Who was he?"

"It's not important anymore." With a determined set to his jaw, he'd shut her down once again.

She decided to forget about it for now. Instead, she took in the rest of the space. The room was decorated in shades of slate grey and black, modern and sleek. The bed itself was simple, king-sized with black sheets, but its setting made her gasp. Three built-in steps led to its raised platform, and the short wall adjacent to it housed a long gas fireplace. Liam walked over to the wall and pressed a button. Flames shot down the length of the fireplace. At a glance, it seemed as if the footboard was made of fire.

She shook her head, awed at this dream bedroom.

Liam blushed. "I know. It's extravagant, but the architect insisted on the fireplace. I don't use it much. It's Vegas, after all. I can turn it off if you want."

"No. It's incredible." She smiled at him. Somehow this room was the perfect symbol of his success in life, in spite of the odds.

Liam came over and took her in his embrace. They stood there, wrapped up in each other, when his desk phone rang. Liam groaned.

"I'd better get that."

She moved over to the fireplace and stared at the gentle flames as he answered his call. Feeling its heat, she closed her eyes and dreamed.

Moments later, he stood behind her, brushing her hair aside and kissing her shoulder. He turned her around and then he kissed her forehead. "A few things need my attention, I'm afraid. I'll have to ravish you later."

Though she'd never admit it to him, she was glad for a breather. "I understand."

"I can do my work from here. I have a spare laptop if you want to check emails or surf."

"It's okay. I should check my messages, but I can use my phone."

"Help yourself to anything in the fridge. I'll just be a couple of hours." He smiled and went to a tidy workspace tucked into another corner of the massive bedroom.

Overwhelmed from seeing how he lived, how he worked, Kate meandered back to the front room. Letting out a breath she hadn't realized she'd been holding, she sat on the couch where she and Liam had first talked.

It was so easy to forget his wealth when they were twisted in the sheets, just a man and a woman, but every time she was shown a new corner of his life, she felt winded. If her dad or that loan shark Vaughan ever got wind of her being here, the demands for money would never stop.

She touched the skin under her bruised eye, wincing. She wondered when it would stop feeling tender. The memory of Vaughan touching her made her bristle with fear and shame. If he found her…

No. She was safe here with Liam. Not that she could stay forever, but for now she had sanctuary.

Thinking of Vaughan caused Kate to remember Lisa. Although Kate hadn't shared the details of the attack yet, she had let her friend know she'd be away for a few days and not to worry. Now that a full week had passed, guilt weighed heavily in her heart. She'd put Rod in charge of the New Horizons meetings until she got back but didn't want to take advantage of his good nature either. Although Kate didn't want to keep her friends in the dark about the attack, she didn't relish the idea of rehashing it just yet.

However, she did want to talk to Lisa about seeing Donny at Vice. Nervous, Kate retrieved her phone from her purse and began typing a text. Changing her mind, she dialed Lisa's number, wanting to hear her voice instead.

Voicemail.

Lisa always picked up when she called. But as the recorded message ended, Kate couldn't help wondering if her friend might be avoiding her.

"Hey Lisa. It's me. I really need to talk to you. A lot's happened." She paused, not wanting to elaborate over voicemail. "Please call me back. Take care." She felt a twinge of unease in her stomach. Within seconds, her unease turned to all-out worry.

She didn't have much time to contemplate the sensation. As she held her phone, it buzzed and she picked it up quickly, hoping Lisa was on the other line. "Hello?"

There was no answer.

"Hello?"

Still nothing, but the memory of Hugo

Vaughan's face haunted her.

"Did you say something, Kate?" Liam called from the other room.

She fought to master her erratic breathing and shaky voice. "Just making some calls." Liam nodded and went back to work.

"Who is this?" she whispered into the phone.

The line went dead. She browsed the call log and found the last number, no caller ID. She dialed it and waited, but a recorded voice came on, providing no further information. Even still, she called Detective Baxter and gave him the number, in case it should lead to Vaughan.

She knew in her bones the loan shark had called her. However, her reasonable side reminded her it could very well have been a wrong number.

Nevertheless, she turned off her phone and slipped it back in her purse. She knew she should tell Liam about the call, but couldn't bring herself to disturb him. She'd taken him away from his work long enough as it was. Besides, he continued to choose to withhold information from her. Now she felt like doing the same.

Instead, she turned on the TV, curled up on the sofa, and stared at the screen.

***

As morning sun gave way to a rare drizzly afternoon, Liam closed his last document, eager to finish his work. It had taken all his willpower to focus on emails and make decisions, when all he wanted was to retrieve Kate from the other room and drag her into his bed. Now he could. He ignited the fireplace. The warm glow from its flames cast a soft light over his darkening bedroom. It might be piss-pouring outside, but inside it was toasty warm.

He moved to the bedroom door and poked his head around the corner. Kate sat quietly, watching some sort of documentary on space in the other room. She stared at the screen, clearly not absorbed in the content, fiddling with the ends of her hair. Watching her, he shed his clothing, feeling his cock swell and thicken in anticipation of the hunt.

Despite the fact their bodies seemed so in tune with one another, he knew he'd alarmed her the last couple of times they'd fucked. He could be a willful son of a bitch and the reticence in her gaze had not been lost on him. But it was only in coming with her that he managed to forget himself for a while. When he lost himself in her body, he forgot about his present obligations, past sins, and future mistakes. He even forgot those damn chest pains.

The moment she tightened under him, lost to the pleasure he created for her, was the closest he'd ever come to heaven.

And quite frankly he was better at fucking than talking about his emotions.

Kate had seen right through him the night he confessed his past to her and he hadn't been at ease since. He'd never let himself be so vulnerable in front of anyone, not since he poured his heart out to his stepmother...and look at the travesty that had caused.

It scared him shitless.

He knew Kate wanted more, wanted honesty and

openness. Hell, he wanted those things too. But he also knew if he allowed himself to be vulnerable with her again, he might fuck it up and lose her altogether. He'd already lost everyone who ever meant anything to him. So the primal beast inside him told him to keep her numb with ecstasy. If she couldn't walk, she couldn't walk away.

Flawed logic to be sure, but right now it was all he had.

As soon as he was nude, he pumped his cock, sucked in a deep breath, then strode into the room.

Kate looked down to his crotch, then slowly back up to his face. Her face lit up with strange emotion. Need, it had to be need, because he felt it too.

He leaned over, picked her up, and carried her into the bedroom, depositing her on his bed. "Now. Take it all off."

She did, not breathing a word. Liam walked over to his closet to retrieve one of his ties. Once her nude form was illuminated by the dancing flames of the fireplace he whispered, "Trust me."

She hesitated, but nodded.

He placed the tie around her eyes, making sure it wasn't too tight. The deep blue of the silk complemented her red hair and the skin that grew pinker with each fraught moment. Everything about her made him want to push his boundaries and explore hers. He wanted to tease her into sexual submission, to take total mastery over her mind and soul.

He wanted to make her his.

"Liam," Kate whispered, tilting her head as if to

catch his scent.

He spread her legs, savoring the sight before him, and slid between them. "I'm here," he said, as he licked at her inner thigh.

He drank her essence, losing track of where they were altogether. She tasted perfect, so bloody perfect, and he could never get enough of her. To have her blindfolded, at his disposal, gave him a heady rush that made his cock swell even more.

He glided his tongue along each sweet fold, savoring her. Kate's body shook, and she made a strangled noise. He looked up, ready to encourage her to shout out her pleasure. However, what he saw made him pounce back up the length of her body so he could see her better.

His tie was wet at the edge where it covered her eyes. A slow trail of tears rolled over her skin. Panicked, he removed the blindfold. Had he freaked her out? "Kate, sweetheart. What is it?"

"I got a call before. I think it was Vaughan."

Fury blazed inside him like the flames in his fireplace. He pulled her into his arms and hugged her. In a hushed voice, she told him about the call and that she'd already phoned the cops. He was glad about that, but enraged Vaughan would try his scare tactics again.

He wanted him dealt with. Yesterday. He urged her to lie down on the bed and held her in his arms. Their bodies felt so right together, and as much as he wanted to be inside her, he held back. Even still, their bodies seemed to have their own minds. Each time one of them moved, the other responded. His cock hardened. Her nipples pebbled. As soon as his hand met with her moist pussy, he could no longer hold back. She whispered his name, so quiet and full of mystery, as he thrust his fingers inside her.

He wanted so much more of her. He wanted to take her, and shake her, and break her, until she was ruined for any other man.

She reached out with a shaking hand and rummaged inside his bedside table, producing a condom. Ripping the package open with her teeth, she pulled it out and sheathed him herself. One kiss, two kisses. A deft turn of his hips, and he penetrated her, thrusting deep.

"I'll keep you safe," he promised, murmuring into her fragrant hair. "Just stay with me."

She clutched his backside and wrapped her legs around him as they crashed into each other, orgasms ripping through them with simultaneous violence.

As her body quaked, he whispered again, "Stay with me."

***

Two days later, Liam sat in a wing chair in his office suite, dressed only in boxers. Kate slept, oblivious to his state of unease. Despite spending every hour together in the past…fuck, he'd lost track of how many days it had been, and despite how much his body craved sleep, he couldn't seem to close his eyes. Even now, at two a.m., it was all he could do to stare out the window at the city lights and listen to the sirens of emergency vehicles as they raced down the Strip.

The air conditioning kicked in. He rested his

head on the back of his chair and shivered as a blast of cool air teased his body. Damn. Maybe it was time they put some real clothes on. They'd been naked together much of the time, throwing on the bathrobes whenever they got cold.

She'd given him her body for days on end, had let him do whatever he wanted with her. He'd held her and caressed her, nibbled and sucked and tweaked her. He'd pinned her down, spanked her, and mastered her beautiful body with his fingers, tongue, and cock. He'd needed her more than he'd needed anything. Although she'd dropped off to sleep now and then, every time he'd so much as crooked a finger in her direction, she'd come and let him take more.

He'd never experienced such greed before. If she'd been cake, he would have glutted himself.

She lay peaceful on the bed, her hair trailing behind her on the pillow, making a slight noise like a kitten's snore. He smiled, oddly comforted by the soft sound. He clearly needed to let her rest for a while.

If only he could.

He got up and walked into the kitchenette to pour himself a fingerful of scotch into a glass tumbler. He moved back into the bedroom and sat on the bed next to Kate's unmoving form. She'd kicked all the sheets off and he couldn't resist running a hand over her bare spine. Her skin already bore goose pimples from the A/C, so he reached for the covers and draped them over her. She made a sleepy noise of appreciation and burrowed in next to his thigh.

As if they'd always slept together. As if they always would.

Liam knew in that moment that he would do anything to keep Kate safe. He'd suspected it when he first saw her. He'd been convinced of it after she'd been attacked by Vaughan. And now, after sharing so much with her, their bond floored him with its simplicity and depth. He wanted her to have a home with him, and not some souped-up office in a casino. A real home, full of love and laughter. The kind which he'd always dreamed about, but feared he'd never have.

I want you out of my home. Do you understand me?

"Oh, yeah, Shauna," he muttered. "I understand. I understand you've lost your power over me."

It was true. Since telling Kate about his childhood, about his feelings of inadequacy, somehow they'd all but fizzled away. Where he used to grow so enraged every time he pictured his stepmother, he now felt only sadness. Sadness for Shauna, because she missed out on having him in her life, or even having the life she'd wanted.

For the first time, he felt ready to forgive. It defied logic, but in listening to him, in sharing herself with him, Kate had taught him there was so much more to life than recrimination or a need to prove his worth. Hadn't he been doing just that in building his casinos, trying to prove how important he was, how special? And all because he'd never heard those words uttered by a ghost of a woman.

With Kate's gentle touches and sweet words, he'd realized he didn't need to prove himself. He only wanted to live up to one standard now, to be the man who would take care of Kate.

Kate.

She was so fucking beautiful whenever he took her, each and every time. Something incredible passed between them every time they touched. She'd seen it too, he could tell. Something profound and mysterious and strangely binding. For years, he'd kept people away. He'd never shared himself completely with anyone. He was too busy maintaining the cult of Liam Doyle and burying his past. But Kate had helped him see the past wasn't clawing its way out of the ground, reaching for him. The past didn't need to be buried again and again.

Of course, he might have already gone and fucked it up a couple of times. He saw the hesitant light in her eyes, knew his intensity scared her. He just didn't know how else to be with her. He could tell she wanted, needed, to talk to him about their pasts, but he was ready to leave the past behind. He didn't want to dwell on hate anymore. He wanted to concentrate on how Kate made him feel. She made him soar. She made him despair. She made him dare to love.

He closed his eyes for a moment, floored by the sentiment.

She must think he was a basket case. Good thing she forgave those peculiarities.

As he thought about the nature of forgiveness, Liam realized there might be room in his heart for one more act of it.

He put down the tumbler of scotch on the bedside table and picked up his cell phone. He dialed and waited until a groggy voice came on the other line.

"Nando? Yeah, I know it's late. Sorry about that." Liam paused. "Look, I want you to drop the suit for Michelle's custody. Yeah, I've changed my mind." He listened to his lawyer's words. "Don't worry about the costs, just bill it to me. Cover theirs as well. It's time to move on. Get some sleep, and thanks." He ended the call before Perreira tried to talk him out of it. Perreira could talk the devil out of devilry.

Liam sat still in bed and waited for true rock bottom to hit. He braced himself for the lump in his throat.

It didn't come.

Yes, he would miss Michelle. Would miss her terribly. But he knew he did the right thing. Andy and Bridget weren't perfect, but they wanted to give their little girl a family, which was more than he often felt he had growing up. He wouldn't rip it away from them.

"Goodbye, Michelle."

Besides, as he looked as Kate, sleeping amidst rumpled sheets, he couldn't help but think he'd found a new family.

She stirred in the bed and reached out a hand to him. He lay next to her, winding his arms about her soft body.

Her lips found his neck and she kissed him. "You did the right thing. I'm proud of you."

He nodded his gratitude and held her until morning.

Chapter Thirteen

Kate took a moment to admire the soft lighting of their surroundings and the opulent, yet understated furnishings. This was a part of Vice Liam had never shown her before. It wasn't even officially open, still blocked off and barred to the public.

"What is this place?"

"It's called Decadence. It's a piano bar. Do you like it?"

"It's beautiful."

He grinned. "I hope to see it open in a month or so. Once I pin down the right talent."

She ran a hand over one of the velvet bar stools that were cheekily constructed to fit two people. "Lucky talent."

His grin expanded into a wide smile and her breath hitched. Damn. They'd slept together, bathed together, and spent the wee hours of the mornings together. He'd taken her every which way, yet her heart still pounded every time he smiled at her, even if her brain still occasionally tried to warn her away.

He shuts you down every time you want to discuss something more important than room service. Run.

Ignoring the voice, she let him lead her, his hand at the small of her back, to a booth at the back of the empty bar where they sat.

"Kate, I brought you here because for the first time in a long while, I'm excited about looking forward. I want you to sing for me. Ever since you told me you performed torch songs, I knew I had to hear you."

"You're kidding, right?" No way he really wanted her to audition. He must be speaking through the haze of lust that had driven them both the past few days.

He gestured to the small platform next to the piano. "I never kid. Except when I do. Come on. If you managed to get me sexed up with a hideous used car jingle, just imagine what you can do in the right setting with the right music."

She looked around the room. With the gleaming grand piano, rich upholstery, and expansive bar filled with colorful liqueurs, Decadence was the piano bar of her dreams. A real launching point for her career. She could already imagine herself on stage, microphone in hand, wearing a sumptuous gown as she crooned.

"Kate, come on. Just a scale, an arpeggio. I want to hear your voice."

"You've already heard it."

"Yes, but I want to hear something other than 'Oh, God, Liam! More, baby, more!'"

She elbowed him in the ribs.

"Don't get me wrong. It's music to my ears." He slid his hand up her thigh, mere centimeters away from her core. He squeezed and her body responded, radiating with warmth. "But I want to hear you sing."

"I don't know." Yes, Liam's nightclub was a thing of beauty, but it still sat in the middle of a Vegas casino, precisely the type of venue she'd avoided for years. She'd had one or two offers to sing in casinos before. Lucrative opportunities, truth be told, but she'd always turned them down. It was one thing to frolic in bed with Liam, but to work for him? To be on the payroll at Vice? It seemed wrong, even unfair to anyone else who might have wanted the job. And the hypocrisy...

"Kate." Liam's low voice made her rebel against her common sense. One word from him, and her libido took up arms against her brain. He nibbled her ear, tracing the shell with his tongue. "I'll keep hounding you until I get what I want."

Of course he will. It's what he does.

Her resistance turned to soup. "Okay, okay." She slid out of the booth and stood, marching to the stage. "You sure are pushy. Do you conduct all your business this way?"

"No, ma'am." Liam leaned back, watching her through hooded eyes. "I've only employed these tactics of persuasion with you."

She stuck out her tongue and sat on the piano bench. With a tentative hand, she stroked the keys and closed her eyes as she struck a familiar chord. Why was it music always sounded more poignant coming from a grand piano? She launched into a melody she'd played for years, wincing when she came to a part that had always stumped her. Avoiding Liam's hawk-like gaze, she took a deep breath, drawing from her diaphragm as she'd been taught, and sang the opening notes of "Smoke Gets In Your Eyes."

She took her time, feeling strangely free even under his intense scrutiny. Ornamenting her phrases, she added a few jazzy syncopations. With him watching, she enjoyed playing with the music, lilting and scooping up to the higher notes, drawing them out to create heartbreaking dissidence. And even though she endeavored to remain distant, not acknowledging Liam's heated looks, in her heart she sang to him and of him. She poured her heart out for him.

Even before she hit the final note, he approached, fire in his eyes. As the note died away, she looked up at him.

He pulled Kate to her feet, his face serious. "You are incredible and you're hired."

"Liam…"

"I mean it. Once the police find Vaughan, I want you to open my club."

He didn't let her respond. Wrapping her in his arms, he claimed her mouth. Tongue, teeth, lips, he took them all and she shook like a leaf in a storm, unwilling to fight him.

She wanted to tell him she couldn't sing at Decadence, at Vice, but the words wouldn't come out. And once his hands slid down her back to knead her bottom, she forgot how words worked.

"Kate," he said on a deep groan. "I need you

now."

Yes, her body shouted, overpowering the brain that yet fought to keep her strong. Her nipples hardened and the pressure in her womb grew frenzied. She clutched at him, her greatest temptation, and moaned into his mouth as their tongues battled. She would give herself to him again, right here. She'd do anything he asked.

She was falling in love with him.

Liam ripped off his shirt, and Kate tugged off her own, tossing it onto the stage. He worked his belt buckle while she threw her bra to the floor. Liam eyed her with hunger and motioned for her to lie back on the piano bench. She did, arching her back at the sensation of cool wood on her skin.

He knelt next to her and cupped her breasts. Rolling her nipples between fingers and thumbs, he plucked them until she flailed and moaned.

"So beautiful," he said. "So goddamn beautiful."

As he was to her, with his sexy eyes and wicked grin. She could look at him forever.

He closed his lips over one nipple and laved it with his tongue. As he suckled, he danced his hand over her belly and slid his fingers over her mound and between her legs. She was already so wet, so primed, he must have felt her moisture right through her jeans. Scratching a fingernail over her denim-clad pussy, he chuckled when she bucked beneath him.

"Far too many clothes." Lifting his head from her breast, he repositioned himself at the other end of the bench by her dangling legs. He unzipped her jeans and tugged them over her hips and pulled them off, along with her panties. Tossing them onto the keyboard, he chuckled when they made a discordant noise.

Liam ran his hands up her legs, spreading them with a determined touch. He lowered his head, breathed in, and smoothed his tongue over her already swollen lips.

Insane pleasure tackled her, rattling through her veins. "Good God."

He teased her with gentle licks, but never sliding deep, never touching her clit. Even so, her sex fluttered and flexed, wanting more, wanting it harder. She dug her hands in his hair, urging him to press on with his intimate kisses.

"You want more, sugar?" he said, lifting his head.

She nodded, desperate for release.

"How bad do you want it?" His fingers glided over her delicate skin.

Just as she was about to tell him to get back to work, or else, he surprised her by tapping her mound, right on her clit.

Her nerve endings exploded in wonderful agony as she experienced a mini-orgasm. Liam didn't give her a chance to recover. Finally rewarding her for her trials, he insinuated his face between her legs and sucked hard.

Her vision grew foggy as she came in his mouth and cried his name over and over.

He continued to lap while two fingers found a home inside her. Stroking, stroking, he did not stop until she'd quieted. Once she did, he continued his ministrations until she tightened under him once more. Shocked she could come again so quickly, she squeezed her eyes shut and went along for the very bumpy ride. He knew just what to do to make her moan, to make her tremble, and as she pondered his power over her, she shattered under him once again.

Before her orgasm had even subsided, he gathered her in his arms and carried her to one of the wide bar stools.

"Lean over, baby. Show me that pretty ass."

She leaned over the stool, glad for the velvet crush on her chest. Liam caressed the globes of her behind and massaged up to her back. She resisted stretching and meowing like a cat, but it was hard not to purr as he manipulated her grateful muscles.

His hands stilled. "Shit. I just realized I don't have a condom."

She stood and turned, eyeing her gorgeous man. As much as she still had reservations about his emotional wellbeing, she wasn't worried about catching anything from him. He'd been meticulous up until now. "It's okay. I'm on the pill. I trust you."

He cupped her face. "I would never do anything to destroy that trust."

She held his hand closer to her cheek, loving his touch. Kate then turned and positioned herself over the stool. "Take me. Now."

She wiggled her bottom for incentive, as if any were needed. Liam groaned and stripped out of his remaining clothes. She looked over her shoulder at the nude god behind her, biting her lip when he touched a reverent hand to her pussy.

"You're so sweet, baby," he said as he wriggled a finger into her core.

"Liam, please. You tease too much."

"There's no such thing as too much teasing, sugar. You know, you look so tempting from this angle, I might get on my knees and eat you out again."

"Liam, fuck me, please."

He slapped her ass. "So unladylike."

Before she could beg, he speared inside her. She shouted in shock and ecstasy as he filled her. He slammed into her over and over, stretching her tight channel as easily as he'd taken her heart. He gripped her hips, digging in with his nails, and she relished the sharp tug on her flesh. Curling over her body, he pistoned into her, his strong muscles powering each debilitating glide.

Her orgasm spiraled into view and her arms and legs went tingly numb.

Kate froze, realizing the numbness wasn't brought on by Liam's thrusts. It was the aura of an impending seizure, the only warning she'd ever received before phasing out.

Only, as always, it happened so fast, too fast to tell him. Her limbs stiffened, she opened her mouth to talk but no words came.

Kate blacked out.

***

Liam had hoped his movements would liquefy her limbs, but realized something was wrong as soon as her entire frame tensed. When guttural noises emerged from her throat, he frantically pulled out and took her off the stool. She moved like an automaton. Her eyes had rolled back in her head and there was spittle on her lips.

Fuck. A seizure.

He remembered a kid from high school who used to suffer from epilepsy. The teacher always said there was no way to stop it. One should just make the person comfortable. Knowing all he could do was help her ride it out, he bundled her to the ground and turned her on her side, facing him.

She shook and sputtered and mumbled strange words. Her fingers dug into his legs. Where her toes should have curled with pleasure, they now stretched as her body was ravaged by the episode.

And he couldn't stop it. He couldn't fucking stop it. She seemed to be in agony and he couldn't do a damn thing. Could only watch and wonder at how much it made his heart hurt.

He ran a hand over her hair. "It's okay, Kate. I've got you. I've got you."

He spoke in gentle tones, belying the frantic pace of his pulse. After the longest minute of his life, her shudders began to subside. The relief that streaked through him was palpable.

Her pretty irises floated back into view and she focused on him, but then she turned away, as if ashamed.

"Hey." He pulled her into his arms and cradled her on his lap. "You went for a little trip. Are you in pain?"

"No."

"Thank God. Can you remember anything?"

"No."

He kissed her brow, letting his lips linger on her clammy skin. Christ, he was just as clammy. Thinking he might have caused her seizure was doing a real number on his sanity. Fuck, to think he might have hurt her…

Had he? He knew he'd been pushing it, pushing her. Guilt stabbed through him, making his chest seize with its familiar pain.

They didn't talk for some time. He was too consumed with the memory of her sightless gaze, her terrible tremors and moans. He wanted to help her, to ensure she never had to suffer like that again.

"What can I do, Kate? Tell me. Should I call an ambulance?"

"There's no need."

"I can call Dr. Chan."

"No, but I should get back to the suite and take my pills." She pulled away, ever so slightly. "I'm usually diligent about taking them, but I forgot the past few days. I've been…distracted."

"Kate, sweetheart. Please tell me I didn't hurt you."

She lifted her head. With her face drawn and pale, she appeared exhausted. When she smiled, it didn't quite reach her eyes. He could have sworn in that moment she retreated from him.

"You didn't. No one knows why the seizures happen. Just tragic timing. Sorry to spoil the moment."

Fuck the moment. He wanted to know he'd have other moments with her, but with the way she looked at him now, he wasn't sure anymore. She looked everywhere, nervous, and colored with what might even be regret.

No, it must be the seizure. Damn, seeing that had done horrible things to him. His heart was still racing. Liam didn't know if he'd ever enjoy another moment of peace, knowing she could drop to the ground at any time. She could collapse in front of a bus, for God's sake. "I want you to see a specialist."

"I've seen them. Lots of them."

"I want you to see another one. I'll get Chan to give you a referral."

"There's no need."

"Of course there's a fucking need." His voice rose with each syllable. Why was he shouting? Maybe because she edged away from him, because she *continued* to edge away from him, rather than sink into his embrace. "You may not have seen what happened, but I did. I don't want you to go through that again."

Kate gazed at him, her cheeks white, her eyes wide. Shit, he was scaring her when he should be comforting her. It seemed the emotion he elicited more than anything in her was fear. This is what came from expressing himself. He didn't know how to do it properly, like a sane person.

"Liam, I know you're trying to help, but I've lived with this a lot longer than you. I'm usually very careful with my medication." Her voice dropped almost to a whisper. "It's been a long time. Please, don't worry about me."

Don't worry about her. Right. He'd never stop now.

***

When Kate saw Lisa's number come up on her cell display the next day, she grew excited. She missed her friend and felt badly about not checking in more frequently. They were so out of the loop with each other. Were Georgie and Sarah doing all right? Was Lisa keeping her head above water? God only knew she had her own updates to share, including her whiling away the hours at Vice with Liam. That wouldn't go over well. Even still, she clicked the keypad, eager to have a good chinwag and determined to bring Lisa up to speed.

"Hey," she said brightly as Lisa picked up. "How are you?"

"Oh, I'm fine."

"I tried to reach you the other day."

"You didn't try very hard. A couple of cryptic 'don't worry about me' messages? Jesus, Kate. It's been almost two weeks. All kinds of things have been going through my head."

"I wanted to talk to you, not a machine. Look, I'm sorry I haven't been in touch more, but there's been a lot going on…"

"Like hanging around with Liam Doyle? Is that what's keeping you so busy?"

Shit. Donny told her. After avoiding his wife's presence for weeks, she should have known he would have made an exception so he could run home and tattle like a child. "Lisa, there's a reason I'm here."

"And I'm assuming it has nothing to do with your pathetic protest, right? Remember when you had morals?" Lisa's voice grew with every syllable. Kate knew her friend was in a fragile place, but her tone still stung.

"Lisa."

"Don't 'Lisa' me. Before Donny told me everything, I was worried sick about you. And all the while, you're playing footsie in Vice. I heard how Doyle came to your rescue. How he held you in his slimy embrace."

"Now wait a minute. You're not even giving me a chance to explain."

"I don't want your explanations, Kate. I want your friendship, and your loyalty. I want you to leave that place now, and come home. I want you to tell Liam Doyle he can go to hell."

"I can't do that. It's not what you think."

"Oh, that's rich," she scoffed. "My life is falling apart, and my best friend is fucking the owner of the casinos my husband lost all our money in. What is *wrong* with you? I know it's been a while since you got laid, but I thought your standards were higher."

"You're just being cruel now. You don't understand."

"I understand perfectly. I understand you're no longer my friend. I understand you will stay away from me and my children, and stay out of my life. Do you hear me?"

"Lisa," she whispered, unable to make her voice any louder. "Don't do this."

"I mean it, Kate. I looked up to you." She let out a sob. "But now, I can't even bear the thought of looking at you." She slammed her phone down and the line went dead.

Kate stared, dazed, and listened to the flat noise. That dial tone would forever be the soundtrack of her life spiraling out of control.

"No," she murmured. "No. She's just hurt right now." Donny might be spouting his vitriol in her ear now, but Lisa was a smart woman. She'd see through what he was doing. Like any compulsive gambler worth his salt, he'd pounced on a chance to make someone else look bad in his stead. Her father had done it dozens of times.

Don't blame me your mother ran out of money to pay the bills. She should have organized the finances better.

It's not my fault your cousin doesn't have enough cash to pay for his knee procedure. Yeah, he loaned me some money, but he should have gotten some insurance.

Don't blame me for going to the casino for a couple of hours of fun. Maybe if the women in my life were more interesting, I'd have stayed home.

Don't blame me. It's not my fault.

Always someone else's problem.

She'd give Lisa some space and try her again in a day or two. It would have to work. The thought of losing her was too much to bear right now.

Thank God she had Liam. He'd been her rock, and she wouldn't let Lisa or anyone else badmouth him. They didn't know him like she did.

Do you really know him at all?

Oh, she hated her fucking inner voice.

She looked at the clock, wondering when he'd

come through the door. He'd gone to work, promising to return in a few hours. She had to admit, she rather enjoyed dwelling in his fantasy suite, but it seemed so empty without him.

When he walked through the door around six, she flew into his arms.

"Hey," he said, kissing her with a tired chuckle. He pried her off long enough to peer into her face and frown. "What happened?"

She told him what Lisa said and his frown grew deeper. When she finished, he just stared at her.

"After everything you did for her and her kids. That sucks, Kate."

"I didn't even bother to let her know I was alive or dead. What was I thinking? I've been a bad friend."

He raised her chin, making her look at him. "You wouldn't know how. Lisa has no idea what you've been through. Remember the reason you came here in the first place. Don't beat yourself up for this. I mean it."

"Maybe I never should have come here. It's been like a dream, but I need to get back to reality."

"You don't mean that."

"Don't I? Liam, despite everything, despite your generosity, it's wrong for me to be here."

His face began to harden. "You're safe here. I don't want you to go."

"But…"

"No buts, Kate." His eyes took on a possessive gleam. "Stay with me."

Even though his face was so serious, so set with determination, his voice cracked. When he looked at her like that, she couldn't say no to him. He was her great vice, her only temptation. People like her dad and Donny might gamble their lives away, but Kate was powerless before Liam's persuasions. He whittled away all her good sense.

"Liam," she said. "I can't hide here with you forever."

He began to breathe heavily, his gaze hovered near her lips, but unfocused. "Yes, you can. I want you to stay, and you know you want it too."

Before she could stop him, he dropped to his knees. He pushed up her shirt and kissed her bare waist. His fingers slid up her legs, under her skirt, pushing it up toward her waist. His face, contorted by desire, made the hairs on her arms stand on end, but she didn't stop him. Dammit, she wanted him even more because of it.

He reached for her panties and dragged them down her legs. Unthinking, she stepped out of them. As she took in the sight of the silky cloth on the floor, Liam pulled her to him and buried his face in her pussy. She cried out as his tongue made hot contact with her skin.

He wasn't gentle. He sucked and bit and demanded her orgasm with every move. As much as she wanted to fall to the floor, to kick and thrash, he held her upright as he continued his ferocious adoration. There was nothing polite about this lovemaking, nothing sweet. Just Liam, showing her how much he needed her, how badly he needed her to come. She banged on his shoulders, eager for him to stop, only to pull at his hair, desperate for him to continue.

He released her pussy lips for one moment and stared at her from the floor. His lips, swollen and wet, seemed to mirror his bright gaze. "You'll stay with me. Now come."

His mouth met with her again, and she reeled under his touch. Heat streaked across her skin, setting her on fire from the inside out. He plunged his tongue into her pussy, staking his claim, and she capitulated. Writhing in his grip, her knees buckled. Horrible, wonderful pressure sliced through her belly, making her ache and squirm. And just when she thought she could take no more, he nibbled on her clit and she exploded into a million pieces. She was sure her head had ended up somewhere in the corner of the room.

Only then did he let her fall to the floor. She lay, dazed, and waited for him to rip at his clothes and fuck her like an animal. But he didn't.

Liam just sat next to her and ran a gentle hand through her hair, a sad smile on his lips. "I won't let you go," he said, pulling her to him.

When she'd first agreed to stay at Vice, Kate had worried he might be a bad influence on her. Now she wondered if she was a bad influence on him. He'd already lost so much. The idea of losing anyone else had turned him into a possessive beast. And she didn't know how to help him other than give him the raw physicality he craved.

Maybe they were each other's vice, after all.

And maybe this feral need in him proved he'd be better off without her.

Chapter Fourteen

That evening, Kate decided she needed to get out of Vice altogether. Liam hadn't been thrilled, still worried about her seizures and Vaughan. However, she accepted his offer of a car and a drive from Wade.

The best medicine for her right now would be to attend a New Horizons meeting. She hadn't been back since the attack, and she missed her pals, especially in light of Lisa's comments. As much as she'd shied away recently, she was now eager to attend and just be there.

Of course, she had every expectation Lisa had given them a run-down on her activities at Vice, and her liaison with Liam. She hoped, however, that they'd listen to her and hear the voice of reason, unlike Lisa. After all, she'd spent years listening to them, supporting them through their trials.

Wade parked outside the building and Kate breathed a sigh of relief as she entered the group room. She understood these people, understood their challenges, and they needed her as much as she needed them.

Eager to see some smiles from some friendly faces, she looked for a free chair and sat down, feeling like the new kid entering class for the first time.

Heads turned in her direction, but not with warm welcome. Rather, her old friends regarded her with apparent distrust.

"Hey, guys," she said quietly, smiling and waving a hand. "I know it's been a while, but…"

They all looked to Rod now. He clenched his jaw, stood, and came over. "Kate, can we speak outside, please?"

She stood and followed him out. "Okay." She had a bad feeling about this.

Once out of earshot of the other group members, he laid it all out for her. "Look. There's been some discussion in the group, and most of us don't feel comfortable with you here right now."

"What?" They couldn't have passed judgment on her already, could they? Not without hearing her side first.

Rod turned a bit red. "Kate, are you going to make me go into detail? I was kind of hoping to spare you the embarrassment."

"Um, too late."

"All right, I'll spell it out for you. Lisa told the group how you've been socializing with Liam Doyle. At Vice."

"Socializing? Well, she was more diplomatic with you than she was with me." As her heart began its sink, she crossed her arms over her chest. "Lisa has the wrong end of the stick, and so do you."

"You left me in charge of the group, and I still have to think of them and how things appear. We have some very fragile egos here."

"Yeah, I know. I'm the leader, remember? The one who brought you all together." Okay, now this was just pissing her off.

"I'm sorry, Kate, but I'm doing what I think is best. Maybe once you sort things out, you can come back."

"Sort things out?" She squawked in disbelief. "Rod, the only reason I'm staying at Vice is because I was *attacked*. Liam saved me. He offered to help."

"You were attacked?"

"Yes." She put up a hand. "You know what? Never mind. I've devoted myself to this group and the minute my life goes to pot, I get booted? Well, then I really don't want to be here."

"Kate, wait…"

"No. You go back to your precious group. I'm sure they'll be lost without their new head honcho." Fleeing before she burst into tears, she raced outside to Wade's waiting car. He opened the back door to the Escalade and she dove inside.

The security guard eyed her warily as he climbed in the driver's seat. "Where to?"

Where to? She had nowhere else to go, no one to turn to other than the man in whose arms she'd come alive, but with whom she'd also lost part of herself. And as much as she wanted to run away from Liam and from everyone else, she was always drawn back to him, like a boomerang.

"Vice. Where else?"

She sighed, noticing how Wade tried to be

stealthy in sending a text, no doubt to Liam.

Liam. As much as she craved him, craved his taste and his touch, this no longer felt right. Maybe it never did. She'd gained a lover, perhaps even someone she could fall in love with, but his acute attentions rattled her. His violent loving made her doubt her sanity. With him, although she'd experienced physical euphoria, it had left her numb and hollow.

He'd lost so much in life, and had made strides, especially by letting go of Michelle. But then he'd transferred those intense needs onto Kate. As much as she was glad she'd helped him with his abandonment issues, she was under no delusion that his demons had been vanquished. Not by a long shot.

He was two men in one. She might have fallen for the owner of those seductive grins, but she was scared of the man behind those dark appetites.

Oh God, I have fallen for him.

No. Impossible. She could never fall for anyone so grasping, so needy. In some ways, he reminded her of her father, someone who always needed more. More money, more friends, more attention. That's what he really got out of his habit, but only for a time. She'd lived with lies and deceit all her life. If this was her new rock bottom, losing her friends, and she had to start over, she owed it to herself to start over in a healthier frame of mind.

What she had with Liam was in no way healthy.

She had to let him go, so they could both let go of the past. It was the only way. They'd been too wrapped up in each other, and it had become too easy to forget the outside world and pretend everything was okay. She couldn't carry on this way, existing just for Liam.

And yet every time she remembered the way he caressed her, she grew weak in the knees. It was all so wrong. Hell, they'd barely had a real date. The night at Franky's seemed so long ago. They'd gone from throwing barbs at one another to him throwing her on the nearest surface and fucking her senseless. Not exactly the basis of a stable relationship. How could she love him?

Maybe because she glimpsed something in him that no one else had ever seen. Even though he'd initially held back from her, he'd revealed his heart. She couldn't forget that moment, as much as he'd walled it back up.

As she expected, by the time they pulled up at Vice, he was standing on the walkway, waiting for them. He was dressed for work, but his pressed shirt was open at the collar with no tie. There were dark circles under his eyes and his handsome face looked strained and pale.

Like an addict.

She slid her compact out of her purse, eyed her reflection, and saw the same qualities in her own face. She'd become a desperate woman, looking for her next fix.

She replaced the mirror in her bag and looked back at him. This wasn't the same playfully cocky Liam Doyle she'd first met. Had that man ever existed? She wasn't sure anymore. All she knew was, even though this Liam scared her, he also drew her like a six-foot magnet. She just didn't know how to relate to him. She had questions he didn't want to answer, and he wanted to explore carnal depths that made her only question him more.

He opened up the car door for her and she slid out. "Hey."

"Hey."

"Wade tells me you had a rough time. I'm sorry."

"It's okay."

"No, it isn't." He let out a sigh and fiddled with one of the buttons on his shirt. "Listen, do you want to go somewhere and talk?"

Talk. Now he wanted to talk. Her heart walloped her insides in a beat she didn't recognize. It was too late for talk.

She needed to do this. It was now or never.

This would be her true rock bottom.

"Kate?"

"You know, Liam, I'd say yes if I thought we were actually going to talk to each other, but that's not going to happen, is it? We'll go back to your room, or some other random room, and just fuck like we always do."

He held her gaze, as if wondering where she was going with this.

"I'm checking out of Vice. I can't be here. Just associating with you, being here in this hotel, has lost me my friends. I was wrong to come in the first place. I got carried away, got tempted by this glitzy world you live in, tempted by you, and now I'm paying for it." She moved past him toward the lobby door.

He reached for her hand. "You can't do that. You

can't go."

"I can and I will."

"Kate, it's not safe for you out there."

She whipped around on him. "Jesus, Liam. It's not safe for me here! Don't you get it? I can't be around you. You make me…want things I can't have."

He drew dangerously close. His voice was deep and soft on her ear. "You can have them. You can have anything you want. I'll get it for you."

"Don't you understand? I never *wanted* you to get me things. I just wanted to know you, to see where things might go. But we've become addicted to each other. You've avoided your work. I've avoided my life. I don't even have a fucking job! We've just lived in a bubble with each other. It's not healthy."

He grabbed her hand and dragged her into a quiet alcove, away from the main entrance. "I don't care if it's healthy or not."

"Don't you get it? I'm your new Michelle. I'm your crutch, and you've become mine."

Liam's mouth fell open.

"I never wanted to be that for you. I want to be something better."

He pulled her to him and lay his forehead against hers. "You are the best thing I've ever known." His fingers clawed against her back, his nails dug into her clothing. He held on as if he was gripping a life preserver. "I can't let you go."

"You'd keep me here against my will?"

Wildness shimmered in his eyes. "What do you think I am? A fucking maniac? I just want to love

252

you," he cried out. "Kate, I love you."

Oh. There they were. The words that would echo in her brain and sear her as she walked away. But she had to do this, for both of them.

"You don't love me, Liam. We don't know each other well enough. You haven't let me get close enough to really know you." There, she said it, even though it made her heart break.

He drew her in and smashed his mouth against hers, thrusting his tongue between her lips and nearly destroyed her resolve.

"I know everything about you," he said. "I've seen your fears and your dreams. I've seen your quirks. I know you cover your mouth with your hand when you chew your food. I know you always tie the left shoe before the right. I know how you play with your hair when you're nervous. I know what makes you laugh and what makes you cry. I know how your body curls into mine when we sleep. I know how to make you whimper with need and how to make your body sing with joy. I know all the important things." He stroked her cheek, his touch more gentle now, but no less desperate. "And the rest I can learn. You're not my crutch, Kate. You're my hope."

Oh, Jesus, keep me strong. The tears broke free and he took turns wiping and kissing them away. She wanted to believe him, to believe their love wasn't sick.

Rock bottom. Her words came back to haunt her. She hated rock fucking bottom.

Who was she kidding? Their affair was doomed from the start. She should never have set foot inside

Liam's office. She'd seen his tattered heart and had wanted to put it back together. He'd glimpsed her bruised soul and had hidden her away. She'd felt like Cinderella with him, but really she was no better than a two-bit Rapunzel, locked away in a tower.

They enabled each other. Their love was like a Vegas casino, bright and lively on the outside, but cloaked in darkness, heedless of time and responsibility. They'd reveled in each other, forgetting the outside world, rather than learning how to function in it.

They couldn't really love each other unless they learned to stand on their own first. She needed to let him go and stop hiding. She needed to hurt him.

Hopefully it wouldn't kill her in the process.

"We're not good for each other, Liam. I can't be with you." She waved her hand, indicating the walls of his casino. "This was never the life I wanted. I lost track of my values. I can't stay. I'll never be able to separate you from what you do. Every meal we eat, I'll see it as coming out of someone else's pocket. Every dollar you spend on me, I'll see it as draining some poor kid's college fund."

"Kate, don't do this."

"You think I want to? I can't look at you and not see Vice. And no matter how much soul-searching I do, I won't be able to stop it." When he moved to brush away her fresh tears, she pushed his hand aside and wiped them herself. "It's time for me to go home."

His face drained. "I won't be able...I can't function without you."

254

"I know, but I think we both need to learn how."

He played with her pinky finger, as if holding onto whatever he could. "What about Vaughan?"

"I'll manage. I did before." She pulled her hand out of his. "Goodbye, Liam."

He didn't answer, but grew paler. She turned and sprinted for the taxi bay before she flew to him, trying to take everything back. She didn't have any of her things, only her purse. The rest she'd ask for later. She couldn't go into his suite to collect them now, or she'd never come out again.

The taxi driver opened the back door and she got inside, barely managing to give the man her address. The driver closed the door and she sat still, waiting for him to start the engine. She didn't look at Liam, but expected him to run up to the car and bang on the window.

He didn't.

As the driver pulled away, she gave in to temptation and turned to look for him.

Like a dream upon waking, he'd already disappeared.

Chapter Fifteen

Kate smiled at the woman auditioning her for the chorus girl job, hoping it looked sincere. She handed her a copy of her headshot and resume, taking a moment to smooth out a wrinkled corner first.

"Do you dance?"

"I'm afraid not."

She raised an eyebrow and then eyeballed her chest. "Comfortable with nudity?"

"Oh. Um, I was told this job involved no nudity, just singing."

"Yeah, they told you wrong. All our girls are topless, but no hoo-hah. It's expected." The woman shrugged, no doubt used to seeing this reaction. "So, you willing to unleash the hounds?"

Shit. This was the fifth audition in the three days since she'd left Liam. And in all of them, the requirements had been the same: show us your tits. Sometimes she thought she lived in bloody Sodom and Gomorrah.

She remembered what Liam said about showgirl

acts being demeaning to women. She certainly felt demeaned. One audition after another, and no producer was interested in her voice, just her cup size. They didn't even care that she couldn't dance, as long as her hooters were hanging out. Any talent beyond that was considered a bonus.

It was enough to make her seek out a nice, boring call center job somewhere, selling aluminum siding or steak knives.

Rock bottom. Rock bottom. This was just one small part of her journey. She would rise from the ashes like a phoenix.

If she could leave Liam standing there alone, ripping out her own heart in the process, she could get through a few embarrassing auditions.

"Look," Kate said, eyeing the faded upholstery and trying to ignore the foul smell emanating from the kitchen. "You have a supper club in the middle of a vibrant city. Not every joint in Vegas needs to provide a strip tease. I have talent and drive. Maybe we could talk about trying a new act." She smiled, willing her positive vibes all over the producer.

The older woman just shook her head and tossed the headshot back across the desk. "Sorry, sweetie. No tits, no dice. In case you hadn't heard, sex sells." She stood up and walked toward the audition room door. "There are plenty of girls in Vegas who are willing to take their clothes off. Some of them can even sing."

As Kate left, she tried hard not to think of Liam's offer to sing at Decadence. It seemed every thought led back to him. Everything she ate reminded her of the sexy breakfasts they'd shared in bed. Every breath she took recalled feeling his in her ear when they made love. Each look of indifference on another person's face forced her to remember his, so full of passion and yearning.

She was beginning to think she hadn't even glimpsed true rock bottom yet. Perhaps it was the difference between the ocean floor and the Marianas Trench.

What about Liam? Was he suffering without her? He'd said he loved her. As much as she wanted to believe it, did believe it, she couldn't shake the feeling they were better off without each other.

Hadn't she always been a loner? Her father's addiction had lost her friends through the years, usually when he'd asked them for handouts. When her mom had taken her own life, Kate had been virtually alone in the world. As sad as her upbringing had been, she'd tried to rise above it, to be an independent woman.

Hiding away with Liam, she'd been on the verge of losing that independence. It had been so nice— no, so wonderful—having him cater to her. But under his roof, she'd become something less than herself. She couldn't lose sight of that.

It was the only thing stopping her from racing back to Vice and burrowing herself into his embrace.

As soon as she walked out of the dingy club, the sun hit her square in the eye, making her squint. She put on a pair of shades and walked to the nearest bus stop.

And still she thought of him.

The hardest part of walking away had been

realizing she never told him she loved him too. And she did.

She knew it in the quiet moments, when the loneliness hung so heavily on her soul it felt like a tumor. She knew it at daybreak when his arms no longer wrapped around her, making her a willing prisoner to his voice, his touch, his very breath.

Unable to tolerate the lights of the Strip, she'd stayed away from it as much as possible. Luckily her auditions had been in out-of-the-way locations. Not that it mattered. Wherever she went, his image still haunted her. Every suit, every flash of navy blue silk, every man who bore the slightest resemblance gave her a lump in her throat. And every second bus stop she passed carried a poster advertising Vice. She couldn't escape him. She didn't want to.

She missed him. It was that simple. But for her sake, as well as his, she had to stay away. The need to stand on her own two feet kept her strong. The desire to see him vanquish his demons kept her on the straight and narrow.

He hadn't called. As much as that hurt, it also gave her a measure of relief. A few syllables from his sensuous mouth and she'd weaken. Cold turkey was always best.

No one needed to know she went home each night and touched herself, trying to recapture some small wisp of their time together. Only then did she permit herself to remember how his stubble teased her inner thigh, and how hot and sweet his mouth tasted.

She stood at the bus stop and remembered how

right it felt to have Liam's fingers tangled in her hair. Lost in thought, she almost missed the man pacing a few meters away. Accustomed to making room for homeless people on the sidewalk, she automatically stepped back as he approached.

Only then did she recognize the auburn hair under his worn hat and that cocky gait.

"Katie-bug." Her father grinned. "I've been worried sick about you."

Kate's lip curled as if of its own volition. "Have you? It would be the first time."

Louis kicked at a beer can next to the bus stop and watched the stale contents drip onto the sidewalk.

"You sent a loan shark to my home, Dad," Kate said. "He beat me up. He punched me and kicked me and threatened to rape me. Did you know he'd do it?"

Louis's face fell, no doubt noticing her faded bruises for the first time. Of course, he'd feel badly. Just not badly enough to do something about it. "Oh, shit. Hugo promised not to get rough. I'm so sorry, Katie."

"You're not sorry for anything," she shouted, not caring if the people walking across the street could hear her. "You're only sorry I didn't give him the money!"

He looked around her but avoided her direct gaze. "Will you…give him the money?"

"I can't fucking believe you!"

"Watch your language, miss."

She refrained from laughing. Her father might have many sins, but he'd always been a stickler when it came to his daughter cussing. To him, women swearing ranked right up there with murder. "Oh, right, because my language is the real issue here." She shook her head. "Have you been following me? Did you trail me today just to find out if I have the cash?"

"I've been watching your apartment here and there. You were gone for a while."

"Yeah. I should have stayed away too."

He drew nearer, his face torn by urges he barely understood. "Katie, I never meant for this to happen. The gambling. Your mom. None of it."

She reached for his hand, noticing how he flinched. It had probably been some time since someone touched him. "Will you let me get you help, Dad? Because I will take you to Gamblers Anonymous right now. I will do whatever it takes, but you have to want it."

For a second, he looked tempted, or at least defeated. But then, with disappointing swiftness, he pulled his hand out of hers. "You don't understand. No one does. I'm in too deep."

"It's never too late."

"Katie, the only way you can help me now is by giving me the money. I can't go to any meetings if I'm dead." He stared at her, his gaze almost heartless as he eyed her pearls. "Maybe if you sold some things, like your choker. Your mom got that from her grandmother. I could get a good price for an antique necklace like that."

Her last shred of hope for him died when he suggested pawning the only memento she had of her mother, his own wife. Had he forgotten her completely? If not, he'd shelved her memory, unable to deal with it. Unable to accept the part he'd played. For him, denial really was just a river in Egypt.

She offered him a sad smile, and did something she never thought she'd do. She reached behind her neck, unclasped the necklace, and handed it to him.

He snatched it out of her hands and thrust it into his pocket as if someone were watching. "You were always a good kid, Katie. I know you probably wouldn't believe me if I told you I was proud of you, but I am. You won't regret helping me. I just have to do this one thing and then I'll get help. I promise."

She might as well have been listening to a tape recording. "Dad, listen to me. We're done. I never want to hear from you again. Ever. I hope you get help. I really do, but it can't come from me anymore. You don't have a daughter anymore, and I don't have a father."

Louis pulled the pearl necklace out of his pocket. For a moment, she thought he was going to give it back, but he shoved it back into his pocket. He rubbed his mouth, turned, and walked down the street.

As he turned the corner, Kate whispered, "Goodbye, Dad."

***

Hugo Vaughan had clearly been paid. Or so Kate assumed. After all, he'd never come back to collect. Whatever price her dad got for the choker, it must have fit the bill to cover his debts. She wasn't sure her mom had ever had the pearls appraised, but she knew the necklace was old and in impeccable condition. She didn't have to work for *Antiques Roadshow* to know it cost a mint.

It was probably the first time she'd wasted a thought on Vaughan since leaving Liam. In a way, she had almost expected the loan shark to show up at her door, demanding more cash. She just hadn't cared. He could come if he wanted. Hell, he could stay for tea and biscuits.

It didn't matter, because every moment away from Liam seemed to ensconce her further down in the hole she kept calling rock bottom, a place she now hated with all her might. She worried about ever being able to claw her way out.

One bright spot was her new job at Percolate, a quaint coffee shop that catered to hipsters and hipster wannabes. She'd walked into the shop, talking a big talk about providing them with some much-needed musical entertainment. The place served great coffee but was far too serious. The manager had offered her a job as a clerk instead, saying she could sing for tips after her shift serving up coffees.

Granted, it wasn't anywhere close to being her dream job, and it certainly paled in comparison to crooning love songs at Decadence, but for now it would have to do. She'd answered ads for every entertainment-related position in the city, but none had panned out. This wasn't such a bad deal. The clerk job offered a bit of money and a whole lot of brain-numbing repetitive work, and at least she could keep her pipes warmed up with the hour of singing she did after the shift.

As she prepared for her shift, she noticed a newspaper lying on the break table. Taking a closer look, she almost gasped. Left open to the entertainment pages, the photo showed Liam surrounded by a bevy of beautiful women at Vice, each of them looking at him with adoration. She looked at the date on the paper and saw it was only one day old.

A stabbing pain assaulted her heart. "Well, you seem to have moved on."

Someone crept up behind her. Her peripheral vision caught a glimpse of blonde dreadlocks and piercings. Cynthia, her nineteen-year-old coworker, motioned toward the article. "Liam Doyle, huh? Fuck me. I would totally let that man shave my pussy."

Kate turned to her, frowning. "Uh…"

Cynthia turned to her. "What? You've never let a man shave you before? It's super-hot."

Kate bit her lip, remembering how much Liam loved playing down there. She decided to keep that juicy memory to herself. "Too much information, that's all."

Cynthia picked up the paper. "Hey, did you hear that guy just…"

"Actually, I'd rather not hear about Liam Doyle. Please." She tried not to look like she was a simpleton.

The girl shrugged. "Suit yourself."

Feeling lower than ever, Kate adjusted her t-shirt, pasted on a smile, and took her station at the counter. Luckily the shop was dead and she didn't have to face anyone right now. She grabbed a wet cloth and proceeded to clean, mentally reviewing her set list of songs for the end of her shift.

The idea of Liam cavorting with socialites made her stomach lurch. Kate took deep breaths and tried to concentrate on her work, sorting prepackaged bags of fair-trade brew. Someone had mixed up the decaf with the strong Columbian and she set about restoring order to the display. The writing on the coffee bags began to blur from her tears. She blinked them away.

You were a fool to think you could be part of his world.

"Hey."

Kate jumped at the soft voice next to her and turned. Kate's eyes widened when she saw Lisa at the counter, Georgie and Sarah at her side. Georgie ran around the counter and hugged her, almost making her burst into tears again, but she held it back so as not to startle the poor kid.

Georgie sniffed her work shirt and said, "Auntie Kate, you smell like Grandma after she comes back from bingo."

Kate let out a laugh, even as Lisa scolded him for the comparison. "You're right, George." Cynthia always smoked out back on her breaks but the smell managed to cling to Kate's clothes anyway.

Lisa turned to her daughter and handed her some change. "Sarah, take your brother and go get a chocolate bar next door."

The girl grabbed her little brother by his collar and hurried out.

"So," said Lisa, sighing.

"So."

"I, um, thought I saw you from outside. Thought I'd grab a coffee."

Kate nodded and poured Lisa her usual black brew. She handed it over. "How are you?"

Lisa took the cup and rummaged in her pocket for change, letting out a puff of air. "We're okay. Day by day, right?" She handed over some change.

"Yup." She ground the toe of her Keds into the floor.

Lisa put down the cup. "Look. Rod said something about you being attacked. Is it true?"

She nodded, not wanting to say more.

"Oh, Kate." Lisa's voice quavered. "I'm sorry."

Her head bobbed up and down. "I'm sorry too."

They hugged and Kate finally gave in to her grief and her fear and cried on Lisa's shoulder. After a couple of minutes, Lisa wrangled herself from their hold and looked at her. "Please tell me Liam Doyle wasn't the one who hit you. Because I will kill him."

"No. Not him. Never him." She gulped back bile. "I love him, Lisa."

Her friend sighed, her eyes crinkling at the corners. "So I see." She narrowed her eyes and peered at her neck. "Where are your pearls?"

"It's a long story."

"Well, I think it's time for a catch up session. Come for a coffee, or something stronger, after your shift?"

She managed a grin. "I'd really like that."

Lisa kissed her on the cheek, and just like that,

some of the weight that had been holding Kate down lifted. She felt she could breathe again. They said a few more words before the kids bounded back inside, eager to return home so they could play videogames. Lisa smiled and said goodbye. Kate waved as they left.

She turned back to the packages of coffee and decided they looked just fine as they were.

***

Lisa handed her what had to be her seventeenth cup of coffee that day, after stirring in cream and two heaping teaspoons of sugar. Kate waited a moment, stared at the mug, and then added another teaspoon of the sweet stuff.

Her friend giggled. "I see we're back on sugar."

"Sugar and I were never meant to be apart." She stirred the hot beverage and licked the spoon, enjoying the tingle on her tongue. "Have you seen Donny?"

Lisa nodded. "When he rushed over to tell me about you and Doyle, he acted pretty excited to be at home. Personally, I think he was just happy seeing someone take the heat for once."

Kate put her hand on Lisa's arm. "But then he disappeared again?"

Lisa gave a short laugh, though it lacked in humor. "Actually, no. Even though I was angry at you, I read him the riot act for trying to get someone else in trouble just to try and get me on his side. We talked. For a long time. I mean really talked."

"You did?"

Lisa nodded. "At first it was the same old song and dance. He was just trying to 'protect' me by pointing out what a shitty friend you were. Sorry, his words."

Kate smiled. "That's okay."

"But then he just went on this crazy rant. Talking about how he hated the world for messing up his life. Our lives. He blamed Doyle, he blamed you, he blamed the security guard who threw him out. He blamed me, and the kids, and my mom. He blamed his boss for not giving him a raise, and his co-workers for undermining him. Then he blamed his car for breaking down and the mechanic for ripping him off. And I think it was around that time he realized he was blaming just about everyone he knew. Except himself."

Kate said nothing, but her eyes widened.

"It just sort of hit him. Like he'd seen himself in a mirror for the first time. I think that's when he realized *he* was the one who messed up our lives."

"Wow. That's sort of huge."

"I know. He broke down after that. Cried for over an hour. That's when we really talked, and for the first time ever he seemed to listen. He's agreed to get help."

"Oh, Lisa. That's such a big step. I'm really happy for you."

"I don't have illusions. I know it'll be a long road. But I want to help him, and more importantly, he wants to as well. We're all seeing a family therapist, and he's started going to Gam-Anon. I think we'll get past this, and for once I don't feel like I'm fooling myself."

They quietly shared their coffee for a time. Kate was still somewhat skeptical about her friend's husband, but Lisa didn't need to hear that right now. She didn't want to tear down all her hopes. But Donny had accepted responsibility, which was more than her father ever did. Maybe there was hope for them after all.

Tired of the silence, Lisa changed the subject back to Kate. "So about you and Doyle?"

She gave her coffee one more absentminded stir, watching the little whorls dissipate. "I don't know. Liam was just…too much for me. Too much money. Too much intensity. Too much sex."

Lisa looked doubtful. "Um, just for the record, there's no such thing as too much sex."

Kate grinned. "There is when it's all you do. Don't get me wrong. It was good. Shouting-from-the-rooftops good. But our whole relationship was based on this bizarre attraction. I don't know if it ever had the potential to get deeper than that. Liam's been hurting for so long, has lost so much in his life. He said he didn't want to lose me, but I think he's just terrified of losing *anything*. It's as if he built this empire of…stuff." She wrinkled her nose. "And there's the whole casino thing. How can I ever get past that?"

"Maybe you don't need to."

"What do you mean?"

"It's his work, not his life. Maybe you just come to an agreement that you never talk work."

"No. I don't want to censor him. Besides, casinos are his life. He practically lives in one."

Lisa tugged at her bottom lip. "Right. The fancy

269

suite with the mile-long fireplace. How could I forget?" The look on her face made it clear she'd already imagined the fantasy suite in minute detail. "Look, Kate, I'm hardly one to lecture another person on choosing a partner. Look at the situation I'm in. But you admitted you and Liam love each other, and I've never seen you cry over anyone before. You've always been the one to help others with their relationships. I think this thing with Liam runs deeper than you know."

Kate shook her head. Was she ready for something that deep? Was he? Not if that newspaper was any indication.

"He already made strides. Damn, you said he dropped the custody suit. Doesn't that prove the man is trying to change?"

It seemed like eons ago. Even though she'd been mostly asleep, she remembered feeling such pride, such relief, on his behalf.

But she knew full well people didn't really change. Look at her father. Look at any number of the other addicts she'd known. She wanted Donny to be the one to prove her wrong, but it didn't mean she wouldn't reserve her judgment. She'd learned long ago it was easier to change her reactions than to compel others to seek help. And where she couldn't affect change, she left.

There was something to be said for keeping one's sanity.

"Kate?"

She gave Lisa half a smile. "I can't ask Liam to give up his career for me. I won't. It's better if I just forget him."

Even as she said the words, they hung at the back of her throat.

Forget him. Ha. It would be easier to forget her own name.

Chapter Sixteen

"I'm not sure I can do this," Kate said on her way into her first New Horizons meeting in weeks.

Lisa rallied behind her. "Of course you can." She steered her friend to one of the well-worn chairs. "Honesty is the best policy, right?"

"Right." She took a deep breath and watched as Rod started the meeting, welcoming new members. After the initial icebreakers, he opened the floor to anyone who wanted to share. Audrey spoke first, updating the group on her struggles with her boyfriend, and then a couple of new members shared their stories.

After thirty odd minutes, Rod turned to Kate with a smile. "It's good to see you back. The floor's yours if you want it, Kate."

"I'd like that." She folded her hands in her lap, looking down. "As some of you know, I recently had a...relationship with Liam Doyle, the owner of the Vice casino. I'm not going to apologize for that. That's a whole other story. I do have to apologize for something else, though. When I started this group, I told you all that I'd cut my dad out of my life. The truth was, I'd been enabling him for years, sending him money. It killed me to do it, but I couldn't stop. I was so scared to cut him off. Afraid of what might happen."

"It's never easy," Lisa said.

"No. But I got help from an unlikely source. Believe it or not, it was Liam Doyle who helped me to be strong. And even though I'm not seeing him anymore, I'll always be grateful to him for that. But that doesn't change the past. I'm sorry I lied to you all."

The room grew silent. A couple of the members traded looks.

Kate stood up. "I'd understand if you want me to leave."

"Hon," said Rod, grinning. "Don't be so dramatic. Have a seat. We'd like you to stay. Besides, we recently received a big donation and are planning on setting up a couple of new groups. I'm not just being a sentimental sap when I say we need you."

Emotion bubbled inside her. Kate hadn't lost her friends after all, and the streak of relief that shot through her made her feel ten years younger.

Unfortunately it did nothing to fill the other gaping hole inside her.

***

Lisa dropped her off at her apartment that night. Kate waved, turned, and sighed. The idea of facing another night alone, without Liam, had her skin bristling. It had been three weeks since she walked away from him and her heart still cried out for him, still wanted him.

Was it right? She wasn't sure anymore.

She just needed to get over this dreadful hump. She still felt his eyes on her everywhere she went. Every so often at Percolate, she'd see a businessman open the door and her heart would leap, only to realize it wasn't him. Whenever she spotted a black Escalade, she fought the urge to wave. She swore she smelled his cologne everywhere, as if he haunted her like a ghost. It both unnerved and thrilled her.

She started up the metal staircase leading to her unit when a noise distracted her.

Peering into the darkness of the backyard, she waited for his wraith to float toward her. Seeing nothing, feeling silly, she took another step.

She had to stop imagining Liam everywhere. At some point, she had to stop looking over her shoulder, hoping he'd appear. It did nothing to help the precious sense of sanity she so cherished.

Sanity. Right now she'd give her right arm for a huge helping of insanity and the chance to hear Liam say he loved her again.

She climbed up the remaining steps and shoved her key into the lock, giving it a hard turn. Once inside, she locked the door behind her, turned on the lights, and threw her purse on the couch. On a mission, she went straight into the kitchen and yanked open the freezer door.

No freaking ice cream. Not even a tablespoon's worth clinging to the lid of an old tub.

She wasn't sure she could make it through the night without some Chunky Monkey.

As she wondered about the hours of the corner store, she resolved to rectify her frozen dairy situation. If she hurried, she might still make it and get back in time for some choice reruns on TV. Sighing, she picked up her purse and keys again and headed to the door. She whipped it open.

Hugo Vaughan stood there, grinning.

Before she could scream or slam the door, he forced his way inside and put a beefy hand over her open mouth, shutting the door behind them.

"Thanks for letting me in, Red. I didn't want to put a shoulder to the door. You know, with my bursitis and all." He looked her up and down. "Lookin' good, Red. You know, I've missed you. Your dad's debt might be settled, but I seem to recall we still have some unfinished business."

God, he reeked of alcohol. Hopefully he was drunk enough that she could find a way out of this. She clawed at the hand over her mouth, trying to cry out.

"Uh uh, Red. Be a good girl and shut the fuck up." He backed her up to the couch and forced her down. She could bite down on his hand, but was afraid of how he might retaliate. A cruel hand tugged at her neckline, ripping at her shirt, and he licked at her neck.

He uncovered her mouth so he could plunge his tongue in. It was too much. She couldn't let this happen. Hadn't she already lost enough? She would not sacrifice her dignity as well.

She bit down. Hard. Vaughan roared in pain and

she gave him a shove. "Get the fuck off me, you filthy bastard," she screamed. She wriggled under him, desperate to bring her knees in contact with his nuts.

Despite being drunk, Vaughan managed to keep her pinned down, his weight crushing her. Clearly, he had done this before. The alcohol may have impaired his judgment, but it hadn't affected his reflexes. He evaded her every squirming attempt at a kick.

He rose up over her, blood dripping down his chin and smiled. "Have your bruises healed yet, bitch? I can give you some new ones." He lifted one hand, poised to strike, and Kate closed her eyes.

At first she thought she heard the sound of his fist cracking against her skull, only she'd felt nothing. Then she opened her eyes and realized the door had been kicked in.

Liam. For real, not the fantasy who'd obsessed her every waking and sleeping thought.

Liam ran forward and pounced on the loan shark, dragging him away. He landed three good punches, his furious words punctuating his movements.

"Fuck. You. Asshole."

By the time he raised his arm for another punch, Detective Baxter and another officer stormed in. They separated Liam and Vaughan. Detective Baxter aimed a furious look at Liam while the other officer pinned Vaughan to the ground and cuffed him.

"What did I tell you about letting us handle this?"

Liam didn't answer. He just glared at Vaughan,

his fists clenched.

The detectives dragged Vaughan outside, reading him his rights, leaving Liam alone with Kate.

For a time neither said a word. He looked so different. He looked like the man who had taken her to Franky's, wearing worn jeans and a black t-shirt, full of rugged appeal. Only tonight he looked disheveled, the dark circles under his eyes told her he hadn't been sleeping. His knuckles were covered in Vaughan's blood.

"How did you…?"

"I put out the word I wanted information on Vaughan. Wade got a tip tonight. Someone at the Golden Nugget recognized him, drunk as a skunk. Bragging about scoring big with a fancy pearl necklace. He made comments about visiting a certain redhead who'd gotten away from him before." His Adam's apple bobbed in his throat. "I called the cops. I just didn't tell them I was already on my way over."

He'd been watching out for her this whole time. God, it sounded as if he had an entire network of casino spies looking out for her.

Liam's blue eyes were marred by red. "Did he hurt you?"

"Not really. Thanks to you." She paused, her throat thick and painful. She opened her mouth, wanting to ask how he'd been.

"Don't. Just don't. I'm…I'm glad you're okay." And without another word, he left her apartment.

When she gave her statement to the police, Liam didn't stick around. He didn't call the rest of the night and neither did she. How could she? What could she say?

When her head hit her pillow late that night, her eyes remained wide open, glued to the dark ceiling. She knew the haunted look on Liam's face would keep her up all night long.

***

A week later at Percolate, Cynthia walked into the break room, huffing mad. "Jesus. If Fred tells me one more time to smile at those goddamn customers, I will shove a bottle of caramel syrup into his mouth. I don't care if he is the new manager. I know my goddamn job."

Kate grinned. "Be patient with the newbies."

"Says the other newbie." Cynthia grabbed a copy of the local paper and thumbed through it while Kate had her egg salad sandwich on nutritionally-poor white bread.

To hell with gluten-free. Since seeing Liam, her emotions had been all over the place, and she'd eaten whatever the hell she'd goddamn wanted. If someone offered a Twinkie/bacon sandwich, she'd wolf it down and ask for seconds.

"Wow," Cynthia said, laying the newspaper on the table. "He really did it."

"Who did what?"

"You know," she said, snapping her tattooed fingers, searching for a name. "Hot stuff who owns those casinos. Liam Boyle."

What? "Doyle. It's Liam Doyle."

"That's it!"

"What's he done, Cynthia?"

278

She peered at Kate. "Where've you been? It's been all over the local headlines."

"What. Has. He. Done?"

"He's sold all his casinos." Cynthia made a face. "Fuck me, Kate. You're in a weird mood. Weirder than usual."

Kate felt all the blood drain from her face. "What?"

"Hadn't you heard? He's been talking to some rich Russian who owns those hot new clubs in New York, Champagne and Liberty. I think he's Russian. I would totally let that dude fuck me too."

As Cynthia prattled on about rumors of Markov being connected to the Russian mob, Kate dropped her sandwich and pushed away from the table.

"Shit. You look like you've seen Amy Winehouse's ghost."

She stood and whipped off her apron, looking around nervously. "Can you tell Fred I can't finish my shift? There's something I have to do."

"Sure thing, spaz lady. I'll tell him you have *feminine* problems. That'll give the kid hives."

Kate raced out of the back room, unsure of what she was going to do, but knowing she had to do it.

***

Wade stood at the front entrance of Vice as she ran toward the door.

"Kate. Long time, no…whoa. Are you okay? Where's the fire?"

"Is he here?"

"Liam? Yeah, he's in his office."

"Please. I need to see him." She gulped for air. Even the run from the taxi bay had winded her. Sometimes the only thing worse than going on a health food diet was going off it again.

"Sure. I'll take you."

She didn't bat an eye at the statues of naked goddesses or the flashing lights from the slots on the way to the elevator. Not even the goddamn ceiling of smoke made her blink. She remained focused, needing to see Liam. She just needed to know…

The door opened into his office, and there he was. Facing away from them, Liam stood at the window, looking out over the Strip. No suit today. Just a rumpled grey t-shirt and faded jeans. His hair seemed a bit longer in back, and from her angle, she spied a bit more beard growth on his jaw.

He still took her breath away, even with his face turned.

Wade called out. "Liam, you have a visitor." He ushered her inside and stepped back into the elevator. As the door closed, he gave her a wink.

Liam turned. His lips parted with a breath. "Kate."

Her heart hammered in her chest. In those torturous seconds, she wanted to fly into his arms. Her eyes watered. Before she could collect her thoughts, a huge sob wracked her chest.

Liam raced over. He grabbed her by the shoulders, holding her gently. "Baby, please don't cry."

"You sold them. Your casinos."

"Yes. My pal Alex took them off my hands."

"Why?"

His lips turned up on one side into a grin that made her belly ache. "I did it for you, Kate. I did it all for you."

Kate pulled away. "But I didn't want this! I didn't want you to throw away your life for me, Liam. These casinos, you built them up from the ground. They're part of you." She crumpled to the carpet and buried her face in her hands.

He joined her on the carpet, sitting in front of her, and pried her hands from her wet face. "Kate, the casinos aren't me. They're bricks and mortar and poker chips. They're illusion and dream."

He tipped up her chin to make her look at him. His Husky eyes no longer bore any hint of fatigue. He looked good. Refreshed. Sexy as hell.

"Look, I sold the casinos for a couple of reasons. I didn't want you to worry, but I've been having some chest pains for a while."

She stared at his chest, wishing she could see right through it to his heart, to see if it was pumping properly.

"My doctor says I'm okay, but too stressed. He's been trying to get me to slow down for a while now, so I am. I let these casinos take over my life. Hell, I have a condo I never see. I'm always here." He stroked her hand, entwining his fingers with hers. "My dad died of heart problems at a young age. I refuse to go down the same road."

Okay, she could accept that reason.

"Secondly," he continued, his deep voice making her feel better already. "Like I told you, I always felt bad about taking Shauna's money to start my business. I've decided I need to forgive her. That's never been easy for me. So in order to finally let her go, I needed to put her money to better use. I'm very comfortable after the sale of the hotels, so I took the amount Shauna gave me and I donated it to New Horizons."

"That was you? Rod told me about the donation, but I never dreamed…Liam, that was a lot of money."

"It's only the beginning. I want to support your group, Kate. It's time I gave back. You were right. I ignored the problems under my own nose for too long. Don't get me wrong. I'm not against casinos, but I want to help the people whose lives have been impacted by them."

"I don't know what to say."

Liam drew closer and pulled her onto his lap. "Then let me say a few more things." He slid his arms around her waist and she wrapped her legs around his hips. "Kate, you told me I needed to hit rock bottom with Michelle. You were right, but that wasn't my true rock bottom. Rock bottom was when I watched you walk away."

"Oh, Liam, I'm so sorry."

"No, don't be. Turns out I have an addictive personality, and you were my addiction. I treated you like my own personal casino. It was too much, too soon. All of it, including the wild animal sex." He grinned and the balls of his cheeks reddened. "Although I did enjoy that part."

"It was okay, I guess," Kate teased.

"Okay, she says." Liam leaned in and teased her earlobe with his teeth. "I really want to start over and see if we can work our way back to the insane monkey sex." She giggled and he danced his fingers under her shirt, smoothing them over her waist. "I do love you, Kate. I don't want to fuck this up."

"I love you too." She gave in to temptation and brushed her lips over his neck and collarbone. "I was miserable without you."

"Me too. Woman, you brought me to my knees. Ask Wade. I was a bear without you."

Even as she laughed, she continued kissing him, letting her tongue trace the long lines of his neck.

Liam gripped her and pushed her back a bit. "Dammit, sugar. If you keep this up, you'll be naked instead of letting me do the honorable thing."

She licked her lips, savoring his taste. "And what would that be?"

He brushed his thumb over her wet lip, his gaze concentrated on her mouth. "I want to take you to dinner. Somewhere other than Vice. I want to discuss our future."

"*Our* future?"

He smiled. "If there's one thing I know, Kate, it's that I'm never going to watch you walk away again. I did last time because I knew you needed a better man. I wanted to be a better man for you. But this time," he said, his voice trembling with a low growl. "You're mine."

The hairs on her arms stood on end at his wonderfully-possessive tone.

"So," he said, kissing her. "Where would you like to eat? I know some nice French restaurants, or maybe a Korean barbeque."

Kate grinned. "How about pizza?"

Liam laughed. "I offer her swanky dining and she wants pizza. Doesn't sound gluten-free."

"Fuck gluten-free. Let's get pizza."

He folded her in his arms and buried his face in the crook of her neck. "Whatever makes you happy."

Chapter Seventeen

An hour and a half later, Kate and Liam sat at the back of Massimo's Pizza Parlor, polishing off the remains of a large double-cheese and pepperoni pizza. Liam sat back, stuffed, and smiled when Kate peeled the pepperonis off his discarded slice and popped them in her mouth. His cock hardened at the sight of that beautiful tongue licking her fingers with glee.

Damn. He so needed to see her naked again.

But business first. He needed to know they were on the same page before he could feel comfortable enough to lose himself in her sweet body. "So, full disclosure from now on?"

She gazed at him for a moment and then wiped her hands. "That would be awesome."

He leaned forward and grabbed her hands, linking them with his own. "I've been seeing a therapist. He's helping me comes to terms with my issues. My need to control my environment. You, Michelle, my work. God, even my *choice* of work. Do you know what one of the oldest sayings of the casino world is, Kate?"

She shook her head.

"'The House always wins.' That's how I treated my life. I needed to be in charge to make up for the times I had no power." He raised one of her hands and kissed it. "I've blamed myself for years for things over which I had no control. Including what happened to me while I was homeless."

She squeezed his hand but didn't say a word.

"I was hungry. I was cold. As a fourteen-year-old boy, I had to deal with big men who wanted to fuck me and women who wanted to buy me. To get by I lost my virginity way too young and learned it was a commodity. People were commodities. I was a commodity. It took me a long time to realize I was wrong."

She tipped her head and gnawed on her bottom lip.

"But I was one of the lucky ones. I was smart enough to get off the streets. When I went back to Aunt Margaret's, it was as someone who'd seen too much, someone who held grudges. I don't want to be that person anymore." He exhaled. "It's still hard for me to share the details, but I've shared more with you than anyone else. Can you be patient with me?"

She nodded, her eyes welling up.

"Thank you." He watched her for a moment, full of fascination and love. "There's one more thing. I want to open a piano bar with you. A proper piano bar, all on its own. With you as the headliner."

"I can't accept that. I can't let you buy me a bar to sing in."

"I wouldn't be. We'd be partners. You can invest as much as you like, but the papers will show we're co-owners. Hearing you sing was the first thing to get me excited in a long time. Not opening Vice, but you. Your talent. I will walk you through every step of the process, but I want you to be my partner. There won't be a single gaming device in the building, I promise."

"This is Vegas. Will people even come if there isn't a slot machine somewhere or if I don't show my boobs?"

"Actually, I don't want to build in Vegas. I've been talking to Alex. He's pointed out some great opportunities in New York. I'd like you to come with me."

"New York." Kate couldn't seem to close her jaw. "I don't know what to say…"

"Say yes." He bit his lip, a silent reminder to himself not to be so pushy. "Or at least say you'll think about it."

It took a few seconds, but soon she bobbed her head. "I want to be with you."

"Then we'll take it slowly and we'll make it happen. I want to make you happy, Kate."

"Then take me home, Liam." Her slow smile made his heart hammer in the best of ways. "Now."

Liam could feel his cheeks in his ears. Not caring that they were in a pizza parlor, he stood, scooped her out of her side of the booth and held her in his arms. Kate laughed as he fished for some money in his pocket and plunked it on the table to cover their meal. Then, kissing her like his life depended on it, he carried her out the door.

***

Somber intensity made Liam's eyes sparkle as they entered her apartment, but Kate could tell something had changed. Gone was the man who had things to prove. Gone was the man who couldn't trust, who needed to bend life to his will. And gone was the little boy who was afraid of being alone.

The need in his eyes no longer filled her with fear. Perhaps because his desire was now tempered with sweet consideration and freedom from his past. His perceived sins no longer held him hostage.

She was glad he'd brought her to her apartment, rather than back to Vice. As much as she felt badly he'd sold his businesses, she knew she didn't need to see the inside of a casino again. Too many memories. Too many ghosts. Like Liam, she'd seen things she never needed to see again.

He embraced her long and hard and she drank him in. The scratch of his beard as he nuzzled her neck. His warm breath as it drifted under her collar. His delicious cologne as it mingled with the scent of his clean skin. He touched all her senses, gave her a heady rush.

Her Liam.

He dug his hands into her hair and looked deep into her eyes. "The last time I saw you here…" Lines of regret furrowed his brow. She remembered how Hugo Vaughan had been all over her.

"Don't dwell on it. The future, remember?"

Since Vaughan's arrest, other women had come forward, accusing him of rape. Detective Baxter had assured her the loan shark would go away for a long time.

Liam brushed his thumb over her cheek. "No one will ever hurt you again, Kate."

"I love you."

"I adore you. C'mere."

He held her against his firm body, his arms molded about her as he covered her mouth with his own. She opened to him and their tongues met in a dance of velvety surrender. He kissed her as if making a pledge to her.

He skimmed his hands over the top half of her body as they kissed, massaging her shoulders, playing with her hair. Tickling her ribcage. She arched into him as her body begged for more intimate touches.

Despite her need, he kept his touch light and sensual, rather than sexual. A few minutes of this took their toll on both of them. Kate panted as he rested his forehead against hers and closed his eyes.

"Christ," he murmured. "I'm trying hard not to rush things, but this might kill me."

She let out a giggle, feeling his pain. "Liam, I want you so much."

"I want you too." He caressed her ribs, his hand straying close to the underside of her breast.

"Then what are you waiting for?"

His eyes narrowed, his gaze piercing. "Just this." Liam reached over to where he'd dumped his jacket and pulled a slim box from out of the inside pocket, handing it to her. "This belongs to you."

Kate already knew what was inside but was too choked up to open it. Liam raised the lid of the box for her. Upon seeing the shimmery strand inside, her tears spilled over. "My mother's pearls."

He took the choker out of the box and fastened it around her neck. "Vaughan left a trail. I just had my men follow it. You didn't think I was going to leave your mom's necklace in some grubby pawn shop, did you?"

She covered her trembling lips with her hand and tried to contain her sobs.

"Hey." Liam smiled and wiped her tears away, holding her until her breathing regulated. "No more tears, okay?"

She nodded. "No more tears."

Within seconds, their outfits lay scattered all over the floor. As soon as he revealed the tantalizing planes of his abdominal muscles, she dropped to her knees and smoothed her tongue over each ripple. His stomach clenched and he buried his fingers in her hair.

"God, Kate."

She gripped him, teasing him further. He swore and lifted her off the floor, then dropped her on the bed. He stood over her, running a hand down her calf.

"Mine," he said as he lowered himself over her, seemingly mystified by their connection.

And he was hers, all hers.

He traced her eyebrow with his thumb. "Forever."

Kate nodded. "Forever."

After worrying they'd never be joined again, he found his way inside her, moving with such aching slowness that she cried out. Letting out a long sigh of ecstasy, she dug her fingernails into his broad back and held on.

Perfection.

Each thrust pitched her higher and his heat warmed her like the sun over the desert.

Their love wasn't wrong after all. They could be good for one another. Would be good. In losing everything, they'd gained the only thing that mattered. Each other.

He rose up on his elbows to gaze at her. He drove them both toward an incinerating climax, and Kate realized she no longer feared his passion. She shared it.

Their bed was no longer a home to vice, to addiction, or fear. Instead, she saw promise in the familiar lines of his face, and hope. As they came together, swallowing each other's sighs, she felt Liam smile against her mouth and her heart soared.

Wherever they went, whatever they did, they would be home.

THE END

Epilogue

Six months later. New York City.

"I don't trust you to keep your eyes closed." Kate reached around Liam's broad shoulders and clapped her hands over his eyes.

Because he was taller, it was too hard to walk through the door that way and her arms jostled. Chuckling, Liam turned and grabbed her wrists. "Looks like you'll just have to trust me. I promise I won't peek until we get inside."

"Do you swear? Because I really want to surprise you."

"I swear. I have no idea what to expect." He dropped a kiss on her nose. "But I will admit I'm not thrilled with the idea you came to scope out this site on your own."

"I wasn't alone. Vanessa was with me."

Liam's eyebrow arched. "I'm glad you had our real estate agent to protect you."

"What? This neighborhood is perfectly safe."

"Neighborhood? We're standing in an alley."

"Not quite an alley, just a dark and lonely street."

"Kate, there's an empty parking lot to our right and an abandoned store front to our left."

"Sure." She waved to the area over her shoulder. "But Broadway is just over there somewhere."

Perhaps it was an exaggeration to say their potential building site was off-off-Broadway. Born and bred in Las Vegas, and only a few months in New York City, Kate was still getting her bearings. However, she knew they were in the realm of Broadway, or so the taxi driver had assured her.

Besides, the old costume emporium was perfect for their supper ' club. She just needed Liam to realize it.

Which meant she needed to get him inside.

"Liam, keep an open mind, okay? I know the place looks rough, but we agreed we wanted character."

He touched a finger to the crumbling door frame. "This has character, all right."

"Come on. Wouldn't it be more fun to restore a venerable old building than to slap up an 'Open' sign in a brand new box? This place has history. I read all about it at the library. As a costume store, it has connections to the theater world. Apparently Liza Minelli came for fittings here back in the day. Oh, and it was a speakeasy during Prohibition. How cool is that?"

Liam drew her into his arms. "I love your enthusiasm. I'm just not so sure about the neighbors."

"Right. About the neighbors." Kate inhaled and exhaled. "Look, I don't want to spend all your money—"

"*Our* money, Kate. It's ours."

Only they were talking about a significant chunk of change, more than Kate had ever handled in her life. Up until a few months ago, she didn't dare buy anything unless it was on sale. That included everything from tins of tuna to new shoes.

Now, thanks to Liam, she was officially a millionaire. Well, she was dating one, anyway.

He cupped her cheek. "We've talked about this. What's mine is yours."

"And what's mine is yours. All five bucks of it. Don't spend it all in one place."

"Kate…"

"I know, I know. Most of the time, I don't even think about the money, I swear. But every so often, I remember how much we're talking about and it's overwhelming."

She was still having trouble getting used to the idea of Liam sharing his wealth with her. It wasn't all that long ago he was her enemy, the man she knew only as Liam Doyle, hot shot developer, casino owner, and toast of Las Vegas. So much had changed since then. As a support group leader for families of compulsive gamblers, Kate had been determined to take him down. She had even staged protests outside his glamorous casino, Vice. However, they'd both been shocked by their savage attraction to one another. Before long, they'd had no choice but to act on it. Their whirlwind romance had turned into something so much deeper.

When Liam had told Kate what he wanted to do with his casinos…

She still couldn't remember that day without bawling. Even now, her eyes welled up.

Understanding, Liam stroked his thumb under her eye to catch her escaping tear. "You're thinking about the casinos again, aren't you?"

"I can't help it."

"I know."

Before Liam, she'd always thought the best vantage point in a casino was the exit. Because of her father's gambling addiction, her family had been destroyed. And yet every time she considered Liam giving up his world for her, the only world he'd ever known, she couldn't control the water works.

His eyes warmed. "I don't regret a thing, sugar. Not a single moment. Everything I did was to ensure our future."

She nodded, her throat scratchy. They'd discussed their future at length and continued to do so. Marriage, children, the whole nine yards. Kate knew Liam's devotion equaled hers.

He just hadn't proposed yet.

He would, she knew it. They'd just been so busy with the relocation from Vegas.

She didn't ever want him to regret his generosity, monetarily and emotionally.

Even though they spent almost every waking moment with each other, working to make their club dream a reality, and even though she spent each night curled up next to his hard body, she often wondered if he'd change his mind. He often told her falling in love with her was the best thing he'd ever done.

A part of her, the darkest, most insecure part, tried to give him an "out" whenever he brought up the topic of marriage. Each time it arose in conversation, and it was always Liam who brought it up, she kept quiet and nodded her approval. She wanted to marry him, more than she wanted her next breath, but she didn't ever want him to feel trapped.

Liam was once photographed wining and dining a Swedish princess and he'd ended up with a Vegas jingle singer.

What if this was all a dream? Being with him had always felt like one, even in their early days.

What if he woke up and realized he'd made a horrible mistake?

Kate would have no choice. She loved him so much she would give him his freedom tomorrow if he wanted it.

It would kill her, but she'd do it if it made him happy.

You're being dumb, Kate. He loves you.

Her caffeine levels were clearly dropping to danger point. She needed a strong espresso.

This wasn't insecurity. This was just fear of the unknown. She and Liam had been through so much change lately and her emotions got the better of her sometimes.

"Are you okay?"

"Yeah."

"Then why so many shadows in your eyes?"

"So many big decisions, that's all."

His hands slid down her back, squeezing her hips. "Don't lose sight of what this is all about. You and me, together. That's all I want, Kate. I don't care if we live in a shack."

"Liar. You would never let me live in a shack."

He rubbed his nose against hers. "This is true. It would have to be a really nice shack before I'd even consider it."

"The Hilton of shacks. The *Vice* of shacks."

"Maybe not quite like Vice, but something like that."

Her soft giggle must not have been convincing enough. Guilt swarmed her once again.

"Hey," he whispered. "Let me kiss those shadows away."

Kate held her breath as he slanted his mouth over hers. A riot of butterflies flapped their wings against her ribcage, trying to get out. She'd expected the headiness, the wonderful giddiness of new love, to disappear but it hadn't. A mere touch from Liam and her nerve endings tingled. A kiss sent them skyrocketing. The best part of all was seeing the way his pupils dilated, turning his pale blue eyes almost black. He always licked his lips after kissing her, as if savoring her taste, as if wanting to keep it inside him.

How could she ever worry about what they had? His adoration was written all over his face and it made her so grateful to be alive and in his arms.

They'd risked everything for each other and they'd won big, as her father used to say on the rare occasions when he didn't empty his wallet at the roulette table.

He ended the kiss on a groan and a nibble on her ear lobe. "Now, before I forget why we came here, tell me what you'd like to do with this site."

She tore herself away from him. "Okay. Bear in mind, this is all pie in the sky."

"I like pie."

"I know this spot's a mess right now, but keep an open mind. I made a few calls. It turns out the parking lot and the empty storefront are also for sale."

"Oh, yeah?" For the first time since the taxi dropped them off, Liam turned toward the block of buildings. He planted his hands on his hips and his eyes narrowed. Kate could see he was in developer-mode.

"If we built our supper club here, we would rejuvenate the entire block. We could bring this dark, little street back to life, Liam."

As he walked back and forth in front of the three lots, Kate held her breath. She wanted him to love the space as much as she did. When she'd wandered down this alley the other day, she'd been entranced. To her, it oozed early New York City, and not in a bad way. The Art Deco touches to the two remaining buildings appealed to the artist in her. The side street looked so forgotten, so flat. She wanted to hook it up to a defibrillator and revive it.

When Liam had declared his intention of making her his partner in a New York supper club, she had thought he was crazy. For some reason, he believed in her talent and wanted her to have a classy singing venue. They'd been on the hunt for the perfect location ever since, but none of the sites they'd seen had piqued their interest.

"If we assumed all three lots, we'd have a

massive space," he said. "You'd want to incorporate the old buildings, I assume? Or, at least, some of the historical features?"

"Yeah. Come inside. You won't believe the details." Smiling from ear to ear, she pushed open the door to the costume warehouse.

Liam slid in ahead of her, his gaze darting from side to side as they entered. No doubt, he expected a horde of junkies to jump out, eager to jab them with their dirty needles. She'd half expected it herself when the real estate agent toured her around the first time. Liam hadn't been available that day, caught up in a meeting with one of his many lawyers.

Their footsteps echoed in the empty room, clicking on the creaky hardwood. Although the building had last been used as a store, it had been cleared out some time ago. Faded Broadway musical posters still clung to several walls, the only indication it was ever a costume store. Crown mouldings ornamented each wall, except for the west wall, a gorgeous expanse of exposed brick. It was the brick that first attracted Kate. In a supper club setting, it would provide such ambience and warmth. If they knocked down the wall between this storefront and the one next to it, they could enlarge the space and buy some of the oversized furniture they'd recently eyed in a design shop. On a larger footprint, the tables and chairs would feel cozy.

Liam dragged his fingers along the brick. "This wall's solid. It's in good condition."

"That's what I thought. Now imagine it, just like

we discussed." She indicated the other side of the room. "We could put plush banquette-style seating all along this side. Mahogany wood everywhere. A single crystal chandelier over the bar. And if we take down the wall separating the two stores, we'd have room for a large dancefloor."

Liam was quiet and thoughtful. His gaze remained glued to her, as if gauging her reactions, rather than analyzing his own. "What else?"

"I see a small stage over there, with red velvet draperies hanging behind it. The stage would curve and extend toward the audience so the performers could interact with them. It would feel as if the artist was singing just to you."

He nodded and continued to walk slowly around the room.

Kate shifted her balance from one foot to the other, waiting for him to say something, anything. After all, Liam was the one with the experience here. She'd never developed a property. Hell, she'd never even bought one before, having only been a renter thus far.

"Of course," she said, "if you see any red flags, please tell me. I didn't notice any cracks in the walls or water stains. The place looks intact to me, but you might see things I don't."

His tease of a grin drove her nuts. "Does it look like I'm waving any red flags?"

"Liam, just tell me. If you think the site is no good, I'll understand."

He walked toward her and it seemed to take a day. Why was she so on edge? Maybe it was because this was the first time she'd felt hope about her career in a long time. Liam believed in her and she wanted to do justice to his beliefs. She didn't want to disappoint him in any way.

He grabbed her hand, slowly stoking her palm. "It's achievable, Kate. I mean, we'll have to do our due diligence and bring in a good inspector to make sure it won't fall down around our heads."

"Absolutely."

"I just have one question."

"Okay."

"Do you love it?"

Her heart somersaulted in her chest. "I loved it from the moment I saw it."

"Then I love it too." He leaned in for another kiss.

"Wait a minute, buster." She held him back with a hand to his chest. "I don't want you going along with this just because I happen to think the exposed brick is pretty. You have to love it too. We're going to be spending a lot of time here."

He patted her bum. "Yeah, and I plan to grope you in each room."

"Be serious, Liam."

"I'm dead serious. You have no idea how often I think of groping you."

She compressed her lips.

"What if I let you in on a secret?"

"What secret?"

His lips grazed the shell of her ear. "I already knew about this place."

"What do you mean?"

"Word travels in my business. I had Vanessa show it to me a week ago." He smiled. "But I wanted you to see it on your own. I didn't want to influence you because I think it's perfect."

Kate's held breath emerged as a squeal. "You do?"

"Yeah."

She jumped up and down. "So we have our club?"

"We have our club."

"Yes!"

He brought her into a bear hug, wrapping his arms around her body.

"God, Kate. You're shaking."

"I know. I've never been so nervous and so excited all at the same time."

"And happy?"

His two words conveyed so much, all their past struggles and all his hopes for a new life with her. Liam had overcome every hardship to get where he was and they'd certainly fought to be together, sometimes even fighting themselves. At the end of the day, she knew all he really wanted in the world was for her to be happy.

Her insecurities could take a flying leap.

"I don't think I can be any happier."

"Oh, yeah?" His eyes flashed. "We'll see about that."

***

When the alarm clock buzzed at seven o'clock, Liam moaned and reached across the bed to pull Kate against him, as he always did. His hand met with cold sheets, rather than her warm, curvy body.

Stifling a bear growl, he smacked the clock button and opened his eyes.

Kate, dressed only in her bra, panties, and one leg of her tights, grimaced. "Sorry. You beat me to the clock."

"Mornin', sugar. Come here."

She sat on the bed, her eyes narrowed in suspicion.

Liam reached over and grabbed the vacant leg of her tights and pulled her over. Laughing, she rolled into bed next to him. He held her before she could wriggle away and buried his nose in her lilac-scented hair. "There. Better." He slid his hand into her panties and cupped her ass. "Much better."

"Liam, we have that meeting with Dev and Lucy today, to look at the upholstery samples. Remember? It's at eight."

He ran his finger along the crease where her ass met her thigh and she wiggled. "I can be quick. Promise."

"You're very tempting but the traffic is nuts and I don't want us to be late." She kissed the base of his neck. "Later?"

"You can count on it. Have you brushed your hair yet?"

"No. Why?"

"So I can mess it up." Liam dug his fingers into her silky, red hair and cradled her skull. Rolling her over, he eased himself between her legs and kissed her.

He really could be quick. God only knew his body was ready.

"You're such a bad influence." Laughing, Kate

extricated herself and got off the bed. She continued to dress, dragging the other leg of her tights on.

Liam lay back and watched her dress. It was almost as good as watching her undress. When she slid into a black dress, he took note of the zipper so he could find it easily that evening. He would take pleasure in easing the slider over her curves.

"That's an evil grin, mister."

"That's because I'm thinking evil thoughts."

Kate blushed and her freckles deepened. So goddamned beautiful. He wished he could paint, just so he could paint her picture.

She was all his.

She pulled her mother's pearl choker out of her jewelry box. The quiet luster of the pearls reminded him of the task he'd have to tackle today, one about which Kate had no idea.

He couldn't wait to see her face.

Hopefully she'd love his creation.

Don't worry, dumbass. She'll love it.

As he stood, the sheets fell from his body, leaving him naked. He moved behind her and helped her fasten her choker. She smiled at him in the mirror above the dresser. "I like your look this morning."

He latched the pearls and kissed the back of her neck. His erection pressed against her sweet ass. "I like yours better." He turned her around in his arms. "Kate, do you mind if I skip this meeting?"

Her brow furrowed. "Too many meetings, huh?"

"Kind of. I managed to double-book myself. It was nice when I had Pearl to take care of my schedule, but now that I'm doing it myself, I'm messing it up. I'm supposed to be meeting with Brad about the bar staff today. We met a couple of good mixologists and we want to lock them down."

"Of course." She stroked his face. Her soft touch made his lower half riot. "I don't want you to get stressed."

"I'm not, I promise."

"Because if there's anything more I can do, I'd like to do it."

"You've already taken on so much. Hell, I appreciate you auditioning the other talent. I never liked that part of the job. I'm out of my element. As a singer, you know what you're doing."

"Let's hope so. The design team will want me to make decisions today. You don't mind me choosing all the upholstery for the club?"

"I have every faith in you."

"I'll stick to the red and purple theme we discussed."

"Sounds great."

She sighed, her hands slipping down his chest. "You are so tempting."

Liam kissed her, moved her away from the dresser and tapped her on the butt. "Get moving, lady, before we both forget our meetings."

Humming, she walked into the bathroom and proceeded to braid her hair.

Liam had to stop himself from grinning as he entered the walk-in closet to choose his clothes.

Today wasn't about locking down mixologists at all. He didn't like lying to Kate, but this would be his only lie to her. It hadn't been easy keeping quiet, not when he wanted to tell her everything on his mind. He didn't like keeping secrets from her.

Of course, some were worth keeping.

Once Kate left for the day, Liam showered and got dressed. After grabbing a quick coffee, he headed outside. As he locked up their house, a sweet Upper West Side brownstone they'd both fallen in love with on their first visit to New York, he hailed a cab.

"Where to?" asked the cabbie.

"Tate's Custom Jewelry on 47th. Do you know it?"

"Yeah, yeah." The cabbie rolled his eyes. "Like I know the adoring face of my own mother. Get in."

Liam chuckled as he got in the cab.

New York. They didn't know him as a big shot here, not everyone anyway, and it was fine by him. The relative anonymity was refreshing. If he'd hailed a cab on the Vegas Strip, the cabbies would have fought over themselves to earn his fare. He might as well enjoy being a regular guy. It probably wouldn't last long. As soon as Kate starting singing in their club, patrons would be busting down the door.

She would finally have the recognition she deserved.

They would, of course, have other talent on hand as well but she would be their headliner. He knew she was nervous. As she often mused aloud, "No one will know who I am."

It wouldn't take long. She'd already prepared her music, vintage love songs that showcased her smoky singing voice. With their new pianist and band accompanying her, she'd sound like an angel.

Men would be throwing her flowers and proposals of marriage as she walked off the stage.

Of course, he'd make sure his proposal beat them to the punch.

The cabbie arrived at the jewelry design store in record time.

"Here you go, mister. That'll be twenty-five." The cabbie put out his hand and nodded at the store. "Looks like some lucky lady is going to get a surprise."

"I'm the lucky one." Liam handed the man a hundred dollar bill. "Wish me luck and keep the change."

With the cabbie still gaping at the tip, Liam strode into Tate's Custom Jewelry. Hopefully he'd made the guy's day with a bit of extra cash.

He'd been given so much and had promised himself his life would be all about paying it forward from now on. The old Liam had been all about accumulation. Accumulating money, casinos, even women from time to time. It felt good to shed that weight. He hadn't realized what a burden it had become. He'd had his reasons, of course, ones he continued to process with the help of his therapist, but none of them seemed to matter as much anymore.

Besides, in losing Kate once, he'd learned she was all he needed to be happy. He'd spend the rest of his days putting a smile on her beautiful face. She'd helped him face his fears and his past, and he owed her everything.

That was why the choice of engagement ring had been a difficult one. He'd already looked at hundreds of them, their diamonds sparkling behind glass cases. None of them had been right.

None of them had been her.

He'd had a special engagement ring designed for her and today he would see it for the first time. If it was to his liking, he'd bring it home.

And spend the next few months trying his hardest to hide it from her. It would kill him not to propose the second he was in the door that night, but he had to stay strong. He had a plan to create a magical night for Kate and he didn't want to spoil it.

Alicia, the sales associate at Tate's, met him at the door. "Liam, nice to see you again. Are you ready to see Kate's ring? I think you'll like it."

Liam nodded. He was ready.

***

Opening night

Liam stood inside the closed door, fiddling with his tie for the hundredth time. There was a crowd outside Crimson, their newly-christened supper club, but the bouncers had been instructed to keep an eye out for a particular car. The party should be arriving any time now, but Liam wanted to make sure he got to them before Kate did.

"Look at you. You're more nervous than I am."

Liam turned upon hearing Kate's voice. *Christ.* "Kate, you look beautiful."

She did a little curtsey. "You like it?"

He ran a hand down her bare arm. "That dress on

you. Jesus, it's life-changing."

Her face erupted in red blotches, making her look even prettier. She hadn't allowed him to even catch a glimpse of her opening night ensemble before this moment. It was worth the wait.

She wore an off-the-shoulder number, a deep purple gown that trailed slightly behind her. Her long red hair was swept off to one side, caught up in a gravity-defying updo. Her mom's pearls had been set aside this evening so she could wear the necklace he'd bought her, a simple silver and amber design that made her hazel eyes sparkle. The makeup artist had given her cat eyes and bold red lips that looked so kissable.

Goddammit, he wanted to kiss her and wear her lipstick all over his face.

Her beauty caused his nerves to sizzle and crackle.

It also made the engagement ring in his suit pocket feel like a boulder.

What if she said no?

Liam had almost asked her to marry him a dozen times since picking up the ring, but had remained strong. His intention all along had been to ask her to marry him on their opening night. Now that it was here, his heart was skittering like a rabbit being chased by a fox.

"You look very handsome," she said, fixing his tie. "I'll have to beat the women off with a stick."

"I'll be too busy carrying my own stick." He grabbed her around the waist and kissed her cheek so he wouldn't mess up her makeup. "You take my breath away. I'm not sure I want you on stage anymore. I just want you back in our bed so I can be the only one looking at you."

"Time for that later. We have a club to open." She gestured to the opulent space behind them. "And a gorgeous one, if I do say so myself."

She was right. Crimson was perfect. It was exactly what they'd envisioned when they began dreaming about it months ago. Liam had never felt so proud, not when he opened Vice or Sin or Luxe. His casinos may have taken more work and money and attention to detail, but Crimson perfectly encapsulated the aura of quiet luxury he'd always strived to achieve with his casino hotels.

Robed in warm shades of red and purple, the club invited one to sit down and stay awhile. Of course, the design team would have scoffed upon hearing him and Kate call the colors "red" and "purple." According to them, the palette was "crimson" and "aubergine." He and Kate had shared some laughs over that but had eventually settled on the name Crimson. Liam had wanted to call the place "Kate's" but she wouldn't hear of it.

Their bar staff stood at the ready, prepared to entice customers with their armada of inventive cocktails. The wait staff, dressed in black, polished the already gleaming mahogany tables. Recessed lights bathed the club in a soft glow while a crystal chandelier sparkled atop the long bar. Their pianist, Ricardo, already seated on stage at the grand piano, played softly to welcome guests. When Kate began her first set at eight o'clock, Ricardo would accompany her while she crooned some of her favorite torch songs.

310

Thanks to a bit of buzz, people were lined up around the block. Word had spread that Liam Doyle had opened up a supper club with his girlfriend, and even some of the Vegas crowd had made the journey to be in attendance.

All they had to do was open the door now.

That, and one last detail.

"You should head back stage," said Liam. "I don't want you to miss your warm up just because of my nerves."

"You're okay?"

He fingered the velvet box in his pocket. "I'm more than okay. How about you?"

"I'm great." She wrapped her arms around him.

He angled his body slightly so she wouldn't feel the jewelry box on his side.

"I love you," she whispered. "Thank you."

"I love you too. And I should be thanking you."

Her eyes bright, Kate hurried backstage.

When she disappeared, Liam expelled a big breath. He texted his head bouncer.

Are they here yet?

They just got here. I'll bring them right in.

A few seconds later, the front door opened. Kate's best friend Lisa walked in, followed her by husband Donny. They both smiled upon seeing the place for the first time.

Liam opened his arms in welcome. "Hi, guys."

"Liam!" Lisa gave him a hug. "It's so good to see you. Thanks for flying us out for the big night."

"My pleasure. How are Georgie and Sarah?"

"Jealous that they couldn't come, but happy to be spending some time with their grandma."

"Good. Nothing wrong with parents having a little getaway." Liam turned to Donny and held out his hand. "How are you, Donny?"

Donny shook his hand but pulled Liam into a hug as well. "I'm great, thanks, man. For everything."

"I'm glad you could be here."

Liam remembered the first time he'd met Donny. He'd been forced to throw him out of Vice. A compulsive gambler, Donny was the reason Lisa had first attended Kate's support group for families of gambling addicts. Donny had been headed down a dark path, the same road Kate's father still trod. They'd made repeated attempts to get Kate's dad into counseling, but he'd resisted every last one. Thankfully, Donny hadn't been so stubborn. Eager to make peace with Lisa and their kids, Georgie and Sarah, he'd accepted Kate and Liam's offer of help. Because he couldn't afford therapy for himself, they paid the bill and it was a small price to pay to reunite a family.

If they couldn't use their money to help the ones they loved, why have money at all?

So far, the therapy was working. Donny hadn't gambled a cent in months. He was even holding down a good job back home in Vegas. Lisa was thrilled, their kids weren't scared anymore and Kate could breathe easily.

"You sure Kate doesn't suspect we're here?" asked Donny.

"Nope. She's completely in the dark."

"I told her we couldn't make it because of Sarah's recital," said Lisa. "Remember? Seeing as the recital happens next month, I assume she'll forgive us a little white lie."

"She'll have to forgive a few white lies." Liam chuckled.

"Speaking of which." Lisa held out her hand. "Can we see it?"

Liam nodded and showed them the ring.

"Oh, Liam." She gasped. "It's perfect. A pearl." Her eyes watered. "For her mom."

"Yeah. And some diamonds around it. I had to throw in a few of those too."

"It looks vintage. She'll love it."

"I hope so."

One of the hostesses approached them. "Liam, would you like me to seat your guests before the door opens?"

"Yes, please, Robin." He turned to Lisa and Donny. "I've put you in the reserved booth near the stage so Kate will see you as soon as she comes out."

"This is so exciting!" Lisa grabbed Donny's hand and they followed Robin to their booth.

Content, Liam gave the door staff the signal to open.

Content. Who was he kidding?

He was ecstatic.

***

Still reeling from the success of the evening,

Kate returned to her dressing room after the show. Her heart was galloping and she needed a breather. Liam had invited every entertainment reporter in the business and Kate had been bombarded with questions after her final set. Of course, most of them just wanted her to pose with Liam but it was more attention than she was used to receiving.

Seeing Lisa and Donny made it all even more exciting. She'd been told they couldn't attend the opening night, and when she spotted the couple in the audience, she'd almost lost it on stage. However, somehow she'd managed to pull herself together and she'd pulled out every musical stop she'd ever learned.

There had been a lot of pleased faces in the audience. Her sense of fulfillment had been greater than anything she'd ever felt while singing jingles for Calvert's Used Automobiles.

Seeing Liam at the back of the club, silently smiling in encouragement, had been the best part of all.

He'd given her a huge bouquet of crimson roses before the show, and they now stood in a vase on her dressing table. She touched the petals of one of the blooms, leaning down to breathe in its scent.

The dressing room door opened. "Don't move. You look so pretty leaning over those roses."

"Liam." She ran to him and threw her arms around his neck. "We did it."

He buried his nose in her hair. "*You* did it. You were awesome, Kate."

"I made a couple of mistakes, but Ricardo covered for me. Nerves."

"Well, I didn't notice and neither did anyone else."

"I hope you're right. Hey, we should change. Lisa and Donny will be waiting."

"Um, actually, I just talked to them. They're going to have a quiet night at their hotel and meet up with us tomorrow."

"Oh." Her face fell. "That's too bad."

"No, it's not. I've been waiting all night long to get you all to myself."

"I like the sound of that."

His smile disappeared and he took a deep breath. His pale eyes sparkling, Liam took her hand in his. He dropped to one knee.

Oh, boy. All the blood seemed to drain out of Kate's head.

When he produced a black velvet box from his pocket, her jaw fell open, and for the life of her, she couldn't clap it shut.

"Kate." His voice was soft, reverent. "You've changed my life. Before you came along, I was hard and dead inside. You looked at a suspicious man and saw a spark of something good, something that I lost long ago. You believed in me at a time when I no longer believed in myself. Because of you, I wanted to be a better man."

Tears filled her eyes. He was always a good man in her eyes, just lost. They'd both been lost without each other.

"I was so proud of you tonight," he continued, "just as I'm proud of you every moment of every day. I want to build a life with you. I want children with you. I want forever with you. Will you make me the happiest man on earth and—"

"Yes!" She pulled him to standing and threw herself at him, kissing him all over the face. "Yes."

He laughed, tears in his eyes. "You didn't even give me a chance to finish. How did you know what I was going to ask?"

She glared at him but it wasn't a real glare because she was smiling too hard.

"I didn't get a chance to show you the ring."

The ring. She'd totally forgotten about a ring.

Liam cracked open the box. "I took a risk and designed it myself, with a lot of help, of course. If it's not to your taste, we can get something else."

Kate gazed upon the shimmering confection of pearl and diamonds. She raised a shaking hand to her mouth.

"Do you like it?"

"I love it. It's beautiful." She didn't even bother to wipe her tears as they cascaded down her cheeks. He'd included a pearl in memory of her mom. "I love you so much."

"I love you, Kate." Liam slid the ring onto her finger and pulled her into his arms. "And I'll never stop showing you just how much."

He already had, every minute of every day. She was the luckiest woman in the world and she knew some would say it was because she'd caught the attention of Liam Doyle, famed businessman.

But that wasn't it.

In their first heady days together, she'd begged him to show her his heart, the real Liam. She'd known there was more to him than fancy suits and luxury hotel suites. In finally getting to know him,

316

his hurts and wounds and dreams, she'd found her own heart.

Their hearts beat together now and it was the most poignant music she'd ever heard.

THE END

ACKNOWLEDGMENTS

From the moment I first set pen to paper with *Vice*, I knew this book was going to be an emotional one. Inspired by my own family's experiences with compulsive gambling, it remains one of my favorite stories and I hope it lives on in the hearts of my readers. It was always important to me to entrust it to good people and I'm so fortunate it has found a home at Limitless Publishing. Thank you to Jennifer O'Neill, Lori Whitwam, and everyone at my Limitless/Crave family. Particular thanks must go to Toni Rakestraw, my wonderful editor. Thank you, Toni, for catching so many of my errors.

Thank you to the members of my fan group, Rosanna Leo's Pride. These are the folks who cheer me daily and who continue to support me in all I do.

If you have a family member who is addicted to gambling, you are not alone. Please reach out to your local chapter of Gam-Anon.

ABOUT THE AUTHOR

Rosanna Leo is a multi-published author of contemporary and paranormal romance. Winner of the Reader's Choice 2015 in Paranormal Romance at The Romance Reviews, Rosanna draws on her love of mythology for her books on Greek gods, selkies and shape shifters.

From Toronto, Canada, Rosanna occupies a house in the suburbs with her long-suffering husband, their two hungry sons and a tabby cat named Sweetie. When not writing, she can be found haunting dusty library stacks or planning her next star-crossed love affair.

A library employee by day, she is honored to be a member of the league of naughty librarians who also happen to write romance.

Facebook:
https://www.facebook.com/rleoauthor1

Twitter:
https://twitter.com/LeoRosanna

Goodreads:
http://www.goodreads.com/author/show/5826852.Rosanna_Leo

Pinterest:
https://www.pinterest.com/rosannaleo/

Instagram:
https://www.instagram.com/rleoauthor/

Bookbub:
https://www.bookbub.com/authors/rosanna-leo

Amazon author page:
https://www.amazon.com/Rosanna-Leo/e/B007X5P4I8

www.ingramcontent.com/pod-product-compliance
Lightning Source LLC
Chambersburg PA
CBHW051955240626
47153CB00005B/1773